The Gutenberg Rubric

NATHAN
EVERETT

The Gutenberg Rubric

Elder Road Books
Bellevue WA

Designed by Nathan Everett

Printed in the United States of America

The Gutenberg Rubric

ONE

THE TECHNICAL TERM for the twinkling of stars is scintillation or, more properly, astronomical scintillation. It is caused by air currents shifting the density of the earth's atmosphere and refracting the light of the stars in different directions. Thus, they seem to the naked eye to move slightly. It is a phenomenon to which the human eye is drawn. Any little twinkle will cause a head to turn.

Take the diamond on the hand of a newly-engaged woman. That sparkle, or gemological scintillation, will catch the eye and draw it to the third finger on the left hand. Diamond cutters spend years learning to shape and polish stones to maximize the refraction of light. The result is mesmerizing.

The twinkling objects that Keith Drucker saw in the late afternoon sunlight as he lay flat on his back on the pavement, ears ringing, were not stars, though they seemed as numerous; nor were they precious stones cut to refractive perfection. What he saw were thousands of tiny bits of glass falling from the sky—glass that moments ago had been part of the soaring atrium entrance of the Kane Memorial Library. This awareness struck him an instant before the glass did.

THE DAY had started so well.

He watched the alarm clock display 5:59 and turned it off before it could ring at 6:00. He'd been awake already for 20 minutes, though this morning he couldn't imagine why he thought 6:00 was a good time to get out of bed. Normally, he was well into his day by 6:30, but his normal day didn't include waking up next to the softly sleeping redhead beside him.

At 43, he didn't think of himself as the type to have a whirlwind romance with a colleague. He didn't consider his bookish appearance and personality sufficient to attract such an incredible woman as Madeline Zayne. They'd known each other for only eight weeks, had been lovers for four, but this was the first time to awaken in the morning in the same bed. He wasn't sure how he had earned such good karma, but he vowed to keep doing whatever it was.

It wasn't that he'd never dated in his years as a scholar, but no one had taken his heart by storm the way Maddie had. He lifted a stray lock of hair from her face and let it fall among the tangled tresses on her pillow. Freckles covered even her eyelids. He wondered for the hundredth time if there was any part of her body that did not have freckles and decided to check at the first opportunity. He was fascinated by the random chaos of color against impossibly fair skin, so translucent he was sure it had never seen sunlight. *Well, "outdoorsy librarian" is an oxymoron*, he supposed.

His fascination got the better of him and he softly touched her cheek, pinpointing one single freckle. She stirred and her eyelids fluttered open. She smiled at him with one side of her mouth. That was the expression that first drew him to her. How can you smile with just one side of your mouth?

"What are you doing?" Maddie asked, rolling slightly toward him. The sheet slipped down off her shoulders, exposing yet another uninterrupted field of freckles. "What?" she asked again.

"I was just thinking that I should count your freckles."

"What?"

"Kind of an inventory," he continued. "How else will I ever know if one goes missing? I think maybe I should name them as well."

"You're crazy!" she laughed. She reached up to give him a light kiss on the lips. "Charming, but crazy."

"One, two, three," he said, touching three random freckles just below her collarbone and pushing aside the ever present locket that held photos of her parents.

"You'll never do it that way," she laughed.

"Why not?" he asked. "Four. Five," he continued, pushing the sheet farther down as he did so.

"It's not organized," Maddie said. "You need a system if you're going to catalog such a large body of work."

"Spoken like a true librarian. Wait a minute. Drat! You made me lose count. Now I'll have to start all over. One. Two."

"This will take forever," she laughed.

"That's a *good* thing." Keith smiled and kissed her.

"Mmmm," she breathed as they moved together.

Waking at 6:00 wasn't so bad if you didn't get out of bed.

KEITH TOOK the long way to work, walking south along the river to the First Avenue Bridge before crossing over and returning north along the East Bank to the library. His apartment was only 15 minutes from the library on foot, but in academia it was better not to show up for work at the same time as the colleague you were sleeping with. Maddie left his apartment 15 minutes before he did and drove directly to her nine o'clock staff meeting.

It had been a wet week, but this morning the sun was shining—a good omen for spring break. It looked like half the students had left early. He usually lectured on Friday morning, but he had cancelled his "History of the Printed Word" class two days ago. In return for the extra day off, his students were to bring a sample of contemporary printing when they returned from break. The sample had to be a piece they considered extraordinary according to the six principles he outlined for them in class. It would be amusing to see how many of his students returned after a week with nothing more than the morning's newspaper.

His cellphone buzzed while he was still on the bridge and he answered it cheerily.

"Granddad! You're up early."

"I'm always up early," the old man said into the phone. "Thought I'd catch you before you were in the library."

"I'm just walking to work now," Keith answered.

"I just wanted to make sure you were taking a break this week," his granddad said. "The last time there was a school vacation and you were working on a project, you got locked in the library for a week."

"It was only overnight, Granddad. I promise I'm taking a break. Umm..." Keith hesitated, then plunged in. "Maddie and I are going to Jamaica for spring break." If his grandfather was surprised it didn't show in his voice.

"I suppose you'll come back with dreadlocks."

"I would if I had enough hair," he laughed. "I'm just hoping not to get sunburned. I don't think Maddie has ever been in the sun."

"Hm. You should probably spend most of your time in your room."

"Granddad!" Keith wasn't as shocked as he sounded on the phone, but he hurried on to change the subject. "I'm looking at an interesting manuscript today. A record of the books in a Carthusian monastery from the 12th to the 19th century. It has some real possibilities."

"What kind of possibilities?"

"The monastery was located near Wurtemburg Mountain in Germany. You know how I like to investigate things from there."

"Don't get your hopes up, son," his grandfather said. "The chance that you'll find what you are looking for is remote. But keep me informed, all the same."

Keith and his grandfather wished each other well and cut the connection as he entered the courtyard surrounding the library.

He and Maddie had had too little time to learn about each other in any way but the professional and the romantic. They shared a deep passion for books, but Keith wondered how she would respond to the rest of his story when he told her.

He had studied typesetting under some of the finest masters of traditional book arts and was a second degree master alchemist. The title always made Keith smile. It was a figurative nod to the alchemical experimentation of Johannes Gutenberg that led to his formula for lead type. The practical study of Gutenberg's experiments in alchemy—preserved by the highly secretive guild Gutenberg founded—had led Keith to the use of spectrographic analysis applied to inks. The five-and-a-half century old guild still preserved the formulae and techniques used to make ink and lead type, something that was almost unknown to the rest of the world now that electronic typesetting dominated the industry.

There were a lot of things they needed to talk about. In spite of the chemistry between the two of them being akin to magic, he didn't know how she would respond to his being involved in an ancient art-form that some considered sorcerous. *Maybe alchemy is something she wants to dabble in, too,* Keith thought. *Maybe she belongs to a secret society. Maybe she'd like to get married.* He let himself drift in his fantasy world as he walked through the commons. He wouldn't rush things. When he suggested a week ago that they go away over spring break together, he thought he might have been pushing it a little. She did hesitate for a minute with a near-panic expression on her face, but then she seemed to shake it off with a firm resolution and suggested that maybe Jamaica would be a nice place. They sat up half the night surfing the Web to find a place to stay and making travel arrangements. The idea of proposing to her on the beach had entered his mind almost immediately and he'd firmly kept pushing it back.

SOME STUDENTS still on campus sat with their feet in the reflecting pool in front of the library, waiting for their last classes. A part of the architect's sense of whimsy, the pool was dotted with concrete pads, inviting visitors to relax in the water. By May the commons surrounding the pool would be awash with chests of beer, frat house barbecues, and sprawled-out students studying to the beat in their personal ear buds. The massive glass panels that fronted the library's atrium would be slid aside, blurring the line between outdoors and indoors, study and leisure.

The library design was homage to the *Biblioteka Alexandrina* in Egypt. The non-glass surfaces of the atrium entrance were covered in mosaic scenes of Egypt, including an image of the ancient Library of Alexandria on the inner wall. He stepped across mosaic Egyptian gods, pyramids, and the Great Sphinx of Giza on the floor of the atrium as he crossed to the coffee kiosk on the far side.

Maddie stepped up from behind a statue of Isis as he got in line to order. To Keith it was as if the goddess had come to life.

"Dr. Drucker, how nice to meet you here this morning," she beamed at him.

"And you, Dr. Zayne," he responded. "May I get you a coffee?"

"Only if I can buy croissants," said Maddie. Keith turned to the barista and began to order.

"I know," nodded the barista, "a vanilla latte and *doppio* espresso with two almond croissants." He nodded and thought he saw Maddie turn slightly pink. Had they been meeting here that often? They sat companionably in two soft chairs that partially obscured an image of jackal-headed Anubis on the floor as they savored their drinks.

"Short staff meeting this morning?" Keith asked. Maddie sighed.

"Short staff, actually," she said. "Two student assistants decided to start spring break a day early and no one else really wants to be here."

"Can't say I blame them," he said quietly. "Want to slip out early?"

"I wish I could," Maddie said wistfully. "The burden of management, you know." She smiled. "I hope you won't mind working without an assistant today."

"Well, I do have a degree in page-turning," Keith laughed. Researchers were seldom given direct access to materials unless a librarian was assigned to assist them. The high-tech workstations in the Whitfield Rare Books Room—fondly referred to as The Whit—generally assured that researchers never actually touched documents nor were left alone with one. It was a policy that he had embraced with good humor, even though in his capacity as consultant it was not strictly required. He found it much easier to record his electronic notes if he was actually talking to a person instead of just to the digital recorder that hung above the examination tables in the lab. He recorded his impressions of each book and made high-resolution photographs of each page.

When they had finished their coffee, they took the elevator up to The Whit. No one else was in the elevator and Keith felt Maddie graze the back of his hand with hers as they stood silently side-by-side.

The Whit was a secure facility perched atop two dozen massive pillars that jutted up through the floors of the main library. It was connected to the rest of the university library only by way of the stairwells and elevator shafts. It had its own power, plumbing, and environmental controls. They passed the sealed case containing a page of the *Mainz Psalter*—a pristine example of historic book art. *Repro*, Keith thought automatically as he walked past. Maddie disappeared into the security vault while Keith checked his computer case in a locker. A few moments later, Maddie returned with a large volume encased in acid-free archival cardboard. The label showed the name of the collection, work, and acquisition date. He had been looking forward to examining this volume all week, and even though he was anxious to be leaving for a tropical paradise with Maddie in the evening, he was excited about spending the day with his other love.

In the study of *incunabula*—printed works of the 15th century—Keith was a big fish in a very small pond. His thesis and post-doctoral research helped establish the use of spectrographic analysis to accurately date and regionalize early books. Each printer mixed his own inks and the composition was as individual as a fingerprint. The *in situ* spectrographic process was non-destructive, unlike other forms of dating that required a sample scraped from the substrate and dissolved in chemicals.

Much of his career had been spent compiling a database of ink-prints from the printers of the 15th century. Other researchers had added profiles of manuscript inks with some samples as old as the Dead Sea Scrolls.

THE COLLECTION the Whit recently acquired was mostly collector-grade volumes of the 17th century with a few older specimens that would fetch a decent price if offered at auction. Keith was acutely aware that his real reason for being at The Whit was to establish the value of a University asset so the Board could determine what to sell and what to keep. So far, only two museum-grade documents had been discovered. It was sad that so many *incunabula* had been destroyed during the 19th and early 20th centuries and the pages sold individually to collectors, but one page in the collection could be worth as much as the rest of the collection combined.

He placed the box on the work table, put a memory card in the digital camera above the table, and positioned the microphone where he wouldn't bump into it as he was working. He put on a new pair of white cotton gloves and opened the box.

"Specimen SOR187," he spoke into the voice-activated microphone, "listed as the catalog of books in the Monastery of St. Luke of the Mountain near Württemberg Mountain in Germany from the founding of the monastery in 1115 A.D. until its dissolution in 1846." With that, he made the first photographs of the book. "The volume is just 20 millimeters thick, but measures 480 millimeters tall and 330 millimeters wide," Keith continued as he measured the book.

Carthusian monasteries like St. Luke's were devoted to silence and the copying of books. By the middle of the 16th century there was little call for hand-copied books because of the rapid spread of printing, but the monks continued to study and copy works as a means of meditation. The practice continued into the 21st century in some Carthusian monasteries. St. Luke's was burned by local villagers after a mysterious epidemic wiped out nearly its entire population in the mid-1800s. Some of its holdings, however, had already been spirited away and hidden by a private collector before burning. Historians assumed most of the books had been burned, but if this catalog proved genuine, it could at least verify what books had once existed within its cloistered walls.

"The binding is Moroccan leather, in excellent condition," he continued. "That leads me to believe the book was bound or rebound late in the 17th century. It is a utilitarian volume." Keith took close-ups of the tooling, commenting on motifs in the leatherwork. He carefully placed the book on the reading stand to open it and photographed the inside cover. He could be random and playful with Maddie, but he was slow and methodical in his analysis of books. Using a thin plastic spatula and a small suction cup, he carefully lifted the pages to count them. The loose papers of the original manuscript had been gathered with new parchment when the volume was bound so there were a number of blank pages in the back of the book, presumably to make room for additions to the monastery's collection.

"The title page is simply drawn with the name of the monastery and a shield on which is a cypher 4 cross, very similar to some 15th century printer's marks. The motto beneath the symbol is in German and reads 'Wächter des Wortes.' An appropriate motto for a scriptorium that translates to 'Guardians of the Word,'" he said into the microphone. He snapped a close-up photo of the arms.

The handwriting in the manuscript changed every few pages, evidence that the job of keeping the record was passed from one monk to another. It was more of a ledger, recording both the manuscripts acquired and supplies for the scriptorium. Keith rolled the spectrometer to the table and sampled the ink from the opening pages. The database of manuscript inks was not as complete as that of printing inks, but the green vitriol content of the faded ink was consistent with samples from other manuscripts of that era. Both handwriting and ink composition changed over the pages, showing the prevailing styles of the centuries. He was already certain that he would be able to authenticate the volume based on the ink and handwriting samples alone, but it would take several days to transcribe the contents and verify that there were no anomalies recorded in the book. Anthropological evidence was as important as the physical evidence. If it recorded acquisition of a book in the 1100s, for example, that was known not to have been written until the 1200s, the book could not be authenticated. *Well, that's a task that will wait until after spring break*, he thought, smiling to himself.

AS EXCITED and anxious as he was to authenticate this volume, Keith took extra care to make sure he didn't miss anything. When he vouched for a document, it was authoritative. If he screwed one up, his reputation and his income would evaporate. He'd seen it happen. There was no forgiveness in the world of rare books. He carefully photographed each page so he could examine it later on his computer at high magnification.

By mid-afternoon, he had reached records of the 1400s. In this particular section, he read and examined each entry carefully as printed books began to show up in the registry. He shook his head. He was beginning to get tired and thought of the late night he had enjoyed with Maddie. He refocused on the catalog.

The number of hand-copied manuscripts in the world fell off rapidly after the introduction of the printing press until by 1500 the art had all but disappeared. According to the catalog, however, the acquisition of new books for the monastery's scriptorium continued unabated. Keith's attention was caught by the last entry on the page: an acquisition of the Wyrich family Gospels, a printed volume containing only the books of Matthew, Mark, Luke, and John. Both the name and the type of book caused him to pause. Any family name in the Gutenberg ancestry was a cause for investigation, though Wyrich was not that uncommon in this region of Germany. There had not been many Bibles printed that included only the Gospels. This could possibly be the second or third part of a Bible that had been bound in volumes. It would be a new line of investigation for him and he took a close-up photograph of the entry for later study.

He turned the page, dislodging a loose sheet of parchment. It was dangerously near sliding off the table onto the floor when he caught it. At first he assumed the page had come loose from the catalog, but quickly realized that the penmanship was different, the parchment was a higher grade and smaller dimensions, and it contained not a list of books, but what looked like part of a letter. He turned off the voice recorder. He didn't like to record thoughts when something surprised him. What he said was part of the permanent record of his examination. He quickly looked through the rest of the book to see if there were any more loose pages, but there were none.

The letter fragment appeared to be about the same age as the page he was examining. He slid the sheet beneath the spectrometer and verified that the ink, though slightly different in composition from that in the book, was definitely consistent with the formulation of inks of that era. The fragment was written in German rather than Latin, like the catalog, and he restrained himself from reading the letter immediately while he checked for other evidence in the book. If the letter fragment had been sandwiched between the pages since the 17th century, there would be some amount of ink transfer or an indentation on the surrounding pages. But his careful scrutiny showed no sign of either.

Finally, he bent over the fragment with a magnifying glass to translate from the German as he read.

Deep in the Mountain of the Gods, Pharaoh's Children protect the Tree of Knowledge. The Master's Key unlocks the Entrance. The Protectors have entrusted us with Knowledge and Art. The Art is in the Ritual. The Knowledge is hidden in the Black River. In Time they will come together and the Wisdom of the Ages will be revealed.

Keith laid the paper down and returned to the pages of the catalog. He glanced at the security camera and saw the red light on the camera go out. The cameras were on a cycle so that one monitor in the library security room could view the lab rooms sequentially. He took more pictures of the letter and of each surrounding page, trying to capture every detail. He removed the memory card and slipped it back into his wallet. He slowly and deliberately closed the book and slid it back into its protective box. Finally, he sat again with the letter fragment and read it thoroughly.

WHEN A VOICE on the public address system announced that the library would close in ten minutes and would be on limited hours for the next week for spring break, Keith broke from his reverie. It wasn't that unusual for him to work through lunch and breaks without being aware of it. He had noticed Maddie had the same single-minded focus. But for the past hour he had been wrestling with a dilemma.

In 1455, just months before The Bible was finished, Gutenberg's financial partner, Johan Fust, sued him for diverting funds to a secret project. When Gutenberg refused to share the project, the courts awarded the entire Bible-printing venture to Fust and left Gutenberg with nothing but his secret. Members of the Worshipful Society of Type Founders and Alchemists once believed Gutenberg's secret project was a book of alchemical instructions that went beyond the metallurgy of "the Guild," as the society called itself. Contemporary members knew that any book Gutenberg created would be priceless, no matter what it contained. There had been no sign of the mysterious book, though, for 500 years. There was only the evidence of Guild lore that indicated it existed.

Gutenberg founded the Worshipful Society of Typefounders and Alchemists with the blessing of Archbishop Dieter von Isenberg. According to Guild tradition, he had dictated the documents and rituals of the Guild to his successor, the Master Printer Peter Schoeffer. Keith was certain that this letter fragment belonged with other letters in the Guild archives. What's more, it could be a key piece in the search for Gutenberg's secret. *Where is the Black River?* he wondered for the hundredth time this afternoon.

The fragment and the others like it in the Guild archives would command a high price on the open market if people knew what it was. But unless the very secretive Guild revealed the rest of its cache, no one could possibly verify that it was the writing of Peter Schoeffer. The fragment was not listed in the inventory of the collection Keith was examining at the library; it *should not* have been there. Somehow the document must have been stolen from the Guild. How many more pages might be missing? Since there was no record of it, he could simply take the fragment with him and no one would ever know. He could then arrange to return it to the Guild. He glanced at the security camera again and began to measure the amount of time the camera was off curing its cycle. He would have 45 seconds between camera bursts. The camera would be on for 15 seconds. If he put the letter in the box while the camera was on, then slipped it out and into hiding while it was off, he could feasibly walk out of the library with the letter.

Maddie would never understand if she found out. Could he convince her to help him return the letter to the Guild? He'd never met anyone more responsible than Maddie. She would not act without the approval of the library board of directors. And she would certainly never do what he was contemplating.

He silently cleaned his glasses with the back of the cotton glove and pushed them firmly back onto his nose.

He simply couldn't betray Maddie's trust. He pointedly turned his back on the security camera and opened the archival box. He would talk to her about it while they were on vacation and explain the importance of returning the letter to the Guild. It was all he could do. He had the high-resolution images to examine and send to the other masters in the Guild. He slipped the fragment back between the covers of the catalog, and then took the boxed manuscript back to the desk in the silent rare books room. No one was there. It appeared, in fact, as though he was the last one in the library. He hesitated. It would have been so easy.

"Maddie?" he called, forgoing their pledge to use their professional titles in the library.

"In the vault," she called back.

"Do you want me to bring the catalog back to you?"

"No, *Doctor* Drucker," she laughed coming out of the concealed room behind the desk. She quickly glanced around the empty room then leaned across the desk to kiss him lightly on the lips. "If you did that, we'd never get out of here," she whispered. "I'll take it from here. Go get your suitcase and pick me up at my house in two hours. I promise I will be ready and waiting."

"I can't ask for better than that." He smiled and then added, "yet."

"Go!" she commanded. "I've got half an hour of cleanup to do before I can leave."

"I'm on my way," he laughed, backing toward the door. The lock buzzed, letting him open the door and Maddie blew him a kiss. Keith retrieved his laptop case from the locker, looked longingly back at her, and entered the elevator. They would have a long talk in Jamaica.

THE SECURITY guard waiting at the door from the library to the atrium showed no traces of impatience as he smiled at the pretty blonde coed leaving the library and struggling with her stack of books. Keith was thankful the guard didn't have to unlock the door just for him. That had happened often enough in the past eight weeks. The girl was through the door and apparently arguing with a boy in the atrium before Keith reached the exit. The boy was gesturing at the stack of books, but he took half of the stack and left the atrium with the girl in the glow of sunset.

The guard chuckled as he threw the bolts on the left door to lock it. "Yessir, he'll have some spring break," he said mostly to himself as Keith approached.

"Looks like she plans to do a lot of reading, doesn't it, Jackson?" Keith asked.

"Yessir, Dr. Drucker," said the guard. "Expect I'll be seeing you studying those old books upstairs during the break, won't I?"

"We're taking a break for a few days," Keith responded. "No more late nights sneaking out past the guard desk," he laughed.

"If I were you, I'd take that lovely Dr. Zayne to a nice sunny place and not think of books for a long time," Jackson said.

"That's a great idea, Jackson," Keith said answered, thinking only of the promising week ahead of him.

"I knew you were studying more than books," Jackson nodded.

"Well don't let on, will you?" Keith said.

"Not a word, Doctor," Jackson said. "Not a word."

"See you in a week, Jackson." Keith headed out through the atrium as Jackson locked the doors behind him. The two young people were already halfway across the pool on the stepping-stones, the boy balancing the books as the girl fumbled in her purse for her car keys.

HE WAS about twenty steps from the library when the explosion rumbled inside the atrium. He turned back, ears ringing, as the ground reverberated. So help him, he didn't intend his first thought to be for the letter fragment. He had already taken a step back toward the library when he thought of Maddie, still up on the sixth floor.

Keith ran toward the building, but was still a few steps away when a second blast blew him backward. As he fell to the pavement, he saw sparkling slivers of glass from the exploding atrium falling from the sky. Before the first splinter hit, he was unconscious.

TWO

A LIGHT SHONE in Keith's eyes. Something held them open and he couldn't block out the light. He tried to speak, but no sound came out. In fact, there was no sound anywhere. When the light went out, he was alone in silent darkness. He must have slept, but there was no sensation of sleeping.

The light came on. How long had it been? He couldn't see anything. It was just light. He heard muffled noises as if he had cotton stuffed in his ears. The noises—*voices*, he thought—were too remote to understand. He wondered briefly if he had been abducted by aliens. That is what people said. You wake up but can't move or see or hear. It would make a great story if he had been abducted. He would tell Maddie. A prickling sensation all over his body, like he was being stuck by pins, became more intense. Suddenly sharp pains stabbed at his face and chest. In a burst of awareness, he remembered being knocked down by the blast and the million shards of glass coming toward him. He could feel them hitting his body and spasmed. There was more urgency in the noises. Then the light and sound faded.

HE COULD hear a soft rustle punctuated by beeps from a machine. Hospital, he thought. The bitter smell of iodine filled his nose. He opened his eyes. Eye. One seemed glued shut. The soft light seemed farther away and he registered vague shapes. He needed his glasses. A shadow moved nearby and a blurry figure approach his bed.

"Maddie," he croaked. He could scarcely hear himself. It wasn't Maddie, but he could almost focus on the face, one feature at a time, as it leaned near. The lips moved and he strained to hear through the feeling of cotton in his ears. *Doctor.* The man came into his focal range. He heard a whisper of sound.

"Welcome back, Dr. Drucker. You've had quite a time of it. You may not be able to hear well right now, but don't let that worry you. Your hearing is returning gradually. It may take a while."

"Maddie," Keith repeated.

"The woman who comes and sits by your bed all day?" the doctor said. "I'm sure she'll be back in the morning." He reached up to adjust the I.V. drip. "We're giving you liquids and nourishment intravenously, and keeping you on painkillers to help you rest. The best thing you can do right now is sleep." In seconds, the darkness returned.

THERE WAS a faraway murmur that he slowly realized was voices. He turned his head toward the sound and opened the eye that he could. Only Maddie could have that color hair, even though he couldn't see her clearly. She was standing in the doorway talking to a man who, though not in focus, had the light hair and bronzed skin of someone who spent too much time in a tanning booth. The man gestured at him. Maddie turned toward Keith and the man walked away.

"Keith! You're awake!" Maddie exclaimed rushing toward him. *She's using her library voice,* he thought. He no more than thought it than it seemed insanely funny. The sound that came out when he laughed, though, was more like he was choking.

"Do you need something?" she asked, drawing closer. "I'll call the doctor." Her voice became louder as she got nearer and Keith remembered the doctor saying his hearing would improve.

"Maddie. You're okay," he managed to say. He was overwhelmed. A tear stung his right cheek. He had dreamed in this most recent sleep; books exploded around Maddie and as the two of them tried to gather up all the pages, she turned into notes from a loose-leaf binder that scattered in the wind. Seeing her was such a relief he couldn't care about his own injuries. He was so afraid he had lost her.

"I'm fine," Maddie said as she leaned in to kiss him lightly on the lips. He winced involuntarily. "I don't know how to touch you; you've got so many little cuts."

"What happened?" he pointed at a nearby water glass with the hand that wasn't connected to a tube and saw that even this hand was bandaged.

"Someone blew up the front of the library," Maddie said as she held the straw to his lips. It hurt a little to suck, but the liquid felt good once it was in his mouth.

"You're okay?" he said, his voice gaining some clarity with the moisture in his mouth.

"It would take a lot more than that to bring down The Whit," she laughed. "I was stuck in the vault for six hours before they overrode the lock-down controls. I was frantic trying to get information about you. There was no smoke or it would have flooded the vault with inert gas. Remind me to find out how long the oxygen tanks will support a person if that happens."

"You're okay," he repeated, reaching toward her.

She stroked his hair gently. Even that hurt a little, but it was worth it just to know she was touching him. "I'm okay and I'm babbling. I was so worried about you, I've been almost insane. You could have been killed."

"You were in there."

"My hero," she said. "Oh God, Keith, I think I'm falling in love with you." It was the first time she had said it aloud and he let the feeling wash over him. He knew he was in love.

"Okay."

"Yes," Maddie affirmed. "Very okay."

"How long?" he asked. "What day is it?"

"It's Monday," Maddie said. "Three days."

"We should be in Jamaica," Keith sighed.

MADDIE WAS already in the chair by his bed when he awoke the next day. His eye felt less filmy, but he still didn't have his glasses to see clearly. The left eye was still bandaged. A larger shard of flying glass had broken that lens of his glasses and pierced the cornea. He would find out today if it was healing. The right lens had actually protected the other eye. He was very lucky, they told him. If he had been in the atrium where the large chunks of glass had fallen, he would certainly have been killed. As it was, he had been hit by the tiny bits of glass that had flown farthest, many of which pierced his clothing and cut his face. The doctors had gone over every inch of his body and done MRI scans to be sure they had removed all the fragments.

The morning and the eye exam passed slowly, but Keith was able to engage more fully. Maddie brought his spare glasses from his apartment and he forced them over the bandages so he could see clearly out of his one good eye. The wounds would itch as they healed, the doctor said, but he was no longer in any serious danger. The eye would take a week or two to heal enough to check his vision thoroughly as the glass had pierced the vitreous humor. In most instances that type of injury healed, but he would need a new corrective prescription. He was able to hear better, but had to concentrate fully to catch everything. Maddie helped bathe his face and it was worth the discomfort to have her kiss his lips once the iodine was completely washed away.

He looked around his hospital room. It was large and private. In fact, he'd almost call it comfortable if it weren't for his injuries. He was pretty sure his meager health insurance wouldn't cover this kind of treatment and had to wonder why he wasn't in a dormitory with half a dozen old men waiting to die.

"I've got to get out of here before it bankrupts me," he said. "Unless the University is paying for my stay?" he added hopefully.

"Actually," Maddie hesitated. "Derek's covered all the expenses."

"Who is Derek?" Keith asked.

"He was here when you woke up yesterday, but he didn't stay around long enough to be introduced," Maddie said.

"So who is he?"

"Derek Zayne, wealthy American playboy and benefactor to those in need," she said lightly.

"Your brother?"

"No, unfortunately," Maddie sighed. "He's my ex. He's a jerk, but a very wealthy jerk who enjoys spreading it around. Somehow he always shows up when I'm... Well, he thinks his money will..." Keith looked at Maddie with a growing unease. He knew she had been married once, but didn't know the ex was still in the picture.

"Your ex is paying for my hospital stay?" he asked, in amazement. "All the more reason to get out of here. What does he expect you to do because he helped me?"

"There's nothing to worry about on that account," Maddie said, seeing the expression on Keith's face. "I divorced Derek over irreconcilable differences, and she's still around."

"Tell me about it," he said, not completely sure that he wanted to know, but feeling compelled to find out.

"It was either divorce him or kill him," Maddie said. "He was a rich, younger man, my brother's age, who swept me off my feet with his charm, wit, and generosity. It wasn't until after we were married that I discovered he possessed two traits that I couldn't tolerate."

"Those were?"

"In spite of his generosity, he is possessive. He couldn't understand that I could spend a day in a library just being with books, and I couldn't make myself be interested in the computers that were the most important thing to him," Maddie said.

"And the other?"

"He likes other women." Keith cringed. It served the guy right to lose Maddie then.

20

"I still don't like the idea of him paying for my hospital stay. I don't need a penthouse suite," he stated as he sat upright. That was a task that was still exhausting. Maddie moved to support him. Her arm around his back felt wonderful. It was bruised but not cut. The glass had all hit him from the front. He turned toward her slightly and the support turned to an embrace as they kissed passionately, ignoring his raw lips.

In the midst of this a nurse entered the room and coughed politely to announce her presence.

"You have a visitor, Mr. Drucker," she said. "I mean another visitor." Keith turned to see a dark-haired, mustachioed man materialize from behind the nurse. He strode across the room with authority and nodded to Keith without offering to shake hands.

"Keith Drucker?" the man said. "I am Special Agent Fry of Homeland Security." He produced a badge to identify himself.

"Pleased to meet you," Keith said. Maddie arranged pillows behind him so he could continue to sit up and look at the Agent more easily.

"And you are Mrs. Drucker?" the agent turned to Maddie.

"Oh. No. I'm not!" Maddie said, a little too emphatically. She was flustered by the assumption. "I'm Madeline Zayne. We're colleagues," she said recovering herself. Keith could not help but notice she had turned bright red. He chuckled to himself.

"Oh, yes," the agent said. "The librarian who was stuck on the sixth floor. Sorry. I'm still getting up to speed. They thought this was some kind of student protest at first but nothing turned up, so the police called the Feds and the Feds called other Feds and eventually somebody called me."

"I always wondered how that worked," Keith mumbled.

"Oh, if you'd been killed we would have been called in much sooner, but injury and property damage don't often get kicked up the ladder," Fry said.

"What gives us the honor?" Keith asked.

Agent Fry ignored the sarcastic question. "I've been talking to people for the past couple of days, but the hospital kept putting me off. They say you are pretty coherent now. Is that so?" he asked.

"I guess so," Keith said. "They've still got me on painkillers with a warning not to operate heavy equipment or sign any contracts, but I'm not taking the heavy sleep drugs they had me on. Of course I'll answer any questions about this that I can."

"I'm noting that medication may affect your memory or recall of details," Fry said as he wrote in his notebook. "That way if a moment of clarity strikes you in the future you will be able to change your statement without repercussion."

"Is this a deposition?"

"No, just questions," Fry answered. "But the government frowns on inaccurate information. It's for both of our protection." Keith looked at the agent. *It must have been hard for him to get a job in Homeland Security with so much suspicion of anyone who looked vaguely Arab*, he thought. He'd known a colleague from Jordan who'd been detained for hours at an airport on suspicions that were never really made clear. Maybe Homeland Security was a little more diligent about examining the reports of agents of Middle Eastern descent.

"You were the most seriously injured person in the attack, though the security guard broke an arm and had a concussion. I stopped to see him earlier and have to say he wasn't getting the same kind of care that you were when I came in," Fry said, smiling slightly. He was obviously trying his best to put them at ease, but Maddie blushed again.

"Perhaps you could start by explaining your relationship?" Agent Fry said.

"We're colleagues, and friends," Keith rescued Maddie. "Dating," he continued when Agent Fry raised an eyebrow.

"You were working together just before the blast?"

"In the same area of the library," Maddie said. "I was still putting things in the vault when Keith left."

"I read that in your statement to the police. Why didn't you wait and leave together?" he asked Keith.

"We haven't exactly told anyone at the library that we're dating," Keith explained. "We always leave separately."

"Fair enough. I understand how office romances can become a subject of gossip." Agent Fry jotted a note and then returned his attention to Keith. "So, no one knows that you are dating and we can't write this off to a fit of jealousy?"

"I don't think so," Keith said. He glanced at Maddie and thought of her mysterious ex. She was vigorously shaking her head.

"Who would want to kill you then?" the agent asked. Keith was startled into momentary confusion. Fry abruptly switched from the office romance tact and was now dead serious. He waited for a reply.

"No one," Keith answered, nonplussed. "Why would anyone want to kill me?"

"Exactly," said the agent. "Who are your enemies?"

"Agent Fry, I examine and authenticate old books for a living. There are only a few dozen people in the world who even care. Certainly there is no one who would consider my work controversial unless I've proven a valuable family heirloom to be a fraud someplace along the line. Most of my work is with libraries and museums. There aren't many private collectors who would get into the picture unless they are selling or donating to a library."

"Like the work you are doing now?" Agent Fry asked.

"Not even that," Keith said. "The collection in The Whit was a bequest to the University. I'm here to put a value on it, yes, but it won't affect the family one way or another. The bequest was made with no strings and no family claims."

"What about your classes?"

"As a guest lecturer, I have one class that meets three times a week," Keith explained. "It is one of a half-dozen that fulfill the University's required Fine Arts elective credit. Most of my 200 students figure it is an easy way to improve their grade point average."

"I spoke to your teaching assistant, so I'm aware of the subject matter. Are you always confrontational in your classes?" Fry pressed. Keith didn't comprehend what the agent was talking about. "Your assistant mentioned a question about the ethics of authenticating documents that might contradict religious teachings." Keith remembered the conversation and nodded.

"I think my response was that I only deal with the authenticity of the document, not with the value of its content," Keith said.

"That's all?"

"It was a pretty minor question and near the end of class."

"Miss Baker quoted you somewhat differently," Fry responded. Looking at his notes, he read, "Dr. Drucker responded by saying that the mythology of one religion was pretty much the same as any other."

"That sounds like something I would say," Keith chuckled. "These kids take themselves so seriously they can't approach artifacts objectively. They need to get past individual beliefs to understand the anthropology of printing."

"And that statement doesn't sound inflammatory to you?" Agent Fry asked.

"Not enough to merit bombing a library. And certainly there would be easier ways to kill me." Keith shook his head. It was absurd. The agent scratched his head.

"Tell me exactly what you remember," Agent Fry instructed Keith.

"I was hurrying to the exit before Jackson—the security guard—locked the door. He wanted to know if we'd be working over the holiday and I said no. I left. About 30 feet from the library, just before I crossed the reflecting pool I felt an explosion. I turned and started back. Then there was a second explosion, closer. It knocked me to the ground and I lost consciousness," Keith said. He had known he would have to tell the story sooner or later, but even in its abbreviated form it brought back the shock and pain in a flood.

"You knew it was an explosion?"

"No. Not at first. I think I filled that detail in from what I've heard."

"Why did you turn to go back?"

"The books… Maddie was still in there," Keith said. He realized it sounded ridiculous that he had thought of the books in the library.

"Did you see anyone else?"

"No. Yes. There was a student who checked out a bunch of books right before I left. Jackson commented that her boyfriend didn't look too happy as they left and I said it looked like she was planning to spend the break reading. They were just on the other side of the reflecting pool when the explosion or whatever went off." Fry opened a brown envelope and produced a grainy black and white photograph. The face of the woman was hidden under the bill of a baseball cap, but the long, light hair was unmistakable.

"Recognize her?" Fry asked.

"Not really," Keith said. "I mean that's the woman I saw leave the library ahead of me, but I never got a look at her face. She walked out and a boy met her in the atrium. I only saw his back. He's shorter than her and thin. They were a few yards ahead of me. They paused to juggle the books as she dug for her car keys, but when the boom hit I turned away from them, so I don't know what happened to them then."

"You saw car keys?"

"They were a good 50 feet away, so I can't swear it was car keys. What else do you dig in your purse for as you are walking toward the parking lot?" Keith paused, suddenly getting the implication of the action. "You don't think…" Fry waved off the partial question.

"A group, or individual, has anonymously and indirectly claimed responsibility for the blast," the agent said bluntly. "It's no one that's been on our radar before and I don't think they formed just to attack you, but you may have inadvertently given them a flashpoint. A note was posted on several Internet forums along with a poor digital photo—probably from a cell phone—of the library just moments after the explosion. But the picture is not from the same perspective as the couple you describe. There had to be another person there."

He produced a second photo. It showed the dust still rising from the library atrium. Keith shook his head.

"I didn't see anyone else."

The Agent handed Maddie a page from the envelope and she held it in front of Keith so he could read it. As they examined the note, Fry absently twisted the ring on his finger. Keith caught the movement, but was too intrigued by the note to pay attention to the agent.

Not all words are equal. There is only one true Tree of Knowledge guarded by holy angels. No key will unlock its secret for the unworthy. Those who seek truth within the chamber of lies face destruction.

Keith kept his expression carefully neutral as he looked up at Agent Fry.

"This sounds vaguely like a threat against all libraries," Keith said.

"Yes," said the agent. "It wouldn't take too many explosions like this to get people to start avoiding libraries."

"You can track things like this, right?" Maddie asked, handing back the note. "Find out who sent it?"

"The messages were posted from at least a dozen different public access computers around the world. Mostly—no doubt with a sense of irony—in libraries," remarked Agent Fry, looking at her intently.

"They have people in a dozen different cities?" Maddie exclaimed.

"Each one with a major library in it," Fry affirmed. "At this time we don't have any good leads other than to stake out the libraries. It could be a new extreme religious splinter group, but the message doesn't mention a specific religion."

"The Tree of Knowledge figures prominently in a number of religious mythologies, and in a number of different forms," Keith said quietly. His mind had already jumped back to the letter fragment he found in the monastery catalog, but he didn't want to mention that. No one else could possibly know about it.

"You don't think it refers to the Garden of Eden?" the agent asked.

"That is the Tree of the Knowledge of Good and Evil," Keith responded. "The Tree of Knowledge is often a symbol representing revelation as opposed to the kind of knowledge that comes from education and study."

Fry nodded and snapped his notepad shut and shoved it in a pocket. "I appreciate your help." He handed each a business card. "Offhand, I'd say you should be careful. It's not impossible that you could be a target rather than an accidental casualty. If you think of anything that might help, please give me a call. Especially if you come up with a possible next target before it gets blown up. Get well soon, Mr. Drucker. Ms. Zayne," he concluded nodding to her. Then he turned and left the room. They could hear the fading sound of his footsteps.

"WOW!" MADDIE SAID into the silence that descended on the room in the agent's absence.

Keith looked at her pensively through his good eye. "Wow indeed. Can you still get into The Whit?" he asked, startling Maddie.

"Yes. Access is restricted, but I have clearance to do maintenance and check systems," Maddie said. "Why?"

"I need you to check out a book before we leave." He threw his bedclothes off and struggled upright.

"Wait. Leave?" Maddie exclaimed.

"I have to get out of here," Keith said. "Get me my clothes, will you please?"

"Keith, you can't just get up and leave a hospital," Maddie said. "Let me call the nurse."

"I don't think we're safe here," Keith said. "I know this sounds insane, but I'm thinking clearly. We need to go see a printer."

"Inkjet or laser?" Maddie wasn't moving. Keith was getting desperate, but he didn't dare to let emotion take control. He needed Maddie to believe him.

"Please." He looked at her pleadingly. "I'll check out properly. If I tell them you will take care of me, there shouldn't be a problem. I just have to ask you to trust me. And give me my clothes." Maddie hesitated a moment longer then turned away. Keith was afraid he had lost, but she walked to his closet and pulled out a tattered jacket and pair of pants.

"I don't think you want to put on what you wore in," Maddie said. "There's probably still glass stuck in the shreds."

"I need something."

"I figured you would eventually, so I picked up your suitcase at the apartment when I got your glasses. You were all packed for a trip, remember?" Maddie asked. She hung the clothes and retrieved Keith's suitcase. He noted that his computer case was also there.

"I'd rather be on that beach with you than sitting here," he said.

"You can't think we're going to Jamaica now," Maddie stated flatly. "You're hardly fit."

"No," Keith responded. "But I really want you to come with me, if you will."

"I'm certainly not letting you out of my sight," she said. "Not now."

THREE

CHECKING OUT OF the hospital was a pain. Keith overrode the doctor's recommendation of a few more days' hospital bed rest. A nurse wrote detailed instructions for Maddie regarding Keith's medication and dressings. The doctor admonished him to be back in a week for a checkup and Keith made the appointment, dutifully promising to be careful to avoid infections. *On that score, I'm safer outside the hospital,* he thought. Nonetheless, his body complained about simply getting out of bed to dress.

Maddie left to get her suitcase and car. Keith was so tired from arguing with his doctor that when she got back to the hospital he acquiesced to being wheeled out in a chair.

As they approached the library, he could see the wrecked atrium across the commons, surrounded now by a chain-link fence. Maddie circled to the parking garage beneath the building, showed her employee ID to the new security guard at the entrance, and parked near the elevator.

"Okay, Mr. Man of Mystery," she said. "What book would you like me to check out for your vacation reading?" When he told her, she looked at him in disbelief. "You've got to be kidding! When you said 'check out a book,' I thought you were serious. I can't check books out of the rare books collection."

"Sign it out as a temporary transfer to the Gutenberg Museum in Mainz, Germany for analysis," he responded. "I know you can do that. Fill out the paperwork for transfer to Dr. Rolf Schneider, Special Collections Curator."

"But there's no shipping available from here this week. I'll have to arrange a pickup."

"I want to show it to you before we ship it," Keith said. "I'd even like to take you there to deliver it in person if we can arrange it." She sat staring at him, and he was compelled to continue. "I don't think it was a coincidence that the blast came right after I looked at that book. I think it was meant to send us a message. It sounds so stupidly cloak and dagger that I can't believe I'm asking you to do this, but I promise that when we get to California I'll be able to explain everything. We'll keep the book safe and if you disagree when you see what I'm talking about, we'll bring it straight back here."

"California?"

Keith nodded.

"You live in California. You're taking me home?"

He nodded again.

"We'll need airplane tickets, and I'm not sure I'm packed right for California. Why don't we go to my place for now and we'll make reservations. You can explain what this is all about when we're relaxed," Maddie suggested.

"Darling, I need to go home. I bought tickets on-line in the hospital while I was waiting to get released. All we need to do is check-in." He paused, almost exhausted. He knew that if she pressed to wait until tomorrow he wouldn't resist, but he made one last plea. "Please. Come with me to California where we'll be safe and have time to figure out what is really going on. I can't explain how important it is. The flight is in just over two hours."

Maddie sat in the car with her hands on the steering wheel looking straight ahead. He was afraid he'd gone too far and realized how new their relationship really was.

"I guess I can live with that," she said. She opened her door and he reached for the handle on his own.

"Stay in the car, Keith," Maddie said, laying a hand on his shoulder. "I won't be long and you still need the rest." He was asleep before she was out of sight.

SHE NUDGED HIM AWAKE in the airport parking ramp.

"Do you need me to get you a chair?" she asked gently. Keith shook himself fully awake. He breathed deeply, dispelling his disorientation.

"I can walk now," he said. "But a chair would get us through security more quickly." They entered the concourse and Maddie flagged down a porter and explained their situation. In minutes, Keith was in a wheelchair. They checked in at a kiosk and went directly to security. As he had predicted they were guided to a special access line and were escorted by the porter to the gate.

"What's in California besides Disneyland? And your home," Maddie asked when they were settled. "I think I deserve to know what's really up."

"I mentioned seeing a printer, didn't I? My grandfather lives with me—or I should say I live with him. He's my number one mentor on book arts and he's pretty worried about me just now. He's only had one call from me since I was injured."

"But…" Maddie's cell phone rang, cutting off the question she was about to ask. She glanced at the caller ID and answered immediately. "Hi, Joey." There was a moment's pause then she began to explain. "I'm sorry, I completely forgot. I'm with Keith and we're picking up our vacation. No. California at the moment. A few days. I'll let you know. Don't worry so much. We'll be fine. I'll call when we get back. Bye." She closed the phone and looked at Keith who was watching with a bemused expression on his face, refusing to ask the question that was hanging over his head.

"Okay," she said. "*That* was my brother. He's a worry-wart. He flew in from Japan the day after the explosion to make sure I was all right. I was supposed to meet him for dinner tonight and I completely forgot to call him."

"I didn't know you have a brother," Keith said. "All the mysterious men in your life."

"He's six years younger than I am," she said. "It's always been me worrying about and taking care of him. Apparently he thinks he needs to return the favor now. Since I'm off with you, he'll probably hit the road again and I'll hear from him from India or Africa or Australia."

"What does he do?"

"He's linguist and freelance interpreter. He speaks half a dozen languages, including three Middle Eastern dialects and Japanese. Sometimes he does work for the State Department," Maddie said proudly. She raised the corner of her mouth in that one-sided smile Keith loved. "I think he's a spy, but I don't know for whom. He was certain foreign terrorists had targeted me because of him."

"I hope I get to meet him sometime," Keith answered.

"We'll see how meeting your family goes, first," she laughed.

"Mr. Drucker," a gate agent said as she came up to him. "We can get you on board now." Keith was rolled down the jetway with Maddie in tow and they settled into their first class seats, Keith's big splurge for their getaway.

IT WAS NEARLY MIDNIGHT by the time they rented a car and Maddie drove into the California desert. They had talked more on the plane, but as Maddie sipped a glass of complimentary champagne, Keith's painkillers dragged him down into sleep again. When they landed, however, he was alert and able to make further arrangements.

He used the GPS and police reports on his computer to warn them of speed traps. On this stretch of almost-deserted highway, 80 was just fast enough not to be passed by most eighteen-wheelers but slow enough to let real speeders take the heat if there were police. Once they were passed by a State trooper cruising in the left lane.

"Tell me about your grandfather so I know what to expect," Maddie suggested as they cruised down the highway. Keith had to agree. It was only fair that he prepare her a little, and talking would keep them both awake for their midnight drive.

"I didn't see him from the time I was 10 until I was 18," Keith answered. "My mother blamed him for my father's death—it was a printing accident—and just didn't make him welcome. I think he blamed himself, too. We wrote to each other regularly, but I was really disappointed when he didn't show up for my high school graduation."

"You can get killed in a printing accident?" Maddie asked.

"He got caught in a web press at the newspaper. He'd taken over Grandfather's job when he retired."

"How awful."

"Mom thought the whole printing industry was evil after that. I was insatiably attracted to it, though. When I graduated, Mom said she had something for me. She was a little embarrassed, but she gave me an envelope addressed to me in my grandfather's handwriting. She said she'd held it until after graduation, but knew I'd be going now. My grandfather had sent me a plane ticket and a hundred dollars. I kissed my mom on the cheek and went to my room to pack."

"How far south does California go?" Maddie asked. It appeared they were headed for the border. "Or are we just eloping to Mexico?"

"Hmmm… Now that's not a bad idea, but I'd like you to meet my family before you jump into things. You may not want to marry me when you see the rest of the gene-pool."

"You said that awfully easily," Maddie whispered quietly. He could see the color rising in her cheeks.

"We've not had much time lately to just be together," Keith answered laying his bandaged left hand on her leg. "But I've thought about the possibility ever since we met."

"Are you trying to scare me?"

"You've survived a bombing, three days by my hospital bed, and a mad dash across the country and into the desert," he said. "Is there something I could do to scare you?"

"Okay, seriously," she said abruptly. "Why your grandfather?"

"It's the ink in his veins," Keith responded. "In our line of work, you and I think of all the scholarly, objective evidence. He thinks of the art and craft and the possibilities. Long before I started my library science degree or applied new technology to the dating of inks, he was able to tell genuine *incunabula* from fake, identify what printing house a work came from, and even the type of press it was printed on. He can mix ink that will exactly mimic any known formulation. And even now—he's in his eighties—he can print some of the finest works you've ever seen. You might not even be able to tell the difference between his and the originals."

"Wait," Maddie interjected. "You mean he's a forger?"

"It was an art form of its own in the 15th and 16th centuries," Keith said calmly. "Usually forgery has to do with handwork, though; you know—paintings and signatures. When it's done with a printing press they call it counterfeiting."

"Your grandfather prints money?" Maddie asked in disbelief.

"No. Never," Keith declared. "He specializes in documents. It's something he's always been interested in. Mostly he prints things that no one cares about. He just does it to experience the feeling of creating a great piece of art. And he has a legitimate business of printing wedding invitations and graduation announcements—in case we ever need that sort of thing."

"Why were you in such a rush to get there?"

"There is a letter," he said carefully. "Actually just a fragment. I found it in the manuscript you so kindly checked out of the library for me."

"There's no listing of a letter fragment in the inventory."

"Precisely," Keith said.

"What does it have to do with your grandfather?"

"Do you remember the message that detective showed us?"

"I didn't memorize it, but I recall it pretty well," Maddie answered.

"I wrote down as much as I could remember while I was waiting to get out of the hospital," Keith said. "I'm pretty sure I got most of it." He pulled a slip of paper from his shirt pocket. "There is one true Tree of Knowledge guarded by angels. No key will unlock its secret for the unworthy. If you seek truth in the chamber of lies, you risk your life," he read. "It's not exact, but I think I got the important parts."

"I don't think it was quite so personal at the end," Maddie said, "but I agree that's the gist of it."

"There are three references to the same imagery in the letter fragment in that book you borrowed," Keith said. "The Tree of Knowledge, its guardians, and the key to unlock the secret. It just doesn't feel like the timing of me finding the letter, the explosion, and the terrorist note could be coincidental."

"Why didn't you tell the detective that?" Maddie asked. Keith noted that she accelerated slightly and her grip on the steering wheel tightened. Keith carefully phrased what he had to say next.

"If my grandfather confirms that the letter is what I think it is, we don't want it in the hands of Homeland Security," Keith said. "We'll all look at it when we get there, but I am absolutely positive it doesn't belong in the collection where it was found. Someone put it there deliberately."

"And you think that same someone bombed the library or that it was an enemy of that someone?" Maddie asked.

"Yes."

"That was an either-or question."

"There might be other options as well, but I'm sure they are connected in some way," Keith answered. "When I found the letter, I realized it was something important, but I put it back in the manuscript so we could talk about it when we were on our vacation. I thought we would be able to figure out together what to do. The blast and drugs drove the idea out of my head until the detective showed us the message.

If my assessment is correct, the fragment was stolen from another collection. And that brings Granddad into it, but not Homeland Security."

Maddie turned on the radio and set it to scan until she found a jazz station. Then she turned the volume up. Keith took the signal that she needed a break from this conversation and absently examined the damage to his computer case with the fingers of his unbandaged hand. He was pricked by something sharp and pulled a glass shard almost as big as the tip of his finger out of the outside pocket of the case. He carefully rolled it around in his hand as an idea came to him. Then he dropped it into his shirt pocket.

MADDIE FOLLOWED KEITH'S DIRECTIONS to what looked like a derelict shack in the devil's backyard nearly two hours later. They had returned to conversation but not about the letter. No cars passed them after they turned off the main highway half an hour before. They traveled deeper into the Colorado Desert under Superstition Mountain. Strange to think of a desert in California being named the Colorado Desert, but the entire region south of the Salton Sea bore that name, including the military reservation.

The shack looked deserted in the quiet darkness when they pulled into the yard. No animals scrambled through the dust that followed them to a stop, and no dogs barked in the distance. Once the car was turned off, the heavy air was still and silent. The shack huddled under the edge of a cliff and only the rusting pickup truck gave the impression that it might be inhabited.

Keith's grandfather burst through the screen door, slamming it back against the siding so that the house seemed to shake. Keith glanced at Maddie, who hung back, but when the old man wrapped Keith in a gentle embrace, he disappeared into his taller grandfather's arms. As soon as the old man released Keith, he swept up Maddie into the same hug.

"So this is the one?" his grandfather asked. "A new flower blooming in the desert! Welcome, Madeline. And thank you for delivering my boy home where I can take care of him properly."

"Thank you," Maddie said, then unable to stop herself she continued, "You certainly live a long way away from things."

The old man's eyes lit up as he grinned.

"You didn't tell her a thing, did you?" he asked.

"Just that I was coming home. I wouldn't spoil your surprise, Granddad," Keith laughed.

"What surprise?" Maddie asked, perplexed. The two men laughed.

"Well, let's get your things and go inside where it's warm," Granddad invited. "Tomorrow it will be close to 90 degrees out here, but nights still get pretty cold."

"Thank you Mr. Drucker," she said politely. "I can manage the bags."

"Now we won't have any of that," he answered. "You just call me Frank. I won't be a Mr. Drucker in the presence of a Dr. Drucker. He laughed as he grabbed both suitcases from the car. Maddie picked up Keith's computer and Frank ushered the two through the screen door.

The room they entered was stuffy with two wooden chairs and a table facing the door. It ran the short length of the shack and was only about eight feet deep. Frank scarcely paused in the room as he swept aside a curtain exposing a hidden doorway and Keith led the way into the real house. Once through, Frank closed a solid door behind them.

Maddie caught her breath. Though not opulent, the living room they were now in was warm and comfortable. A few pieces of inviting furniture were placed near the gas fireplace and a dining table was set for three.

"This is beautiful!" Maddie exclaimed.

"Not such an old hermit as you might think," Frank said, turning off the television. Maddie looked around at the shelves of books in the soft lighting. She realized there were no windows in the room, but illumination came from lights in the cove of the ceiling.

"You're underground!" she exclaimed, suddenly realizing what it meant. "Your house is built into the rock."

"Mostly right," Keith said. "Actually it's built in a cave. Granddad managed to cover the entire entrance with the shack after he built his house inside."

"Took a bit of engineering to make sure I had fresh water, electricity, and plumbing, I'll tell you," Frank beamed. "But I had help. Trickiest part was getting a television signal."

"There's a satellite dish up on the top of the cliff with the cable running down concealed in the rocks," Keith explained. It was obvious that he was as proud of the engineering as his grandfather was.

"Let me show you to your room, Madeline," Frank said. "Keith can sleep out here on the sofa. I want to take a look at those dressings."

"It's okay," Maddie said. "I don't mind sharing."

"Now see here," Frank said, "I don't have any old fashioned notions about couples who aren't married. But in my home, no young woman is going to be brought thirty miles out into the desert and forced to share a room with any man. If you choose to invite him in, that's your business; but the room is yours."

Maddie smiled and gave Frank a hug. "Thank you," she said. "Now, let's get Keith a pain pill and into my bed. I think we're both exhausted." Frank turned to Keith.

"How you ever got this lucky…" he mumbled.

FOUR

"IT'S YOUR JOB to know where she is, Joey. How goddamned hard can it be to keep track of a librarian?"

"She's somewhere in California," Yousef answered. The imposing frame of his former brother-in-law towered over him and it made him nervous. "She's my sister. She doesn't tell me everything."

"And you couldn't follow her?"

"I figured I could track her cell phone later, but she's off the grid. She must have shut it off for the flight and never turned it back on. You know how she is." Yousef was getting tired of the role of being Derek's watchdog over his sister. Of course he'd wanted to be close to her after the explosion, but it irritated him every time Derek asked for information about her.

He couldn't remember what had drawn them together in college in the first place, and regretted a little having ever introduced Derek and Maddie. Derek was everything Yousef was not—tall, tan, muscular, and rich—a man who took pride in his body and expected everyone else to admire it. Yousef was short and slight. His father's genes had left him light-skinned with a spray of freckles across his nose. Sometimes he wished he looked more Persian like his mother. It would fit his name better.

Derek had been a year ahead of Yousef in college and had all but adopted him the first week of school. If Yousef had difficulty with physics, Derek tutored him. In exchange Yousef helped Derek with Latin. When Yousef's computer was stolen, Derek bought him a new laptop, much better than the desktop model that was stolen. He said he did it because he *could* do it and that Yousef should never think of the giver, but focus on what the gift would enable Yousef to contribute to humanity one day. It made Yousef focus on his studies and even strive to understand the programming that engaged Derek. It was all for the greater good of humanity. Somehow, that seemed to have changed.

Yousef wasn't the only student to benefit from Derek's generosity. Many people who had received something from Derek, though, were shunned by him in a few months. They seemed to feel that they could go back for whatever they wanted whenever they wanted. Yousef never presumed on Derek's generosity and that seemed to please Derek immensely. When Yousef introduced Derek to his sister, it had cemented a relationship that far outlasted the short marriage.

"She was traveling with Keith Drucker."

"That dude is like a lightning rod for trouble," Derek answered. "How can your sister's boyfriend be the only one hurt in an explosion that took off the entire front of the library? She could get killed hanging around him."

"She likes him. He's a nice guy." Yousef defended Keith, even though they had never met.

"That didn't keep him from sleeping with my wife," Derek muttered.

"Ex-wife," Yousef corrected. "You're divorced."

"Yeah, whatever" Derek said, tapping keys on his computer. "Okay, they're near El Centro, California."

"How do you know?"

"It isn't what you know, it's who you know that counts," Derek said. "I still have some sources that you don't."

"Why bother to have me follow her?"

"I want you near her."

"Now?"

"No. It would be too suspicious if she walked down the street in Almost-Mexico, California and saw her brother coming toward her," Derek said. "There must be some spa out there that they went to for the guy's health." Derek poured himself a drink, but didn't bother to invite Yousef to join him. His mother's aversion to alcohol had rubbed off on Yousef and he never touched it. But as Derek drank, Yousef scanned the room, looking for any sign that they were being watched. *It's Derek's office. Of course we're being watched,* Yousef thought. *That's what Derek does.*

"Remember playing 'gossip' back in college?" Derek asked. Yousef nodded. It was Derek's game, but Yousef had discovered that he was quite good at it. They collected names of people, places, and activities. On the weekend they drew one of each. "Charles Crawford scored in Hartford," could be a sentence. The task would be for each to find the right place to plant the gossip in such a way that it would become an accepted fact by the next weekend. If the gossip was traced back to the originator, however, the game was over. Permanently.

The trick, Yousef discovered immediately, was not to be malicious. There were multiple definitions of the word "scored," for example. Scored a point in a game, scored with a girl, scored some pot, scored on a test, scored a sheet of paper. If Yousef chose the right combination of meanings, the subject might pick up the gossip himself and begin to believe it.

"The kids are all clumsy today," Derek continued. "They batter each other on Facebook and text messages until no one believes anything or someone kills herself. Either way, everyone knows who is responsible. When we work our magic, we have to make sure no one knows it's us casting the spell."

"I don't play anymore," Yousef said.

"Yeah. That's too bad," Derek said. "You were the best. So you just keep track of the pieces and I'll play the game. Keep your phone on and watch for your sister to come back on the grid. There's nothing interesting in California. She'll be safe there. But I want to be the first one to know when she moves. Tell Sophie. I want the two of you ready to go wherever they head next. I'm willing to give them a couple of days, but the clock is ticking now and we need another demonstration soon. We'll take the jet if we need to." Yousef nodded his head and turned to leave. "Don't worry, Little Brother. I haven't forgotten my promise, and neither should you. We keep those we love safe." Yousef turned back to look at Derek who smiled warmly back at him. He left the office and went home. Derek was right. Yousef felt safer when he was near.

DEREK WATCHED THE door for a minute after Yousef left, just to make sure he wasn't coming right back in. Finally satisfied he picked up his phone and said brusquely, "Sophie, get in here." The slender blonde that entered from a side door to Derek's office was really nothing like the nymph that attached herself to him years ago. At ten feet, she could make you believe she was still a teenaged California surfer girl. But closer, you saw the hardness and fanaticism of a much older woman.

"Are you going to keep me safe?" she asked mockingly.

"Who said I loved you? I'm more concerned about keeping people safe from you." Derek said. "You were supposed to wait until everyone was clear of the library before you set off that blast. You've set us back a week already."

"Yeah, yeah. You gave me that lecture already. Use fewer explosives and make sure people are further away," Sophie said. "You are such a pussy. If we are going to make people afraid to go to a library, then someone's going to get hurt."

"What were you doing inside? These books you checked out aren't relevant to anything. You could have been recognized. Your picture is all over the security cameras."

"Not a one got a look at my face. Do you think I'm that careless? And even if they look up my student ID they won't see me. I know how to keep from being recognized. People who are afraid of libraries depend on the Web for information. We own the Web. Get focused," Sophie lectured him.

"I'm focused on the goal. You've forgotten that. You're so focused on blowing things up you've forgotten why."

"The great altruist speaks," Sophie said. "We're going to have a dictatorship, but it will be a benevolent dictatorship. Hypocrite! We're inciting a revolution, and in revolutions people get killed. Or did you forget our little escapade in Tunisia."

"You've spent too much time with video games," Derek snapped. "Just be ready to travel when Drucker reappears. And don't hurt him. I need him to solve the codex. The more heat we put on him the more he will be compelled to finish the job. Left to their own devices these academics would sit around and think about the problem for a few years instead of actually trying to solve it. We need an incontrovertible source of religious history. That's the key to bringing down religious and national boundaries. I knew the first time Yousef showed that letter fragment to me that it was the map to that source."

"Poor Yousef—a pawn in your little game who gets nothing for all his efforts to find the family treasure." Sophie poured herself a drink and swallowed it at once. "Nothing but me."

YOUSEF STEPPED INSIDE the darkened entry of Sophie's apartment, closed the door and stood listening. It was a habit he developed while serving in Iraq. He listened wherever he went. If there was a voice—even the slightest whisper—it could be trouble. But other things made noises, too. Extra clocks, a different hum in the heating vents, a rattle in the refrigerator motor. Any of these could indicate a listening device or even an explosive in the apartment. He inventoried each sound and checked it against his memory. He heard a faint click from the direction of the kitchen. He stood in silence, straining to hear it again.

He felt guilty about telling Maddie he'd been in Japan. She wouldn't understand why he'd been in the same town as her for so long without telling her. She would be especially upset when she found out he was living with someone and hadn't told her. But Derek said it was better that way for now.

Yousef didn't really like sharing an apartment. It wasn't so much the idea of sharing with Sophie, as the fact that it was *her* apartment and he had no control over it. Anyone might have been here since he left this morning. Of course, having Sophie *in* the apartment with him went a long way toward mitigating his discomfort.

Derek had introduced his assistant to Yousef and Yousef was smitten. She was their age, or maybe a little older—she wouldn't say—but she was young and intense at heart, and still a beautiful woman. She was nothing at all like the women he had known most of his life, and she proved it to him the first night they were together. She burned with a fervor that overwhelmed him. Where Yousef was cautious and shy, Sophie was bold to the point of being reckless. Yousef's heart still jumped when he thought about her racing a train to the railroad crossing and flying across it just ahead of looming death. In general, he avoided riding with her now if he could help it. She brought the same boldness of her driving to their bed. Yousef was overwhelmed and a little scared by her passion.

There was the click again. Yousef reached behind him and pulled the door slowly open. He slipped out as narrow a gap as he could and closed the door silently behind him. He stood in the hall waiting for an explosion from the kitchen that would rock the building and blow the exterior wall out of the third story apartment. He tensed as he edged toward the stairwell a few steps away.

DEREK SAT in his darkened office. Sophie had finally left. For as much as she drank, she scarcely showed signs of inebriation. He watched from his office window for her motorcycle to pull out of the garage eight floors below before he finally relaxed. Palming her off on Joey had given him the first peace he'd known in ten years. How could a man as rich and powerful as Derek be so weak around this woman? Even his father had been wrapped around her finger.

When Derek's father died, Derek inherited the business and his father's corner office. The first time he sat at his father's desk, the second door in the office opened and Sophie walked in. Derek had always assumed it was an executive washroom for his father's use only and had not yet had time to investigate. She introduced herself as his personal assistant. He said he had an admin in front of his office and Sophie should see her to make an appointment. But he had quickly been disabused of that notion.

Sophie had been his father's personal assistant—mistress?—and was determined to be his as well. Her office had a separate door and both locked from inside. She was not employed by the company. She was employed by the president of the company. She gave adequate reasons to Derek to let him know that her employment was not negotiable. She came with the office.

Derek still wondered if his father's sudden death had something to do with Sophie. Had he displeased her? Derek fully believed that she was capable of anything. Most of his master plan came from her files. He was accustomed to manipulating information to his advantage, but it had grown and changed. The stakes had gone up and he would have to decide what to do about Sophie soon.

FIVE

FRANK ALREADY HAD COFFEE brewed when Keith and Maddie awoke in the morning. He sat Keith at the dining room table to redress his wounds while Maddie went to take a shower.

"Bad cuts on your hand, but it looks like it will heal," Frank said softly. "I'm worried about your eye, though."

"My right hand was protected by my computer case when I fell," Keith said. "The case covered some other vital parts, too. But my left hand was flat on the pavement when the shit hit. Luckily my mouth was closed."

"Don't understand why people would do this," Frank said.

"That's why we needed to come here as quickly as possible, Granddad. It's about the other Gutenberg. We have a new clue," Keith said, pointing to the archival box on the table.

"Are you sure you want to go there?" Frank asked. "It's been hidden for 600 years. Maybe it should stay hidden."

"Finding this means someone else knows, too," Keith said. "Someone else is looking." He opened the box and lifted the pages of the book just enough to remove the letter fragment. Frank pulled a pair of latex gloves from a box in the kitchen and reached for the fragment.

"If your rare books curator found you handling these documents without gloves she would be very upset," Frank said as he took the letter. "What does she think of it? Have you verified that it's genuine?"

"Maddie hasn't seen it yet. It all happened just before the explosion. Spectrographic analysis indicated late 1400s," Keith said. "I thought we could finish it here."

"It was just loose in the manuscript?" Frank asked.

"Yes. This is a catalog of books that were in a monastery near Württemberg Mountain," Keith responded. "It was stuck between two pages of the catalog. I verified about half the book as being genuine, but haven't checked every page after the late 1400s where this was inserted. But this letter hadn't been there since the 1400s. The book was rebound around 1680 or so. You can tell by the stitching in the leather. There's no residual impression of the letter on the pages surrounding where I found it. It hadn't been in the book more than a few years at most."

"And you think there is some significance to it being where it was?" Frank asked.

"Open the book and I'll show you where I found it." Frank began turning the pages, commenting on the quality and importance of the manuscript. As he found the page that Keith pointed out, Maddie entered the room and gasped.

"What are you doing with that open here? We need a controlled environment!" she exclaimed.

"Sorry to start without you," Keith said turning toward her. He was arrested by the image of Maddie standing in the doorway. Frank, too, seemed speechless.

She was dressed in a sea-green pāreu, wrapped around her waist and drawn up and tied behind her neck. It left a mile of leg and acres of flesh exposed. Keith gazed open-mouthed. Maddie stared at the book open between Frank and Keith.

"Wow!" Keith said, breathlessly.

"Wow, indeed," Frank agreed. "Are you cold, Madeline?" he asked. "I don't usually turn the heat on during the day."

Maddie looked at her pāreu and grinned at Frank.

"We were on our way to Jamaica when they blew up the library," she said. "I'm afraid I didn't repack."

"Little island, little clothes," Frank said. "You'll probably want to go into town and buy something warmer. I'll keep the heat on."

"Maddie's right," Keith said, changing the subject back to the book. "We should have taken this to the lab."

"Well, it's not too late," Frank said. "Forgive our enthusiasm for getting right to the book," he said to Maddie. If you wouldn't mind helping to transport it, we'll take it to a proper facility. He pointed to the box of latex gloves and Maddie snapped a pair on before closing up the book and boxing it. She paused to look at the letter fragment before putting it in the box as well.

Frank opened a door into a cozy study lined with bookshelves. Opposite a small secretary at one side stood a library table with reading stand, camera, and electronic equipment. The setup, in fact, was very similar to the reading rooms in The Whit. Maddie crossed to the stand and sniffed the air.

"There's a filtration system that ionizes the air to remove particles," Keith said. "It's where I did most of the research for my thesis." Maddie nodded approvingly. She unboxed the book, placing it carefully on the reading stand.

"Where were you?" she asked, taking charge of opening the pages. Keith quickly explained the section of the book they were looking at and what he was looking for. Frank crowded in on the other side of Maddie with a magnifying glass and looked at the entry Keith pointed to.

"Wyrich family Gospels," Frank read. "What makes you think that could have anything to do with it? You think Gutenberg printed a Gospel?"

"It's possible," Keith pondered. "But what if Gutenberg's secret wasn't a book he printed, but one he owned. It could be his mother's family Bible. They may not have been able to afford a whole Bible. If it shows names of his grandparents with dates that correspond, that could be what's missing."

"So where is it?" Frank asked.

"That's a problem," Keith sighed. "We have to find it."

"Well, there you are, back to what the Guild has been hunting for 500 years," Frank said.

"It's a different age now, Granddad," Keith said. "We have different tools."

"This thing, you mean?" Frank said, pointing to Keith's laptop bag. "What can it do?"

"Do you remember Rob Nelson?" Keith asked.

"Yes. I had great hopes for that boy," Frank said with a hint of disappointment in his voice. "I thought he'd be your equal in the Guild until he got seduced away by computer technology."

"He's doing quite well in that field," Keith said. "And he's written me a program to help in on-line searches. It's called a spider—kind of a super search engine. I enter keywords into it and it gives me results after searching the entire Web. The longer it runs the more results it returns."

"You are looking for a real book," Frank said. "Paper and leather and ink, not some electrons floating around in outer space." Frank had never been a big fan of computer technology. It had destroyed print, as Keith had heard him say on numerous occasions.

"It will show me any references that have been made to the real book," Keith went on. "I just need to tap into the dish and send out the query."

"Well, it's still there," Frank conceded. "Won't hurt to find out if somebody mentioned this fabulously rare book of the 15th century on SpaceBook or YouHoo."

"Granddad, you're getting all technical on me now."

"Do it!" the old man commanded. "I want to examine the letter. Care to join me, Miss Zayne?" he asked Maddie politely.

"Perhaps you could tell me about the Guild and this secret project you mentioned," she said. "It seems to be something Keith neglected to tell me." Maddie smiled at him and soon the two were bent over the letter and Frank was telling her about the ancient Guild to which he and Keith belonged.

Keith sat at his computer and started to design his search.

THIS ROOM was more home to Keith than anywhere he had lived in the past twenty years; it always gave him pleasure to return to it. On his first visit to his grandfather, the old man had brought him to this room and shown him to a desk. Keith divided his time between study at the desk and work in the shop.

Frank had a small but exquisite collection of early American printing, including flawless specimens of Ben Franklin's *Poor Richard's Almanac* and Thomas Payne's *Common Sense*. He said it was a great reminder that the press brought freedom with it wherever it arrived.

Keith devised several keywords that would help him locate references to the book, including the way it would be classified in a library. The Wyrich Family Gospels would probably be in a private collection, but if it had been sold there might be a registry entry or sales record in someone's database. He cross-referenced the keywords with an index of names and places that were relevant in the Gutenberg saga. He was so intent on getting his search parameters set up correctly that he didn't hear Maddie come up behind him. Frank had left the study to make lunch.

"Keith?" she said softly from a few steps behind him. He started and spun to face her.

"You take my breath away, darling," he said looking up at her through his one good eye. "Even when you aren't startling me half to death." Maddie was still dressed in her island wrap, but she seemed hesitant and a bit in awe. "What is it, Maddie?"

"Keith, your grandfather has a copy of the *Mainz Psalter* in a glass case," she said, pointing to a case in the bookshelves beside the desk. She shook her head in disbelief. Keith had forgotten all about the pristine volume his grandfather kept in a museum case. He realized it must look very suspicious to Maddie. "There are only ten of these known to be in existence," Maddie continued, "and this one isn't documented. It must be worth three million dollars, at least." Keith smiled and hugged her. Her fresh scent nearly overwhelmed him.

"It would be," he said, kissing her ear, "if it were genuine."

"You can't be serious!" Maddie exclaimed, dragging him with her to the case. "This is a counterfeit?"

"One of the best ever printed. It looks perfect, but it wouldn't withstand carbon-14 dating. It's only about fifty years old," Keith laughed. "Spectrographically, though the inks are almost indistinguishable from the originals. Granddad made me test my analysis theories by dating this piece."

"But it's perfect," she said. "Your grandfather printed it?"

"He won a rather profitable competition with it," Keith said. "It was before electronic publishing, and cold type was still just starting. Everybody was moving to offset lithography and the Guild decided to hold a competition among the members to see who could reproduce a historic work with the greatest accuracy. The Guild chose the *Mainz Psalter* as one of the greatest examples of *incunabula*. The prize was $100,000 at a time when that wasn't a common salary."

"And your grandfather won?"

"By a unanimous decision," Keith affirmed. "There was only one close contender as I understand it. He did pretty well, too. His copy was broken up and sold as limited edition artwork and may have made him more than Granddad's did. There was one hanging in the library. I mean your library. I hope it wasn't harmed in the explosion."

"So that's where it came from," Maddie whispered. "He really was a great printer."

"Was and still is," Keith responded.

"Only members of the Guild were in the competition?"

"Yes. They were the best in the world at the time. There hasn't been a similar competition since."

"In order to make a copy that exact," Maddie mused, "he must have had access to an original. How did he manage that?"

"The Guild has a copy," Keith said. "Not one of the ten. Each printer in the competition was given equal access to the original."

"They let them touch it?" Maddie exclaimed in disbelief.

"Let me assure you, the Guild's copy is in perfect condition."

"You've seen it?" Maddie asked.

"When I became a Master in the Guild I was given the tour of the private archives. A lot of my work creating the database of print-ers' inks is based on analysis I did in the Guild library. It is one of the best cared-for collections in the world—and most secret. The *Psalter* is unbound—leaves straight from the press of Peter Schoeffer."

"Information overload. So in addition to being a scholar and *incu-nabulist*," Maddie said, "you are also a Master Printer?"

"Not exactly," Keith said. "Different guild. For now, let's say I'm a Master Typesetter. Nothing compared to Granddad, but I was his apprentice out here for five years."

"How did he teach you typesetting clear out here?" Maddie asked.

"That's his secret, not mine," Keith responded, placing another kiss on her ear. "I've forgotten where I was. Let's see." Keith spun her around and pointed to a freckle on her arm. "Four," he said. "Five, six," he continued randomly pointing at freckles. Maddie silenced him with a kiss which went on until they heard Frank clearing his throat at the door.

"Internet search isn't what it used to be," the old man said. "Who's for burritos?"

Keith and Maddie broke their embrace. Keith was flushed almost as red as Maddie. They followed Frank to the dining table where he served the Southwestern staple.

"GRANDDAD," KEITH SAID when they finished lunch and he had taken the prescribed painkillers. "Maddie would like to see the shop."

"Well, that can be arranged," Frank said. "Maybe I'll get a new shop apprentice."

"I've always been fascinated by typesetting and printing," Maddie said. "I started reading about it when I was a little girl."

Frank led the way to the back of the house. The last door at the end of the hall opened into a dark cavern. A second door opened ahead of her and she stepped into a wonderland of antique printing equip-ment. The shop was as immaculate as the rest of Frank's house and library. Three hand-operated presses, typesetting equipment, and trays of metal type lined the room. Shelves held books and magazines Frank had printed over the years. Maddie looked at the shelf of samples.

"You printed all this by yourself?" Maddie asked, astounded.

"It's hard to get help out here in the desert," Frank laughed. "Of course, once they were inside I'd never be able to let them out again." He laughed and ignored Maddie's quick glance at the door. Frank moved from tray to tray of type as if greeting old friends. "This is the type I used on the *Psalter*," he said, holding up a handful of metal bits. "Keith told you about it, didn't he? Not much use for black letter these days, but I've never been able to bring myself to melt it down. The real trick was that particular characters had to be used in specific places. The slight imperfection of one bit of type might show up on only the first, tenth, and seventeenth pages. I had to be sure that I had precisely that bit of type in that particular position."

"How long did it take you?" Maddie asked. "It sounds impossible."

"Nearly three years," Frank said. "Three master typesetters working side-by-side in identical set-ups held to the same working hours that Peter Schoeffer and his staff would have had in 1459. It was a life-changing experience. Of course, it took us longer than it did Schoeffer," he chuckled.

"What Gutenberg saw in the Mainz Bible after which he patterned his type was the variation in the letters written by the scribe. No one ever writes the same letter twice in exactly the same way. But the type from the 42-line was used and reused, so in spite of some 250 different characters that he cast, the exact same character anomalies show up repeatedly." Frank handed two bits of lead type to Maddie and pointed out a small crack in one of the letters. The other was perfect. "The same is true of the new type font Schoeffer used for the Psalter. It was a little more elegant than the earlier Gutenberg type, but if one metal character had a tiny flaw, it reappeared in the printed work each time that bit of metal was set. I had to make sure my type-case replicated Schoeffer's, and that the individual characters were used in the same places."

"That's amazing," Maddie enthused. "What about paper? What did you use?"

"We have a lot of research on the subject within the Guild. It's vellum, of course, and came from Northern Italy where Schoeffer, like Gutenberg before him, acquired most of his substrate. It's the one sure giveaway regarding the age of the book under glass. The aging process for animal skin is clearly identifiable. Under proper conditions, you'd be able to tell that the vellum is only about 50 or 60 years old."

"This place looks like half print shop and half chemistry lab," Maddie said as she began exploring the shop.

"Typefounding is an alchemical science," Frank said.

"We create the physical manifestation of ideas and dreams," Maddie mused. Frank turned suddenly to Keith.

"I'm impressed," Frank said. "One would think you had read *The Printer's Devil*."

"The magazine?" Maddie asked. "I read every issue. In fact, I think it was responsible for my becoming a librarian. There is simply no way to read that magazine and not fall in love with books. I wonder what happened to it."

"The subscription base was too small to keep up the labor of producing it," Frank said. "Newer, more cost efficient ways had to be found to educate the next generation. We simply couldn't keep producing the magazine every quarter for the number of subscribers."

"We?" Maddie asked, turning to Frank. "Were you involved in *The Printer's Devil?*" Keith approached Maddie and turned her toward the shelves of samples in Frank's workshop. Frank went immediately to a file cabinet and began riffling through folders.

"Granddad is *The Printer's Devil*," Keith said softly. He lifted a stack of uncut signatures from the shelf to show to Maddie. "Every issue of the magazine that was produced is right here," Keith went on. "It's the reason this workshop exists."

"It was such a wonderful magazine," Maddie said.

"How did you happen to come by them," Keith asked.

"They started coming to me in the mail when I was little, back in South Carolina," Maddie said. "It was near the time my dad died and it was like having a connection with him. He loved books, too. Kind of an archaeologist, I guess. He was killed in Iran about the time the embassy was taken over. I was 12."

"What happened to your copies?" Keith asked.

"I wanted to keep them forever," Maddie said. "But I started sharing them with my little brother when he was old enough to make sense of them. He ended up taking them all."

"Is your brother a librarian, too?" Frank asked. Maddie hesitated, choosing her words carefully.

"He's a linguist and translator," Maddie said. "He does freelance work for the State Department sometimes, but personally, I don't think it's all translating for foreign dignitaries. He is incredibly paranoid and always believes someone is following him."

"You know what they say," Keith said. "It's not paranoia if they really are after you." Maddie punched him lightly and smiled.

"Madeline," Frank said cautiously, "I have only one Madeline in my subscriber list, but Zayne is not her last name."

"I suppose there hasn't been time for Keith to tell you all the background," she answered. "I was married at the time I completed my doctorate. After the divorce, I didn't change my name back for career reasons. My maiden name was Wadsworth." Frank returned to the card file and examined an entry. His shoulders were hunched forward and Keith was puzzled over his sudden cautiousness. Still, the name Wadsworth rang a bell, but Keith's mind wasn't working fast enough to solve the puzzle.

"Madeline, how would you like to be a printer's devil yourself?" Frank asked, returning the card to its cabinet.

"You mean be an apprentice in a print shop? Don't I need some kind of indoctrination first?" Maddie asked.

"That was the purpose of the magazine," Frank said. "So I don't see any problem in teaching you the next level. At this stage, we have to do whatever we can to preserve the knowledge and culture of the Guild." Keith nodded.

"Can we get back to the fragment?" Keith asked Frank. "I know you and Maddie were working on the letter while I was working on the search parameters."

"No question. The letter is from the mid-1400s," Frank said.

"I'll even vouch for that," Maddie confirmed. "I can't believe you didn't come running to me as soon as you found it."

"I'm still puzzled though," Frank said. "According to your spectrometer, there's a phthalocyanine dye the page."

"What does it say?" Keith asked, astounded.

"What do you mean?" Maddie asked.

"Phthalocyanine is a basic ingredient of invisible ink," Keith said.

"That's the thing," Frank responded. "It doesn't say anything. It covers the entire page in a very light coating. It's detectable on the front, but not the back. I can't see any reason for it other than possibly trying to treat the page to see if there were secret messages on it."

"What about the paleography?" Keith asked his grandfather. Maddie looked at him questioningly.

"What would you compare this handwriting to?" Maddie asked.

"Other letters by the same person. Letters that are in the Guild archives. I am 99% positive that the handwriting is an exact match," Frank said.

"Which means?" Maddie asked.

"Which means that this document is part of the initiation mysteries of the third degree mastery in the Guild," Keith said. Then he added, "Written by Peter Schoeffer."

SIX

MADDIE AND FRANK decided to complete the ink analysis of the Carthusian manuscript while he instructed her in Guild lore as his new apprentice. Frank said he wanted to check the manuscript for any later transfers of the Wyrich Gospels that might have been mentioned in the records. Keith was so exhausted, however, that he left the workshop and collapsed in bed for a nap.

He awoke with Maddie snuggled close beside him. He took a quick inventory of his wounds and realized that most of the small cuts that peppered his body and face didn't hurt, but with the healing process were itching fiercely. The dozen stitches in his left hand ached and his left eye was covered and puffy. Beside him, Maddie was comparably perfect. He hesitated to wake her, not knowing if it was day or night. Keith could hardly wait to check his search results to see if he could locate the other missing document. He was not excited enough about the search, however, to pull himself out of bed and leave Maddie sleeping. When he kissed her shoulder she stirred and snuggled closer to him. He settled back beneath the covers and she welcomed him into her careful embrace.

"Cyanide," Maddie whispered to him.

"How romantic," he answered. "Are we making a suicide pact?"

"No," she answered. "It's what killed the Carthusian monks."

"They were poisoned?"

"By the ink," Maddie confirmed. "The final two pages of the manuscript show an increase in the level of cyanide in the ink."

"The monks copying manuscripts would ingest small amounts of ink each day as they touched their pens to their tongues when they wrote," Keith said, reconstructing the scenario in his mind. He shuddered. "That sounds like a long slow death."

"The catalog also records the receipt of supplies for the scriptorium," Maddie added. "The last delivery of ink came with a manuscript and request for two hand-written copies. The entries with cyanide in the ink cover about four years, right up until the last entry."

"Talk about a poison pen," Keith said. "What was the manuscript?"

"Something called 'The Wisdom of Ptolemy,' according to the record. There was a short description saying it was a treatise on Egyptian history and Ptolemy's power over demons."

"That doesn't ring a bell," Keith said. "I wonder what they were using that introduced cyanide into the ink. It's certainly not common in inks of the 19th century. The records we have say the monastery's fatal epidemic occurred in 1852. The property was burned because the people in the nearby village believed it was infected with a plague."

"Which means that the level of cyanide in the blood built to a fatal level over those four years before everyone started dropping dead," Maddie said. "Spooky. But here's something more spooky. The last entry in the catalog was the return of the manuscript and its copies to the original owner along with what was recorded only as 'and many other important works.'"

"Sounds like they emptied the scriptorium to protect the books from the inevitable burning that would come when all the monks died."

"Yes," Maddie affirmed. "But I'm afraid it also means that unless the monks considered the Wyrich gospels to be an important work, it was probably still in the monastery when it was burned, and whatever Gutenberg's secret was probably went up in flames."

IN THE AFTERNOON, Keith resumed his search. He was refreshed after the nap and feeling better after taking painkillers, but it was still difficult to read the thousands of results with just one good eye. Normally, he would scan results before starting to pare them down to see if anything jumped out. With his difficulty reading, he decided to run comparisons on the search results electronically, winnowing out obviously false returns with his friend's search algorithms. While the reports were being generated, he checked to see if there was anything new regarding the bombing of the library.

"Say, Maddie," he called to her from the study. "We made the news, sort of."

Both Maddie and Frank came from the living room where they had been discussing the finer points of document dating and authentication.

"What's up?" she asked.

"Take a look at this. I haven't read it all yet," Keith answered. "You can fill in the details for me."

"It's an analysis of the bombing of the Kane Memorial Library and says it appears to be 'part of a new wave of global *biblio-terrorism*' sweeping the world. It reports half a dozen attacks on libraries in the past year and lumps in book burnings from Hitler forward. At one point, the analyst even goes so far as to cite instances of people defacing books by crossing out words and writing in the margins. Is this for real?"

"Who wrote a thing like that?" Frank asked.

"There's no by-line," Maddie answered, "It just says that according to authorities, 'the attack on the Kane Memorial Library should not be considered an isolated event. Any library could be a target.' Whoa!"

"I won't believe that until I see it in print," Frank said.

"It almost sounds like a challenge," Maddie said.

"Or a warning," Keith added.

"Warning to whom?" Maddie asked.

"Us? Or maybe to the world? Stay away from libraries." Keith swung around in his chair so his one good eye could take in Maddie standing over him. He almost lost his train of thought just looking at her. She nudged him and he went on. "Maybe I'm seeing things where nothing exists, but it's got too much in common with the note the agent showed us," Keith went on. "Read this last paragraph." They all looked at the screen to read the last statement.

Since the Garden of Eden, there have been governments and religions intent on keeping humanity away from the tree of knowledge. But key to the story is the fact that you can't know what you are missing until after you've eaten the fruit.

"I'm not sure if it's directed to us or not," Maddie said at last. "But 'tree of knowledge' and 'key' in an article about 'biblio-terrorism' gives me the willies. I'm a little concerned about walking back into work Monday morning like nothing happened."

"The damage was pretty superficial," Keith said. "They didn't really get explosives into where they would do damage to the books. The façade and atrium were badly damaged, but as far as we know, no books were harmed. It was like they tried to do it in a hurry and didn't get their explosives to the right places."

"Or like they wanted to harm the library, but not the books?" Maddie asked.

Frank had been quiet during this exchange and Keith noticed that he looked as if his thoughts were far away. His eyes fell on the *Psalter* in its glass case.

"Are you okay, Granddad?" Keith asked.

"Yes," the old man hesitated. "Yes, yes," he repeated. "I was just thinking what a shame you kids missed your vacation to Jamaica." The non sequitur startled both Keith and Maddie. Maddie smiled and went to touch Frank's arm.

"I'm thinking that we're going to have lots of opportunities to take a vacation together," she said gently.

"Well I certainly hope so," Frank said. "None of this summer romance stuff. You're both too old. I was just wondering if you could take another week off work, Madeline."

"You think we should go to Jamaica now? I guess the sun might help these cuts heal," Keith said.

"I wasn't exactly thinking Jamaica," Frank said. "How about Mainz?"

Keith was silent. He had told Maddie they might take the book to Mainz, but hadn't been so sure that they needed to after they got to Frank's laboratory. "Well, I'd like to see the Gutenberg Museum," Maddie said. "I understand it has a wonderful collection of rare books."

"If you include both the museum library and the Guild, the collection of unique manuscripts and *incunabula* is probably more extensive than any other in the world, including the British Library," Frank said. "I know Keith is aching to give you the tour."

"As much as I've been aching from everything else," Keith said. The hasty exit from the hospital and cross-country flight had taken its toll. Every time he took a pain pill he could hardly keep his eyes open.

"All the documents aren't in the library or museum?" Maddie asked, genuinely shocked at Frank's statement.

"Many are considered Guild secrets," Frank interjected. "They have been in the same hands for nearly six hundred years."

"Still, it seems that the world should know," Maddie said.

"Perhaps so," Keith responded, "but once they were given to the world, as you say, who would have access to them?"

"Scholars and archivists," Maddie answered quickly.

"Exactly the people who have access to them now," Keith responded. "We make sure that appropriate knowledge is disseminated to the world, and there is a debate in every generation about making the entire collection public. Some of the documents have to do with the secrets and rituals of the Guild, and as such to release them would effectively destroy the Guild."

"For all our care, however," Frank said, "there are documents that have gone missing over the years. We have delved into this matter, searching the world for them, but once they are out of our care, they are very hard to locate again, or to re-acquire."

"I get that you think the letter fragment Keith found is a missing document of the Guild," Maddie said. "But how did it end up in a collection we just happened to acquire at the Whit?"

"We didn't even know the document was missing," Frank acknowledged. He sighed.

"See, that is what I'm talking about," Maddie argued. "In a real library or museum, documents like that wouldn't just disappear."

"Even within the Guild," Keith said, "not all documents are available to all members. Certain items are seen only by those who have reached the highest level of mastery."

"So we can check with a master at that level in Germany and confirm its origin?" Maddie suggested. "If it isn't part of the Guild's rightful collection, then it belongs in my library or a museum."

"We have no masters at that level at this time," Keith said. Maddie opened her mouth to protest, but Frank jumped in.

"Just because we don't currently have a master of that level, doesn't mean we won't have," he said. "Unlike many secret organizations, the Guild doesn't require elevation to be granted by people who are already at that level. We have very specific tests that determine if an individual is worthy to be raised to the next level."

"Oh," said Maddie in sudden enlightenment. "Like your *Psalter*."

"Yes, like that," Frank said, "but the Psalter was a competition to determine who would get to *try* to attain the next level. It wasn't the test itself. The actual test was last taken by your grandfather, Madeline." Both Maddie and Keith were speechless at this comment. They glanced at each other but did not find words to respond to Frank's revelation. He went on. "I assume that Errol Wadsworth was your grandfather.

Please correct me if I am wrong." Maddie nodded, confirming Frank's assumption.

"You knew my grandfather?" Madeline asked quietly.

"Errol Wadsworth worked side-by-side with me for three years as we competed for the *Psalter* prize," Frank said. "We were competitors, but also good friends. "Errol was never quite the same after his initiation to the third degree mastery. He was a true master and when he vanished from the Guild it was a loss from which we never really recovered. The only contact we had was when he submitted your name as a subscriber to *The Printer's Devil*."

"Do you mean that the reproduction pages of the *Psalter* that I've seen are my own grandfather's work?" Maddie asked.

"What happened to Errol?" Frank asked. "Is he still alive?"

"If you can call it that." Maddie dropped her head. "He has Alzheimer's. No one can believe he is still alive. He's been deteriorating steadily for thirty years. Now he's in a locked ward so he can't wander away and hurt himself. When we were kids, he would tell us stories, but we always thought they were just stories that old men tell. He was always telling us about great manuscripts and hidden treasures."

"I'm sorry to hear that he's not well," Frank said. "I'd like to visit him sometime before the end."

"Since we're going to Germany next," Keith said, "it would be a great opportunity for Maddie to be formally presented to the Guild." No one seemed to notice how easily they had all jumped to the assumption that they were, indeed, going to Mainz.

"Actually," Frank said, "I think Maddie could be initiated as a journeyman. I haven't been to Mainz in a few years myself."

"Don't I need more training?" Maddie asked.

"Between *The Printer's Devil* and your grandfather's stories, I'm pretty sure you're ready," Keith said. "I'm just sad you weren't found years ago. For lots of reasons," he added.

"As it happens," Maddie said, kissing Keith lightly on his forehead, "I can get at least the next week off and possibly the one after.

They are running the library on skeleton staff with no official access to rare books until the damage is assessed and repairs are underway. I could take an extra week. Or two," she added, looking at Keith. "Just to advance my studies, mind you. Are you feeling up to the trip?"

"I promise, I'll advance your studies," Keith said smiling at Maddie. "And if I've got a good supply of pills, I think I can make the trip all right. Do you think we can arrange things, Granddad?" he said turning to the old man.

"There's only a few of us left, Keith," Frank said. "It shouldn't be that hard to get us together for this. I'll make some calls."

"THE WISDOM OF PTOLEMY," Frank explained as they ate dinner in El Centro, "is the name of the last book that the monks received just before the ink changed in the catalog to a formula laced with cyanide."

"And the only book named in the last entry," Maddie added.

"The evidence suggests that the monk who brought the book intended it to be the last project the monastery completed," Frank said.

"All these things we've seen and surmised make a fascinating story," Keith said, "but are they really all connected? We've got a page from a letter by Peter Schoeffer, a gospel that might have belonged to Gutenberg's grandparents, and a manuscript called 'The Wisdom of Ptolemy' that might have been accompanied by cyanide laced ink. I'm having trouble connecting the dots."

"Maybe they are not connected," Frank said. "But I think we need more trusted brainpower gathered together to do the analysis, and perhaps a third degree Master. That is why I think we need to go to Mainz."

"You'd really undertake the trial after all these years, granddad?" Keith answered.

"If it was necessary," Frank answered. "Of course if all goes well, it might not be necessary."

"Maybe not, but we'd all like to read a book called *The Wisdom of Ptolemy*," Keith said. "I can't think of another mention of such a work in anything I've ever read. Do you suppose it actually refers to a book written by one of the eight Ptolemys? Or is it a bit of esoterica that a cult of the middle ages wrote?"

"My guess is that it refers to a writing of Ptolemy Soter, the first of that name," Frank said. "Of course, anyone could write something and credit it to him, but the entry has a couple of clues that make it more interesting than others of that time or the next two pages."

"For instance?" Maddie asked around a mouthful of beans and rice.

"Well, here's what it says," Frank said, pulling a notecard from his pocket. "I copied it out in case you wanted to hear it at dinner. '*The Wisdom of Ptolemy*, received from Brother Alexander of Anatoly. Request one copy and one for the scriptorium. This book contains the Key of Pharaoh, said to unlock the gates of Eden and the power of Armageddon.' Pretty heady stuff," Frank concluded.

"Everything mentions the Tree of Knowledge and the Master's Key in one way or another," Keith said.

"In this case Pharaoh's Key and Eden, where the Tree of the Knowledge of Good and Evil is supposed to be," Maddie supplied. "Why the reference to Armageddon, though?"

"Perhaps as a warning that the power to open the gates of Eden is also sufficient to end the world?" Frank suggested.

"Frank, could that be the great manuscript and treasure that my grandfather tried to convince us was real?" Maddie asked. "That's what my father was searching for when he was killed. I'm not sure I want to inherit a treasure-hunting gene. There's been enough of that in my family and I'll stick to libraries if you don't mind."

"What happened?" Keith asked.

"My father believed the stories," Maddie said. "Based on Errol's stories, he hunted for the treasure in Egypt. That's where I was born, during the 7-day war with Israel. My mother died in it."

"I'm sorry, Maddie," Keith said. "It must have been hard not to have a mother."

"Oh, not as bad as you might expect," Maddie said wistfully. "I never knew her. All I have is the picture I carry of the two in this sealed locket. My Aunt Virginia took care of me for the first five years. Then Dad came back from one of his trips to the Middle East with Lily. For a while we all settled down in South Carolina like a family and my brother was born. But it wasn't long before Dad was off again. He had moved his 'research' from Egypt to Iran where he and Lily had met. Then, he was killed during the revolution in '79. For all I know that's what my brother, Yousef, spends his time doing in the Middle East. I don't want to be one of the treasure-hunters."

"I don't think it will be a problem," Keith said. "The librarian who wrote the catalog entry has taken something of Egyptian origin and superimposed Hebrew and Christian mythology over it. There is no reason for that. He's putting his own editorial spin on it or else the work is a medieval mystery text and not the work of Ptolemy Soter."

"You're probably right," Maddie said, "but I don't like having so many references to something that we have already associated with bombing a library and nearly killing you. We have the letter fragment, the note Agent Fry showed us, the news article, and now this. It just makes me uncomfortable, like I'm being caught up in something I can't control."

"We'll get help in Mainz," Frank said. "In fact, I think we should go in the morning."

Maddie excused herself to use the restroom and Keith used the opportunity to hand Frank the glass shard he'd recovered from his computer case. He always knew he could depend on his grandfather, but when the old man heard what Keith wanted, he seemed reluctant.

"Are you sure about this?" Frank asked.

"No. But when I am sure, I don't want to be delayed."

"Well, that makes sense. Better to be prepared. I'll take care of it."

THEY SHOPPED for warmer clothes before returning to Frank's home. Frank insisted on buying Maddie a gray wool coat because Germany would be much colder than the desert in April. When they returned to the house, Keith immediately checked on his search results. Frank sat at the dining table, describing the journeyman initiation to Maddie. They were deep in the meaning of printer's marks when Keith came out of the study looking dazed.

"Keith! What is it, darling?" Maddie exclaimed, rushing to him. Frank stood staring at his grandson.

"I think I've found the other Gutenberg," Keith said hoarsely. "Granddad, we need to make a stop before we go to Germany."

SEVEN

FRANK LEFT KEITH AND MADDIE at the San Diego airport, going straight to Mainz himself to arrange the Guild meeting, while the couple went to Salt Lake City. Keith had found two almost identical notices in a genealogical chat archive that had been retired for over ten years. The postings were apparently for the same book with the same phrasing and description. One citation was to the Family History Library in Salt Lake City and the other to the National Historic and Genealogical Archives in Indianapolis. They decided to go to Salt Lake first since it was closest, but Maddie left messages for a friend who worked at the NHGA to ask for help in locating the book.

Salt Lake proved to be a dead end. The librarians could find no record of a Gospel that matched the description in the notice. "I'm sorry," the librarian said as she shook her head. "It's not that unusual to have people mix us up with the NHGA. Probably, the person who posted these notices either wasn't sure which one or posted one then posted the other when they found out the first was incorrect. They should really make note of that kind of thing. Would you like me to call NHGA for you?"

"That's okay," Maddie said. "I've already put in a call to them and I expect I'll hear back soon." They thanked the librarian and left.

"We could have flown straight to Indianapolis," Keith said. "Now we won't be able to get to the NHGA until morning."

"Well, let's head for the airport. We've got the 11:00 flight, and even if it is too late to get there tonight, we can get some rest in Indianapolis and be at the NGHA when it opens in the morning," Maddie said.

"Always looking on the bright side, aren't you?" Keith said. "How did I ever manage to find such a good sport?"

"It is kind of like a game, isn't it?" Maddie asked. "You find a clue here and follow it to there. I've decided to make the best of it and just keep following the clues... and you."

THE COUPLE ARRIVED in Indianapolis at 6:00, had dinner, and collapsed in their hotel room. Keith was tired of traveling with his injuries and examined his pain medication carefully to see that he would have enough for a trip to Germany. Random, blinding light flashes in his bandaged eye left him disoriented and his head throbbing. The number of pills in the bottle was dropping at an alarming rate. He was not much company as Maddie bathed the eye and bandaged it, then applied a cool washcloth to his forehead.

In the morning, Keith and Maddie walked to the National Historical and Genealogical Archives about a block away. Maddie was thankful for the new wool coat and warm clothes Frank had insisted on. It might get warm later in the day, but it was just above freezing when they left the hotel. They were just two of the crowd of genealogical researchers lined up waiting to look at some of the billion plus family records, books, and microfilms kept in the building. They met their guide at the information desk at 9:00 sharp. Leslie Hayden, the librarian who showed Keith and Maddie around the collection, was friendly and outgoing. Though much older than Maddie, the two had done their undergraduate work together years before. Leslie exemplified the dedicated and friendly staff the Archives were known for.

"Of course, what you are really looking for isn't on any of these floors," Leslie said as they completed the tour of the second basement. "The rare books that you want to see are on the next level down. Isn't it funny how your rare book collection is on stilts six stories above ground and ours is buried three stories below? We're really worlds apart!"

They were worlds apart in more ways than the locations. Maddie's collection of rare books was carefully acquired from estates and wealthy families, sometimes from churches, or other universities. Each purchase was deliberate and evaluated both before and after the transaction. Most of the Archive's acquisitions were donated by individuals who had a few family heirlooms to dispose of. Anything that had a family name in it was actively solicited. The speed of intake was such that the typical book was catalogued and shelved with just one criterion: old or new. If the book appeared to be over 150 years old, it was deemed too valuable to be shelved in general collections and was sent to the stacks, which in this case were located underground. Its treatment in the stacks was little different than that in the public portion of the library, but restricted access meant there was less handling of the volumes.

It was amazing to Keith that there were so many people in the public portion of the library whose method of research was to go down the shelves and pull every volume off and examine it. No doubt it was likely to turn up an unexpected reference, but the task was tantamount to cataloguing Maddie's freckles—a thought that brought a smile to his lips.

"This portion of the library is off-limits to the general public," Leslie said, "but since you are visiting scholars and librarians yourself, I got you special dispensation." She led them to a small room with shelves on all walls and a table running down the middle. "Have a seat here," Leslie said, "and I'll go fetch the book you want to look at."

Maddie sat at the table and Keith nearly collapsed at her side.

"Are you okay, darling?" she asked him. What could he say? Maybe checking himself out of the hospital so quickly and then bouncing cross-country hadn't been such a good idea. Just last night,

Maddie had discovered another bruise on his back that seemed to be growing instead of shrinking. And the headaches were certainly aggravated by the number of hours he had spent staring one-eyed at his computer screen.

He closed his eye and rested, leaning against Maddie.

In an impossibly short time, Leslie arrived with the book they had requested. It came in a plain canvas bag with a reference number stamped on the side. The catalog description had simply said, "Old Bible, inscribed 'In memory Elyssa and Bjorn Wyrich—undated.'"

"We have hundreds of these old Bibles in the stacks," Leslie said as she laid the book on the table. "If it's in a canvas bag like this, then usually its condition isn't too good. So be careful with it and if any pages fall out, try to stuff them back in the right order. You probably won't need to look at anything but the first few pages. Usually that's where the family records are kept. Let me know if you need anything else and just drop it off at the information desk when you are finished." Leslie left them alone with the book.

"Just stuff the pages back in the right order?" Maddie asked incredulously. "I can't believe Leslie is so cavalier about it."

"The value of the documents here is in the data about families," Keith said. "The books themselves are no more than containers. Like she said, they have hundreds of old Bibles. It's where people kept family information. We can count ourselves lucky that they don't just cut the dedication pages out and discard the rest."

"Still…."

They opened the ties on the canvas bag and slid a worn and tattered leather-bound volume out onto the table. Maddie gasped when she saw the binding and held out a hand to stop Keith from opening it. She rummaged in her purse for a moment and pulled out two pairs of lightweight white cotton gloves. She handed a pair to Keith and pulled on the other herself.

"It's probably a little late for this," Keith said, pulling a glove over his bandages. "This book is worn to the point of falling apart."

"There's no sense in contributing to its deterioration," Maddie responded. "Here. Let me open the pages. I know how to handle these."

"Dr. Zayne," Keith smiled. "May I remind you that I, too, have studied the care and preservation of texts?"

"Yes, Dr. Drucker," Maddie said, blushing a little. "But your degrees were done with two hands. Besides, you didn't bring any tools with you." She returned to her open purse and withdrew two velvet page weights, a small suction cup, and a thin Mylar bookmark. With these at her side she gently propped the book on a reading stand on the table and opened the cover.

It was huge in length and breadth, but thin in depth compared to other Bibles of the era Keith had seen. As worn as the volume was outside however, it was pristine on the inside. Pencil marks on the inside front cover identified the acquisition date and library call number. The book had been donated in 1983. The rest of the words were smeared beyond recognition.

"Pencil!" Maddie exclaimed. "I don't believe it."

"It's pretty common," Keith said. "Lots of books are identified in pencil because of the belief that it causes the least damage. They don't think about how the graphite smears and leaves prints. It's interesting that this is plain-bound. Most of this sort from the 16th century have marbled book paper on the inside covers. This appears to be a fairly coarse rag paper."

"Yes, but the facing page is vellum," Maddie said. "It looks like the survival of the book might be due to the quality of the paper it was printed on." Maddie applied the tiny suction cup to a corner of the facing page and lifted it enough to slide the Mylar strip between it and the next page. She released the suction cup and raised the page with the Mylar bookmark. They stared at the page in startled silence.

After a blank sheet, a beautiful, hand-painted dedication page bore the inscription mentioned in the catalog. Keith quickly pulled out a small digital camera and fumbled to get a picture of the page. Maddie took the camera and carefully focused on the page, following Keith's instructions regarding angle and framing. Beyond the dedication page, the vellum sheets were crisp and the simply illuminated chapter heads were elegant. The book contained only the four Gospels. A blank back leaf was the last thing between the tattered covers.

"Is this your grandfather's work?" Maddie asked. "It's almost as if a new book was bound in an old binding," Maddie speculated. "It can't really be what it appears to be, can it?"

"If you mean the Gospels from a Bamberg 36-line Bible," Keith responded, feeling suddenly rejuvenated, "then yes, it could be."

"But there is no known record of such a book having been printed," Maddie protested.

"Actually, there is," Keith said. "Most of the 42-line Bibles were bound in two volumes with a few bound in three. But the extra 200 pages of the 36-line Bamberg made it suitable for four-volume binding. This could simply be the third of four volumes, the others lost."

"How did you ever find it?"

"The search I did cross-referenced names of Gutenberg's known associates and the significant locations around Württemberg ," Keith said. "It was no small task."

"What name came up?" Maddie asked.

"At various points in the catalog, donors were listed. One of the monastery's benefactors was a Baron von Hussen. The Baron's wife was Marie Humery. There is no direct evidence of a relationship with Gutenberg's second partner, but the name was enough to bring up a flag in the search routines."

The search results generated from the spiders connected names and places that would have taken Keith days or months to find in any traditional way. Much to his surprise, the von Hussens had appeared on one of the many ship manifests from the Württemberg migration to America in the middle of the 19th century. It was the settlement of the estate of a great grandson in 1983 that led to the donation of the book to the NHGA. Keith was certain the book was the same one mentioned in the catalog.

"Who are Elyssa and Bjorn Wyrich?" Maddie asked. "The name sounds sort of familiar."

"They would be Johannes Gänsfleisch von Gutenberg's grandparents on his mother's side," Keith said.

"Hmmm." Maddie pondered. "That means there has to be a disconnect someplace. The Bamberg 36-line wasn't printed until at least 1460. Gutenberg's grandparents must have been long gone by then."

"This is a memorial page. It says 'In memory Elyssa and Bjorn Wyrich, husband and wife, interred in Bamberg,'" Keith said. "Perhaps Gutenberg's grandparents played an important role in his life while he was young. Look at the last part of the inscription." Maddie looked over his shoulder.

"My German isn't good," she said. "Is that the name of a priest?"

"Dieter von Isenberg, Gutenberg's friend and priest, who apparently interred his grandparents. By the time of the Bamberg Bible, Dieter von Isenberg had ascended to the position of Archbishop of Mainz," Keith said.

"That's it," Maddie interrupted. "The Mainzer wars. He was ousted by Adolf somebody who was the Archbishop that recognized Gutenberg's contribution and gave him a pension."

"Yes, but Dieter outlived his rival and became Archbishop again upon Adolf's death," Keith finished. "Dieter was never removed from Adolf's court. He was simply deemed too radical a reformist to hold the position. Adolf attacked on the Pope's orders. In spite of about 400 citizen casualties, Adolf seemed to be a fair leader when his position was secure. The treatment of Gutenberg was a good example of that, but was probably suggested by Dieter."

"So where does that leave us?" Maddie asked. "I got a lot of instruction from Frank yesterday, but it all left more questions."

"Guild lore says that Gutenberg was entrusted with a secret that had to be protected for a future age," Keith said. "He divided clues to the secret and hid them in two places. One was in the rituals of the Guild itself. That's why the page we examined at

Granddad's is so important. If we lose part of the key, we can't complete the secret."

"Sounds very mystical," Maddie laughed.

"Well, guilds all had secret rituals and things they were supposed to protect," Keith said. "Wait until your Journeyman initiation. One of the reasons the Guild didn't elevate another third degree Master after Errol is because no one knows where the other half of the mystery is hidden. A second degree master is elevated about once every fifty years in order to make sure the rituals still work, but no one has ever found the other half of the secret."

"And you've been looking for it all your life?" Maddie asked.

"Sounds pathetic when you put it that way," Keith winced. "What we know is that there were Guild rituals and the other codex. It has always been surmised that he was secretly printing this other book at the same time as the Bible, and that was the cause of the falling out with Johan Fust, his financier. The hiding place has remained a mystery."

"But now you think you might have found the other Gutenberg," Maddie surmised.

"I've been thinking for quite some time that perhaps it wasn't another book that Gutenberg printed, but was one that he owned," Keith said. "The assumption about the secret project is entirely conjectural. What got me thinking about this particular book were not the names of the people in it, but the name Johan Humery."

"Did Germans have any other names besides Johan? Who was this one?" Maddie asked.

"The immediate answer is that he was the person who gave this book to the monastery for safe-keeping."

"I'll bite," Maddie laughed as they turned and examined another page. "What is the long story?"

"Conrad Humery was Gutenberg's second business partner in Mainz, after he returned from his exile when Adolf became archbishop," Keith said. "Humery was Gutenberg's sole heir and inherited everything in the estate. Presumably, Johan was a grandson and either father or brother of Baroness von Hussen."

"So the fact that he had a Bible—or Gospel—that matches the type of the Bamberg Bible…"

"That Gutenberg designed and probably sold to the printer of Bamberg," Keith added.

"And the fact that it contains the names of Gutenberg's grandparents," Maddie continued, "leads you to believe Gutenberg owned it."

"It seems reasonable," Keith answered.

"We can't even verify that it is that old," Maddie said.

"No," Keith responded. "That is why I need you to work a little more magic."

"What?"

"Go request this book on behalf of your library to examine it under laboratory conditions," Keith said. "We can have it shipped, but see if you can get it expedited so we can take it with us."

"Back to The Whit," Maddie said flatly.

"No. To Mainz," Keith answered.

Maddie sat and thought about the request as she turned through a few more flawless pages.

"If we verify that this is not only a book printed from the Bamberg type at the same time as the three volume Bible, but was also owned by Gutenberg with his family names in it," Maddie said, "what would it be worth?"

"About $14 million," he answered. "There isn't a library in the world that couldn't use an extra $14 million."

"And I suppose you know one that would pay for it." Keith just smiled back at Maddie. She scooted her chair back. "This could take a while," she said. "Don't bleed on any pages." She left the room.

Keith doubted that she would be successful, but the task promised to give him at least an hour to examine the book alone. There was something else he had noticed about this strange volume that he wanted to investigate, and Maddie would not have approved.

He returned to the inside front cover. He thought it was strange that the cover paper was plain instead of marbled, and that it was a rag paper and not vellum like the remainder of the book. He also noticed that the paper had come loose at the bottom of the binding and the padding pages had slipped down to expose an edge. He could be wrong, he supposed, but the padding pages looked like vellum.

He carefully inserted the plastic book mark under the edge of the cover paper and began to work it around, loosening the rest of the edge as he went. Soon he was able to lift the edge up just enough to insinuate the suction cup beneath the book paper and grasp the first of the padding pages. What he pulled out was one of printing's rarest finds. He held in his hand the rubric for the Bamberg Bible. As he continued to extract sheets of padding, first from the front cover and then loosening the cover paper from the back cover, he found twelve perfect velum sheets of printing.

These sheets would make no sense to an average person. They contained what appeared to be a random collection of letters, finely printed in columns and lines that mimicked the design of the Bible itself. These were the missing letters of the printed Bible. Even though Peter Schoeffer was including engraved initials printed in color in the *Psalter* of 1459, the Bamberg Bible was printed with blanks where a scribe was supposed to paint the graceful illuminations and red letters that appeared in the final work. The rubric was the guide that told what letter went in the next blank spot on the page. The rubric was normally printed on lower grade paper, sometimes bound into the book, but more often discarded with the scribe's notations scribbled on it. This was a rubric for the entire Bible—not just the Gospels—printed on fine velum and hidden in the cover of the book.

Keith was certain that he had found the real codex.

He intended to make every effort to acquire this Bible on behalf of the Gutenberg Museum in Mainz, but he had to get the rubric out of the library and to Mainz as quickly as he could.

While Keith was contemplating his problem, Maddie burst through the door. Keith must have looked ready to pass out, judging from Maddie's reaction to seeing him. She rushed to him and felt his head as though he had suddenly contracted a fever in addition to his wounds.

"We need to leave, Keith," she said before realizing what she was looking at. "You're sick." She paused seeing the loose pages lying on the library table. "What is this? What have you done?"

"The secret of the book was hidden in the covers. They're perfect," Keith said. He could see Maddie struggling with the act of vandalism and the importance of the discovery that Keith was communicating to her. Her excitement was apparently winning out when she abruptly repeated herself.

"We have to leave now."

"Our flight isn't for hours yet," Keith protested. "And I have to figure out how to get these loaned to us right away."

"It'll never happen," Maddie said. "Even getting the interlibrary loan of the book is going to take an act of God." She grabbed her coat from the back of the chair where it had been deposited when they came into the room. "Gather the pages up," she commanded. As Keith complied, she laid her coat open on the table and began tearing out a seam in the lining. "Put the book back in the canvas bag." Keith obeyed and Maddie inserted the pages of the rubric behind the lining of her new coat. She put her coat on and marched Keith with the canvas bag out the door to the information desk.

"Please tell Leslie that we're sorry we missed her when we left," Maddie told the woman at the information desk pleasantly. "I'm afraid we have to run to the airport. Better get that right back in the vault—I mean stacks—where it belongs."

She turned and hurried Keith out the door as quickly as she could. They nearly ran back to their hotel room to remove the pages from Maddie's coat lining and place them in the archival box in which they were carrying the monastery manuscript. Then they checked out of the hotel and caught a cab for the airport.

Once they were through security and waiting at the gate—for two hours, Keith noted—he turned to Maddie and confronted her.

"What on earth inspired you to take those pages and rush out of the library, Maddie?" Keith asked.

"Darling—" Maddie said softly, "and you are my darling—you aren't thinking clearly. I know that with your injuries and the drugs things move too fast sometimes." Keith had to admit she was right about that. He resisted the impulse to check his watch to see if he could take another painkiller yet. *But…* "In spite of their name, the NHGA isn't a public library, or a university library, or a government archive. It's privately held and isn't a part of any of our interlibrary loan systems. It could take months to get the book transferred, no matter how many forms I fill out or to whom I talk. If they even had an inkling the book is as valuable as it is or that you found a rubric in it, it would never be allowed out of the archives. These people might not be as skilled as you and I at evaluating what they have, but they are jealous about keeping it. I had to get us out of there as quickly as possible so there was no chance they'd discover what we know."

She's right, Keith thought. *If I were thinking clearly, I'd have acted more quickly, too.*

He took another pill without looking to see what time it was and was scarcely aware when the gate agent wheeled his chair down the jetway and Maddie settled him into his seat. After changing planes in Washington, D.C., they relaxed for the overnight flight to Frankfurt.

Eight

ROBERT FRY RUBBED HIS EYES and tried to think when he had last slept. His investigation of the Kane Library bombing had been hampered by lack of staff and too many bases to cover for his little division of Homeland Security. He did as much of the footwork work as anyone. A list of the ten most likely libraries in the U.S. that might be targets was being watched closely by his small team. The top candidates were libraries from which the note claiming responsibility for the first explosion had been posted to news forums. Others were on the list because of the type of collections they held, the name attached to the library, or their sheer size. A series of phone calls from his office had reached most of the head librarians and fortunately they took the threat seriously. It seemed like such a stretch to think that terrorists might target libraries, but already a series of Internet articles had appeared speculating government involvement and denouncing the attack on the Kane. Conspiracy theorists were coming out of the woodwork.

The Library of Congress and the National Archives were nearly impregnable, but conspicuous pieces in their collections had been temporarily removed under the guise of conducting maintenance on the climate control for their displays. The Declaration of Independence, Constitution of the United States, and the Two Volume Gutenberg Bible were no longer in their cases, but were in a vault deep beneath

Washington, D.C. Very respectable duplicates had replaced originals of some historic documents. Twice the usual number of guards patrolled the perimeter of the library and security had been tightened at every entrance.

Management of the New York Public Library knew only that government agents patrolled its premises. The larger public libraries had taken steps to protect their most precious works. Universities had taken advantage of the attack on the Kane Memorial Library to approach their boards with requests for better security and monitoring of their prized possessions. The ten regional branches of the National Archives each had federal security guards, but the buildings that housed the collections were by-and-large warehouses with no historic or architectural significance. Fry dismissed them as likely candidates for attack.

There were a few good-natured jokes in his office. A colleague brought his partner in cuffs saying he'd written in the margins of a book and was being charged with biblio-terrorism. Everyone had a good laugh but they were taking the work seriously. The worst part was waiting for another move. They tracked all the leads they had, but little was forthcoming. They waited and watched.

Nearly a million people in the United States had top secret clearance, a third of which were independent contractors. The network of intelligence agents was so massive that no one knew exactly what any other branch was responsible for. Over a hundred congressional committees and subcommittees monitored the activity of Homeland Security alone, and it was only one of sixteen different intelligence agencies. Obviously, not everyone was as concerned about the security of libraries as Robert Fry was.

"Rob, you should see this," his chief said, entering his office without knocking. "We've got another hit."

"Which one?" Fry asked quickly.

"Not on your list," the chief said with a hint of disappointment and censure. "Indianapolis. The National Historical and Genealogical Archives."

"Way down the list," Fry said. He never thought that library would make the top ten, let alone be the next target. "How bad is it?" The chief sat at the conference table in the situation room. Leroy Anderson, Fry's second was already in the room and turned on a monitor."

"Ten minutes after closing, a tourist was filming his family outside the Archives where they had spent the day. This is what he caught," Anderson said. They watched as two small explosions burst behind the pillars in front of the Library behind a woman and two children who were thrown to the ground by the blast. It looked like the film had paused for a fraction of a second, then the portico and façade of the building collapsed. Dust rose into the air and settled rapidly, smothering the small fires that sprang from the points of explosion. The camera was moving rapidly toward the building, no longer focused on the damage, but bobbing along as if at the side of the cameraman who put it down to tend to his family. They could hear his call to 911 as he frantically tried to explain that his family had been injured when a library exploded. The video was still running when the ambulance and fire department arrived, then went blank.

"His battery died," Anderson said.

"Any indication of who was responsible?" Fry asked.

"Not yet. We've got a flag out on any forum or email sent with indicators from this location or the key words from the first message," Anderson said.

"What are our chances of finding something?" the chief asked.

"We flag 1.5 billion messages and forum posts a day as it is," Anderson said. "Adding a few keywords won't speed or slow down the search. But we are better at picking up the right messages after the fact than before. We'll get something."

"Get Hu onto this," Fry said. "As soon as we spot a message that claims credit, track it back to the original IP address. I'm betting it will come from overseas. Compile a list of every international call out of Indianapolis within the bracket of the explosion and when the message appears. Correlate that information with the IP address. They have to find out when the bomb went off before they can post a message. Is any of this on TV yet? As soon as it hits the airwaves we lose the edge. I want a list of every name we've entered since the Kane bombing. Find out where every person is who is on that list and whether any of them were in Indianapolis. Get plane tickets, credit card charges, phone records. Anyone who has come on our radar in the past week... make that ten days to be safe... who was in Indianapolis any time in the past twenty-four hours. Get public records and Internet searches. I want to know which ones were in Indianapolis today.

"We're on it," Anderson said. He left the room yelling names, starting with Agent Hu.

"Get out there," the chief said. "You are the only one with a chance of seeing the pattern. Don't worry about security at the other libraries. I'll shake people loose for numbers 11-20."

"Chief, we can't do it that way," Fry said. "We've got to pinpoint what they are after. We can't guard every library. There's 3,200 of them named Carnegie alone. If we spread ourselves out trying to cover everything we'll leave something really valuable vulnerable."

"And your suggestion?" the chief asked.

"Put all forces on the high-value targets. Send notices to every-one else to button up their valuables like we did at the Library of Congress," Fry said. "We've been lucky with these two. The terrorists didn't penetrate the building. All the explosives were set outside. Lots of cosmetic damage, but nothing structural. Let's not let them get deep inside the Library of Congress or New York Public. Let's keep them on the perimeter."

"I'll take care of troop deployment," the chief said. "Get on a plane."

"I'm gone," Fry said. He stopped in his office just long enough to arm himself and then he was on his way to Indianapolis.

HOMELAND SECURITY DEPENDS on local agents to respond to emergencies rather than moving agents from place to place. It was an exceptional sign of Fry's importance to this investigation that he was loaded into an Air Force jet and hustled across the country. There was scarcely enough time to get a nap in before he was unloaded at Wier Cook International Airport. A nondescript black car met him on the tarmac and swept him into the heart of Indianapolis. The area around the library north of Monument Circle was cordoned off and the National Guard stood at attention around the block. Spotlights were trained on the damaged building and forensics experts were sifting through the rubble. Search dogs still prowled the area. Fry flashed his I.D. and walked purposefully toward the front of the building.

"Rob!" called one of the agents sifting through rubble. Fry recognized Zach Taylor, the local field agent.

"What's the word, Zach?" Fry asked.

"Two very low yield devices, placed high on the front pillars," Zach reported crisply. "Could have been planted anytime in the last week. Even a gardener wouldn't have noticed. Blended into the stonework. Took out the central pillars and the portico crashed down. Otherwise, no damage and no serious injuries."

"What about the family that was video-taping outside?" Fry asked.

"Fell down more out of fright than from the blast itself. Minor cuts and abrasions," Zach said.

"You say they are low yield?"

"If it had been any less it wouldn't have broken through the pillar at all. It was just enough to bow them out enough to snap. Weight did the rest," Zach said.

"Timing device?"

"No, radio receivers. Different signals to set off each charge one at a time. Not exactly efficient. Speaks to being set up quickly—possibly today. Forensics will get us a report by morning, but anyone with a line of sight could have set the blast."

"Good work, Zach. Locals on it?"

"Yeah, but they're not complaining about us taking the lead. Someone high up gave them the message."

Agent Fry stood at the site and scanned the surrounding area. At one time the monument had been the tallest structure in the city, but now hotels rose above the historic monolith. He looked toward the grassy mall north of The Circle. It extended eight blocks north of the Circle and was dotted with memorials and museums.

"What's that building?" he asked, pointing across the street.

"Hotel Sanford," Zach responded. "We've canvassed it, but no one saw anything."

Fry could imagine someone looking down from a window just at the time of the explosion. To his left, a parking garage rose five floors, each with a vantage from which a radio signal could have been sent. Even the top of the monument was in line of sight of the blast. A tourist inside could have set it. Fry's eyes continued into the sky where he saw a contrail.

"How close would the signal have to be?" Fry asked Agent Taylor.

"Not sure exactly," Zach responded. "I'm guessing within 200 yards—very likely less. We'll get the info from forensics."

"Let's get air traffic as well," Fry said. "Helicopters? Tours? What's that down there?"

"The canal. Lots of tour boats, canoes, paddle boats. No commercial traffic anymore," Zach responded.

"Geez. How do you protect a place like this?" Fry asked.

"How do you even know it needs protecting?"

"Keep me posted if you find anything interesting," Fry said. "I need to get a view from higher up." He turned and walked across the street and circled around to the front of the hotel.

When he was inside, he found the staff as friendly as Zach had indicated. They didn't hesitate when Fry asked to see the guest log. He asked for a floor plan with room numbers and scanned quickly looking for any name on the roster that rang a bell, but paying special attention to the rooms in the back of the hotel on floors three through eight. He quickly shot a picture of the register and emailed it to his office for comparison with the massive lists they were compiling. His phone rang just as he was getting ready to return the register to the desk clerk. He held onto it as he answered the phone.

"Fry here."

"This is Anderson. We've got a note," he said. "It was posted on one of the usual message boards. We're tracking down the posting location, but it's looking like Egypt."

"Give me the note," Fry said calmly. He listened then commanded, "Send it to my phone. I've got to get back to the site."

"There's one other thing," Anderson said. "We've got a match on people that were in both locations."

This could be good or it could be a wild chase, Fry thought. He flipped back a page in the hotel registry printout as he listened to his colleague. "Tell me."

"You won't like it," Anderson responded. "Two witnesses to the Kane bombing were in Indianapolis today." The words were scarcely spoken when Fry saw the names on the registry from the day before. "Madeline Zayne," the two agents said at the same time. "And Keith Drucker," Anderson finished.

"They checked out of the hotel shortly after noon according to the hotel records," Fry said. "Where are they now?"

"Their flight should arrive in Frankfurt, Germany shortly," Anderson said. "We've put a watch but do not apprehend bulletin on them."

"What time did their flight leave?" Fry asked.

"Two-fortyseven p.m. Eastern Standard from Indianapolis. The flight from Dulles went at 7:15."

"The explosion here was at 6:15 p.m.," Fry said. "They would have been in… Wait. Did you say they changed planes in D.C.?"

"That's right." Images of national monuments flashed through Fry's head.

"I don't like this. Get a crew on scrubbing the pillars, porticos, and entrances of the Archives and the Library of Congress," Fry said. "If Drucker and Zayne were in D.C. at 6:15, they couldn't have set off the explosions here in Indianapolis. But the bomber could be following them around."

"Drucker and Zayne couldn't have," Anderson said. "But her brother's flight wasn't until 8:00."

"Her brother was here, too?"

"Her half-brother. We've had him on a watch list for two years," Anderson said. "He's part Iranian. Did freelance work for the State Department on and off over the past several years, then dropped out of sight the last few months."

"Why didn't I know anything about that before now?" Fry shouted into the phone.

"We just put it together," Anderson said. "He's using an Iranian passport under the name Yousef Hassan."

"Pick him up."

"We can't," Anderson responded. "His flight left Chicago for Egypt about two hours ago. It will take us forever to get through Egyptian red tape. You going after him?"

Fry thought hard for a moment before answering. One sibling that made her living taking care of rare books and one who got his kicks blowing up libraries? Talk about yin and yang. But if the brother was needling the sister by attacking wherever she was, he'd be following her to Europe. Fry had to be there first.

"No. You follow him. Egypt is the home of the very concept of libraries. Tell the chief I'm on my way to Germany," Fry said. "And Leroy, have Hu get me every detail about where Drucker and Zayne are traveling."

Fry disconnected and walked outside, then dialed Keith Drucker's phone number. There was no answer and Fry left a terse message. The car that brought him from the base was still parked at the blocked street next to the library. He slid into the back seat and directed the driver to Weir Cook Airport. He kept trying first Keith's phone and then Maddie's, leaving messages and sending texts.

If he read them right, they were truly horrified about the bombing of the library, but he had a feeling they weren't telling him everything. Why get out of his hospital bed to visit a library 800 miles away?

He needed to be where Drucker and Zayne were. And they were a long way from vacationing in Jamaica.

NINE

KEITH SPRANG AWAKE when the plane touched down in Frankfurt and felt fantastic—at least by comparison. Things weren't hurting as badly and he was thinking clearly when they stood to get off the plane. He waved away the offered wheelchair and they walked through passport control with the only difficulty being a border agent curious about his bandages. Keith was scanned and then they both passed through into Germany. They were met on the other side of passport control by a tall man to whom Keith spoke in German. Keith greeted him as Günther and they were escorted to a waiting Mercedes. Günther tossed their bags in the trunk and got in the front to drive. Maddie kept the archival box containing the stolen pages and manuscript with her. Inside the car, Frank was waiting for them.

"No trouble getting that through Customs?" he asked, pointing at the box.

"None at all," Keith said. "They were more concerned that I might be carrying drugs under my bandages than that I was transporting stolen manuscripts."

"They can be strange about transporting antiquities," Frank said, "but printing seldom raises an eyebrow." Frank paused and looked at Keith strangely. "What do you mean stolen?"

"You've brought manuscripts in before?" Maddie interrupted.

"In and out," Keith said. "Usually we've had certificates and authorization to transport early printing, but there have been instances..."

"Speaking of which... stolen?" Frank repeated.

Keith had his phone open. No sooner had the phone found a signal than it began to chime with text messages.

"Somebody wants to reach us," Keith said.

"Who is it?" asked Maddie.

"About a dozen messages from Agent Fry demanding that we call him at once. Either we're suspects or something else has happened."

"Well, don't ignore it," Frank said. "What did you steal?"

Keith entered the number. "You probably have messages on your phone, too, Maddie," he said as he waited for it to connect.

"I don't know if I even have service in Europe," Maddie said as she pulled her phone from her bag and powered it on. By the time her phone started chiming with incoming text messages, Keith had Agent Fry on his line.

"Where the hell are you?" Agent Fry demanded at once.

"In Germany," Keith responded.

"I hope you aren't visiting any libraries."

"Not exactly," Keith said. "We are investigating some old manuscripts. What's up?"

"Don't pretend you don't know about the bombing at the National Historical and Genealogical Archives," the agent growled.

"Wait! Bombing of what? We were just there," Keith said.

"Imagine that!" Fry shouted. "You were just at the Kane Memorial Library when it blew up. You were just at the NHGA when it blew up. What library are you heading for now?"

"We're headed into Mainz, Germany to the Gutenberg Museum," Keith answered. "You don't really think we had anything to do with this, do you?"

"Anything to do with it? Yes. Responsible for it? No," Agent Fry said. "The NHGA was bombed just after you visited it. Same kind of explosives and trigger. Exactly what got you out of a hospital bed to travel to Indiana?"

"I went to see my grandfather and while we were there we…" Keith hesitated. He didn't really want to go into any detail about what they were really after. "We were doing some family research and decided to go visit the library," he finished lamely.

"And this family research has taken you to Germany now?" Agent Fry asked.

"We're visiting friends," Keith answered. "My PhD advisor lives here. We have some questions about an old manuscript."

"And will your visit include any libraries?" Fry pushed.

"Yes," Keith answered.

"Well don't," Fry said. "I think the bomber is following you. I don't know why or how, but I have a feeling you do."

"What gives you that idea?"

"The latest note," Fry said. "Somehow I think this is going to be important to you and I don't know why. I have a notion to have you picked up and put in protective custody until I get there. I am leaving in 20 minutes so give me your hotel name and I will meet you there as soon as I arrive."

"We're on our way to Mainz," Keith said. "We're staying at the Sheraton. It's just two blocks from the museum."

"There will be plain-clothes police in the hotel," the agent said. "They are there for your protection. I want to be there before you enter that museum."

Keith nodded his head as he looked at his grandfather and Maddie and then realized that the agent couldn't hear him.

"Can we visit a friend?" Keith asked.

"I don't see any problem with that," Fry said. "But don't try to lose the agents who will be following you."

"What does this note say?" Keith asked.

"I'll tell you when I get there," Fry said. "Do not go to the Gutenberg. Understand?"

"Yes." Fry broke the connection before Keith could ask anything else.

"This is going to be more difficult than I thought," Keith said. "Homeland Security thinks we are being followed by the biblio-terrorists. They don't want us to go to the museum until Agent Fry gets here. He wants us to stay in the hotel, but said we could go to a friend's house." Keith looked meaningfully at Frank. Frank nodded.

"I'll make the arrangements," Frank said. "Why don't I drop you at the hotel and take the package with me. That way when you walk over to Dr. Schneider's house you won't be carrying anything suspicious—or stolen."

"It's some pages we found at the NHGA," Keith explained sheepishly. "We didn't have time to check them out properly."

"You two may be a bad influence on each other," Frank said shaking his head.

"Do we have time for a nap before we do anything else?" Maddie asked around a yawn she couldn't seem to stifle.

"That's a good idea," Frank said. "An hour nap, then a cup of strong coffee, and then come to meet us."

"I'M SORRY I can't take you into the museum this afternoon," Keith said. "I was looking forward to showing you the exhibits. I thought perhaps you'd like to pull a page from the Gutenberg press."

"You're kidding, right?" Maddie asked.

"There is no evidence that the press was *the* one Gutenberg or Schoeffer used," Keith responded. "But there is a print shop set up in the museum that is pretty authentic with a press representative of the same era. You'll love it."

"Well, tomorrow after Agent Fry gets here we can go in," Maddie sighed. After a few moments, Maddie asked, "What are we really doing here, Keith?"

"I think you know," he said. "We're looking for the secret concealed in the Gutenberg rubric."

"You know something you haven't told me," she said. "You might not know what the secret reveals, but you know what it is."

"That's only partly true," he said. He closed his computer and stretched out on the bed next to her. "Unfortunately, over the years we've learned not to talk about our suspicions. People would discredit our personal qualifications in whatever work we were doing."

"It's all about alchemy, then."

"Yes," Keith responded, "but probably not what you would expect."

"Tell me."

"I've told you that there were two parts of Gutenberg's mystery. He hid part of the secret in the mysterious other book and part of it in the rituals of the guild. But that only explains how he was hiding the secret," Keith said. "Nothing really says what he was hiding."

"You mean that you don't actually know what you're looking for?"

"We know there is a book or books or manuscript involved. According to the stories, it or they contain a big secret Gutenberg held."

"What was he, Colonel Sanders?" she laughed. He joined her. He knew very well why these stories were never told outside the Guild. But now that he'd started telling her he couldn't back down just because she gave a predictable response.

"The proper name of the Guild is The Worshipful Society of Typefounders and Alchemists," Keith said.

"You don't really think there's an alchemical formula that will turn lead into gold," Maddie said

"Not lead into gold alchemy," Keith said. "Gutenberg was protecting something he considered too dangerous to share, but too important not to. He was sued three times that we know of, twice over a secret project he kept from his partners."

"I only really know two things about alchemy," Maddie said. "The transmutation of base metals into rare metals, and the so-called philosopher's stone that gave eternal life."

"I'm sure some of the early members of the Guild hoped that was what it would lead to," Keith said. "Gutenberg was a metallurgist and alchemist, true, but he was as close as we can come to a chemist in the pre-Newton world. He combined elements in unexpected ways that surprise even modern chemists. His ink, for example, has never been surpassed for blackness and permanence. Its composition shows minute traces of various heavy metals in it. His formula for lead type was used pretty much intact for 500 years until phototypesetting began to take over the industry. Guild lore says that he could mix the formula for lead type without using scales."

"So, you are saying that perhaps he invented or discovered some other alloy?" she asked.

"Alchemy changes the state of a substance," Keith said hesitantly.

"What do you mean by the state? You mean like water, can turn to ice, or steam?"

"Sort of," Keith said. "But those are strictly a liquid, solid, gas function of temperature. They aren't permanent states. I should say allotrope instead of state. It's more like turning sand into glass. You can look into the sand all you want but you won't see through it. But when you melt it and it re-solidifies, suddenly you are looking right through the sand. And it stays that way. It doesn't turn back into sand. It has to do with how the molecules line up with each other."

"There's more to glass than just melted sand."

"You *can* make glass out of just sand or silica, but you have to heat it to over 4000 degrees. If you add sodium carbonate to the sand though, it reduces the melting point to only 1500 degrees. Some upscale restaurants cook steaks over an 1800 degree flame," he said.

"So you could make glass in a kitchen."

"A form of glass. But soda lime glass is water soluble, so it makes a pretty poor window," Keith laughed.

"What else do you add?"

"It depends on the type of glass you want to ultimately have. Mostly heavy metals. Most commonly, you add lead for crystal, boron if you want to make the glass impervious to heat, barium, magnesium, or other things. Glass ends up being about three quarters silica and the rest a combination of other elements," Keith said. "When there is lead or other heavy metals in the mix, it lowers the melting point, too—down to about 1400 degrees.

"Then you could say that making glass is a form of alchemy."

"It uses many of the same principles and even has some of the same ingredients as lead type. Each of the elements has a higher melting point than the combination of the elements together." He loved this subject and was as likely to go on talking about it all afternoon as to take a nap. She smiled at him and moved closer.

"I've got an example," she said. "The closer I get to you, the lower my melting point becomes."

"That's more than chemistry," Keith said.

"Show me." Eventually they slept.

TEN

AFTER THEIR NAP, Keith and Maddie stopped in the hotel restaurant and ordered black coffee. He looked around the café as they waited for the coffee to be delivered. A man in a gray suit too small for the width of his shoulders sat at a nearby table and seemed never to take his eyes off of them. Another man slouched near the entrance to the café reading a newspaper. A young man stood in the lobby engaged in texting on his cell phone. Two women sat at a sidewalk table sipping coffee and talking animatedly.

"It would be a lot more comforting having a bodyguard if I knew which one it was," he whispered. "Any of these people could be either a security guard or a terrorist. They should all wear nametags."

"Whatever happened to the days when the good guys wore white hats and the bad guys wore black ones?" Maddie agreed. "In fact, whatever happened to good coffee?"

"It wasn't supposed to be good coffee," Keith answered. "Just strong. Come on. We're only a few blocks from Dr. Schneider's house."

"Why are we going there? We could have stayed in bed."

"Dr. Schneider has access to certain tools that we need," Keith said. "Let's just say that the Guild is an underground society."

They stopped at the door of a house in a long row of buildings so close together that they touched. A ramp led up to the door in addition to the steps. Answering Keith's knock, a man in a wheelchair opened the door. As he slipped inside, Keith looked behind him to see which of the people he had spotted were following him. He saw three people, but none looked familiar.

"Guten Morgen, Herr Doktor Drucker," the old man said to Keith. The two talked casually in German for a few moments and then Keith turned to Maddie.

"Herr Doktor Schneider, hier ist Fraulein Doktor Zayne. Doktor Zayne, Herr Doktor Rolf Schneider." Maddie mumbled a quick "Guten Morgen" to the old man in Kennedy-esque German.

"Do not worry, Dr. Zayne," said Dr. Schneider. "I speak English and welcome the opportunity to use it."

"Dr. Schneider was my advisor in antiquities when I came to study in Germany," Keith said to Maddie. "There's no one better qualified to help us decipher whatever it is that Gutenberg left us."

She smiled and warmly shook the old man's hand.

"I'm very pleased to meet someone who was so influential to Keith, Dr. Schneider," she said.

"Können wir du sprachen?" Dr. Schneider said. Maddie raised an eyebrow at Keith for a translation. "Use first names," Dr. Schneider continued. "Please call me Rolf. There is no need for academic formalities in my kitchen. Come and have coffee and tell me what you have found. We have not opened the box in your absence. Frank would not hear of it." At the mention of his name, Frank stepped through the kitchen door and embraced the couple.

"Yes, please call me Madeleine," she said as Frank led her back into the kitchen. They sipped coffee from Rolf's countertop espresso machine with satisfaction. It was much better than the hotel coffee.

"We have a clue to the puzzle," Keith said when they were served. "We have a page of the Schoeffer manuscript that talks about a treasure revealed in the other Gutenberg. And we have the other Gutenberg."

"And you stole it?"

"It was an emergency. All we needed were the padding sheets. They are a rubric for the 36-line Bible," Keith explained. "They were behind plain rag book papers in a bound copy of the Bamberg Gospels."

"And what makes you think that all you needed was the rubric?" Frank asked. "We may still need to wait for an official transfer of the Gospels to an evaluation center in order to complete the puzzle."

"I don't think so," Keith said. He hungrily accepted biscuits from the tin being offered. It was almost time for lunch, but Keith was starving for breakfast. "The Gospels were identical in every way to any other 36-line Bamberg. It just happened to be only the first four books of the New Testament."

"What made you think the rubric was the key?" Maddie asked.

"There were three things," Keith said. "First, a vellum copy of the rubric was bound into the cover. Vellum would normally have been scraped and reused or it would have been bound into the book as final pages as we've seen on a number of occasions."

"Not exactly conclusive," Frank said, noncommittally.

"That brings me to the second item," Keith said. "The bound book was only the first four books of the New Testament—The Gospels— but the rubric is the full 12 pages of the Bible copy sheets. And they are unused—no scribe crossed out letters or made annotations. So, the message, whatever it is, must be in the rubric, and if the Bible is needed at all, only the Gospels will be required. I seem to recall that there is a 36-line New Testament in the collection."

"Lots of speculation going on there," Frank said.

"Which brings me to point three," Keith said. He was used to this skepticism from his grandfather. It was the way they worked together when Keith was beginning his dissertation. Frank may have had no more than a high school education, but his probing questions and demand for more proof drove Keith to some of his best work. "I think there's an anomaly in the rubric."

"Now we're getting somewhere," Frank said. "Without that we could use any rubric for the Bamberg and any set of Gospels. What's the nature of the anomaly?"

"You didn't tell me there was an anomaly," Maddie said.

"It wasn't an issue when we took the pages."

"What is it?" Rolf asked.

"There are nicks in some of the characters," Keith said. "The printing is pristine. The substrate is crisp and clean, but randomly throughout the page, the characters have tiny wedges taken out of them. I didn't have time to check every page, but the nicks occurred frequently enough on the first page that it stood out."

"And what does that mean?" Frank asked.

"I haven't the faintest idea," Keith said. "It just struck me that such a beautiful piece of work shouldn't have damaged characters in it. I know what you went through to shape characters in exactly the way Schoeffer's type was worn. But these are a regular shape. There must be a message buried in it somewhere."

"We should start by just reading the letters that are nicked," Maddie volunteered. "Maybe they spell something out."

"There's enough of them," Keith admitted, "and we should definitely check that. I'm guessing that we'll find that there aren't enough different letters to make out a message when taken in order."

"Why not?" Maddie asked.

"Think of the rubric in terms of first letters of chapters," Keith said. "Occasionally there is an entire line of text that will be inked in red, but mostly it is the grand capitals that are left to be filled in by the scribe. In English, the most common letter that begins a sentence is 'T.' I've never done an exact study of it, but I would guess that in German it is 'D.' The rubric for a Latin New Testament has more 'Es' and 'Is' than all the other letters of the alphabet combined."

"You say the nicks are wedge-shaped?" Frank asked.

"Yes," Keith said. He wanted desperately to pull a page of the rubric from the archival box for the four of them to look at, but good document preservation instincts kept them sealed in the box until they could be opened and examined under proper conditions. "It struck me that all the nicks are uniform in size and shape," Keith said.

"Like arrow-heads," Frank speculated. "Same size and shape, but not all pointing the same direction? Could be a path we have to follow."

"Did he actually have to cast type in each letter shape?" Maddie asked. "I know he did a lot of different versions of the same character to accommodate mimicking the scribes and making the lines come out even."

"We'll have to get it under high magnification," Keith said, "but I'm guessing the nicks were made after the characters were cast, and maybe even after they were set. It would be awfully hard to predict and cast characters that had to be set in a specific order through the body."

"So we need the laboratory," Rolf said. "I see no reason to wait." He led them to a door that Maddie had assumed was a closet, but when opened revealed a small elevator. "If you would not mind using the stairs," Rolf said, "I will meet you below." Next to the elevator was a second door that led to a stairway descending in the adjacent space. Keith surprised Maddie, however, by opening yet another door at the bottom of the stairs and leading her and Frank down a much longer set of stairs.

"Rolf guards one of the entrances to the Guild laboratory," Keith said to Maddie.

"How many entrances are there?" Maddie asked. Frank chuckled behind her.

Keith glanced back at Maddie, remembering his own first time descending to the lab. He had entered through the museum and thought they were going into the basement, but the stairway went down six flights with no doors.

"I'm not sure," Keith told Maddie, "During the war, everything was at risk. The museum was actually bombed. The caretakers had to find ways to protect the collection, first from the Nazis who were burning what they called seditious texts, then from the bombings, and finally from the Allies who saw victory over Germany as a way to gain a huge number of valuable artworks and spirit them out of the country. It was a wonder that any of the collection survived intact. You know that a Gutenberg Bible that went missing during the war recently surfaced in Russia. It was taken away and hidden during the entire Communist era and the Russians refused to return it to the museum from which it was stolen during or soon after the war. Part of the strategy here in Mainz was to wall off rooms and create a maze in the catacombs under the city. Nothing leads directly to anything anymore, but Rolf has a connecting laboratory just under his house. Other passages might wind for a mile before you connect to the hidden rooms."

"Were you in Germany during the war, Frank?" Maddie asked.

"No. My family emigrated from here to the United States when I was only seven. But they maintained strong ties back here."

They reached the bottom of the staircase and Frank opened a door on the right.

The laboratory they entered was as well-equipped and modern as the one Maddie worked in. She gasped when she saw it.

"Part of the work of the Guild," Keith explained, "is the preservation of the art of printing as represented by the great works that have come from the press. This is actually a kind of teaching facility where Guild members learn every aspect of the printing arts, including hot-metal typesetting, cold-type, and even computer typography."

"Keith is responsible for having introduced computers into the lab," Frank said. "Most of my generation was not enthused about it. But it is part of the comprehensive package. It all has to do with the preservation of the word."

Rolf was already in the room, an elevator door open behind him. "Now let us see this new discovery," he said.

"Yes," said Keith, clumsily donning white gloves from a drawer. Keith offered gloves to Maddie, but she had already pulled a pair from her purse and was opening the archival box.

"Rolf, Maddie is an expert in handling old documents," Keith said. "Could I suggest that she arrange the pages for us to look at?" Maddie smiled at Keith.

"Wunderbar!" Rolf said. "It is difficult for me to move the documents from this chair. It is such a pleasure to have another professional in our work."

The team was established. Frank sat to the side, occasionally asking a question or offering an opinion on a typographic characteristic, but letting the three scholars examine and discuss the work. The process involved spectral analysis of the ink, carbon dating a scraping from the vellum, and high resolution digital photography of the pages so that they could be examined under magnification.

Keith and Rolf had progressed far past the student/teacher phase of their relationship and were colleagues who knew how to work well with each other. They spoke freely, easily shifting from English to German and back with occasional Latin phrases thrown in. When Maddie used an Italian phrase to ask for clarification of a German one, they began including Italian in their mix as they discussed the documents in front of them.

Verification that they were dealing with a genuine Bamberg rubric came after comparisons of the ink mix and vellum age with documented analysis of existing copies of the 36-line Bible late in the day. But that merely meant that deciphering the code—if there was one—was still ahead of them. It was not long before they had eliminated the idea of simply compiling the nicked letters in order and reading them. The frequency of letter usage made a substitution code—basically a cryptogram—equally unlikely. A heated discussion on whether the direction of the nicks in the characters meant anything yielded no resolution. There did not seem to be a pattern or logic behind linking the letters together using the nicks as directional indicators.

When the work moved away from the actual documents to computer images of them that were manipulated on-screen, Maddie gathered up the originals and returned them to the portfolio. Keith and Rolf were bouncing ideas back and forth at an incredible speed.

Frank laid a hand gently on Maddie's shoulder and said softly, "Finding it hard to compete?" Keith glanced up and smiled at Maddie.

"I'm trying not to feel like I need to," she answered.

"Let's take a break," Frank said, much to Keith's relief. As stimulating as the work was, he was finding it increasingly difficult to focus. His head was pounding and the light flashes in his left eye distracted him from the image on-screen. "I'd like to officially welcome Maddie to the Worshipful Society of Typefounders and Alchemists."

Rolf began applause and Keith and Frank joined him. Maddie grinned and curtsied.

"Why, thank you very much," she laughed.

"It is time to formally accept Dr. Madeline Zayne, granddaughter of Master Alchemist Errol Wadsworth, as my apprentice and to begin her initiation into the Black Arts," Frank said. Maddie furrowed her brow as she heard this. The term seemed to puzzle her. "Printing is the black art," Frank explained to her. "Because of the ink. We've never actually sacrificed a virgin." Maddie looked startled at first and then laughed as she picked up on the black humor. "You are, however, about to learn both the art of printing and the science of alchemy," Frank concluded. "Disciplines in which your grandfather achieved the highest mastery.

"I knew my grandfather was a printer, but I had no idea he was part of this," Maddie said. "Is it very difficult to learn?" she asked, turning to him.

"You speak Italian?" he asked.

"Yes," she answered.

"An easy language to learn, but a difficult one to master. It's the same with alchemy. Easy to learn how to heat metals to the right temperature and what portions to mix. Very difficult to master actually blending them at the right stages."

"Sounds like espresso," she laughed. "You can have a machine grind the coffee to exactly the right fineness, heat the water to exactly the right temperature, and force it through the grounds at exactly the right pressure. But it will never compare to a shot pulled by a really good barista."

"Yes," laughed Frank in response. "Ordinarily we would ask your grandfather if he would sponsor you, but you've told us that he is too infirm to be of help."

"How well did you know my grandfather?" Maddie asked.

"We spent nearly three years in the same chamber working on the Psalter," Frank said. "In the Guild, we count each other as brothers and sisters."

"You've had women in the Guild before?" she asked.

"Not many," Frank admitted, "but a few. It doesn't seem sensible to most women."

"What doesn't?" Maddie persisted.

"Things like swearing you to secrecy before I answer that question," Frank smiled. "And you have to ask me to do that." Maddie hesitated and then nodded her head. Keith watched the proceeding with nostalgia as he remembered the day he arrived in California to begin his own initiation with his grandfather. He was right. Most women Keith knew would never swear an oath of secrecy before they knew what they were keeping secret. It was a paradox. Maddie, after a minute's consideration, turned to Frank and looked him squarely in the eye.

"Frank, will you sponsor me for membership in the Guild?" she asked. "I am ready to swear the oath of secrecy." Frank smiled.

"I'm glad that was a carefully considered answer," he said. "This is now an official act of the Guild then. I will sponsor you and administer this oath." Rolf opened a drawer in his desk and removed a small vial and spoon such as would be used for measuring minute amounts of elements used in mixing ink and metals.

"Taking a small amount of printer's ink on your tongue and swallowing it is symbolic of taking the craft and its knowledge into your body and mind. Will you accept this sacrament?" Maddie grimaced, but closed her eyes and opened her mouth. Keith could see she was thinking of the cyanide in the ink at the monastery. Frank touched her tongue with the spoon of ink. She grimaced, but swallowed it down and opened her eyes.

"Now repeat after me," Frank said. "By the ink that runs in my veins, I swear…"

"By the ink that runs in my veins, I swear…" repeated Maddie.

…that I shall keep and maintain the secrets of the Worshipful Society of Typefounders and Alchemists as they have been kept since the day that Johannes von Gutenberg gave them to Peter Schoeffer. I swear that the ink I mix will stay forever black; that the type I set will be true and square; and that I will honor my masters and learn what they have to teach me. May the ink in my blood turn to poison if ever I am forsworn in this oath.

Maddie stood with a puzzled look on her face when she had finished the oath, then smiled.

"I've just had the strangest feeling of déjà vu," she said to Frank. "Once my grandfather was helping me draw a poster for a school project—maybe first or second grade—and he reached over and touched a felt-tip marker to my tongue. He said that now we both had ink in our veins. He drew something on my arm and said that all the members of our club had a tattoo. He showed me the tattoo on back of his shoulder. I always thought it was something to do with the Navy or such."

"Each of us has a tattoo," Frank said. "It is part of the journeyman's ritual—if you choose to go that far. It is typically placed on the left shoulder blade."

"I've seen Keith's flags on his shoulder," Maddie said.

"Shields," Keith interrupted. "Each of the tattoos is a printer's mark from the days of the *incunabula*. The shields were the mark used by Schoeffer and Fust. A bit is added at each elevation."

"I remember an anchor on Errol," Maddie said. "That's why I always thought it was from the Navy."

"The anchor and dolphin of Aldus Manutius," Frank said. "The last of the printer's marks of the first half century of printing. Now you are ready to learn some of the secrets of the Guild."

"Are there really secrets so valuable they can't be shared outside the Guild?" she asked. "Every society wants to believe it has secrets that would change the world if they got out. Look at the Freemasons. Or even the CIA. The secrets they guard are never as potent as the members want desperately to believe. Is the Guild so different?"

"There is never as much power in knowing a secret as in keeping it," said Frank. "Take the whole concept of black arts. We call printing and typesetting black arts because of the color of ink. We talk about ink in our veins and running like rivers from the presses. It is all a metaphor for putting ink on the page."

Maddie suddenly got a far-away look in her eyes as she processed what he was saying. Frank paused as he saw her lose focus. She suddenly turned to him.

"That's it!" she exclaimed. "Black ink running like a river from the presses. All a metaphor for putting ink on the page. The Black River. It's in the letter fragment. The secret is hidden in the Black River. In the ink on the page."

The ritual came to an abrupt end as the team huddled over the pages of the rubric again to discuss what the clue might mean and how Gutenberg could hide a secret in the ink on the page. Of course the mere fact that the letters were notched could be all that was meant in which case they were no further along than they had been. But they were sure there must be some other clue, perhaps in the formulation of the ink itself. Maddie examined one of the pages of the rubric under high magnification, a task Keith was unable to focus on with his single eye. He huddled near her suggesting things to look for.

Eventually, Keith slumped in his chair from exhaustion.

"I'm shot," he said. "If I don't get food and drugs sometime soon, I'm going to pass out."

"And no wonder," Frank said, looking at his watch. "It's nearly midnight. We should never have let you stay down here so long."

"There is food in the kitchen," Rolf said. "We can leave everything here in the lab until tomorrow." Maddie carefully boxed up the rubric and manuscripts before she turned to the stairs. Keith was standing at the door looking up.

"Rolf," she said quietly, "can Keith use the elevator to go back up? I don't think he can make the stairs." It was only half an hour later that Maddie and Keith stumbled into their room and collapsed on the bed. Sleep claimed them immediately.

ELEVEN

FRY WAS ON THE GROUND and buzzed on caffeine. He was at least twelve hours behind Drucker and Zayne, but Intelligence showed no sign of Zayne's brother being in the same area. German security was on alert and even though they doubted Fry's assessment, they considered the Gutenberg Museum too precious a treasure not to protect.

There was only one significant shrine to ancient works in Germany. The three great repositories of Europe were the Vatican, the British Library, and the Gutenberg Museum. If Drucker and Zayne were headed to the Gutenberg, then so were the terrorists.

A driver and an interpreter met him at the airport. Fry was fluent in Farsi, but was not familiar with German. He needed to communicate clearly with his international counterparts and Homeland Security had come through with just the sort of person to whom both Fry and the Germans could relate. Gretchen Holtz was a tall blonde with obvious Nordic heritage. A woman of restrained good looks, she dressed professionally in a conservative suit with moderate heels. Fry speculated that she might be a world of fun when she was off-duty, but on-duty she was a serious agent for the United States Government.

"What's our status?" Fry asked once they were in the car.

"The *Bundeskriminalamt* or BKA has guards patrolling the Platz and area immediately surrounding the museum and library," Gretchen said, pulling a folder and map out of her briefcase. "Bomb-sniffing dogs have gone over every inch of the exterior to check for anything that could have been planted before the alert. All negative. Based on the previous *modus operandi*, guards were doubled during the time immediately before and after closing. Nothing threatening was spotted. They are waiting for a full briefing as soon as you get to Mainz."

"What about Drucker and Zayne?"

"They arrived, checked into their hotel and left about three hours later," Gretchen continued. "They went to the home of Dr. Rolf Schneider, a respected antiquarian and professor. Drucker studied under him in college. They have not yet left the home to return to the hotel."

"If they aren't back by the time we finish with the BKA, we'll visit them there," Fry said.

"There is one other thing."

"Yes?"

"Dr. Drucker's grandfather is also staying at the home of Dr. Schneider," Gretchen said. "We do not have a record of their relationship, but the senior Drucker did not check into a hotel. He arrived a day before Drucker and Zayne." Fry considered the news. Keith had told him they visited his grandfather in California when he checked out of the hospital, but didn't mention the old man was meeting them in Germany. Fry hated it when whole families were involved in a case. If the people of interest were all unrelated, you could draw conclusions based on their meetings. But if they were all related, there were hundreds of reasons they might get together. Perhaps they were simply on a genealogical expedition as Keith had suggested. But with Madeline Zayne's brother in Indianapolis at the same time they were, it suggested things were more complicated. They had no record of the brother being near the Kane Library as yet, but the search had just begun.

"Drucker is a German name, isn't it?" Fry asked Gretchen.

"Ja. It means 'printer,'" she replied.

"Do all German names mean something?" he pressed.

"Many do, or did at one time," Gretchen answered. "Holtz is a derivative of the word for woodcutter. It doesn't mean that we become what our names suggest, anymore than people in America named Smith shoe horses or that people named Fry are cooks."

Agent Fry laughed in return. "You may have noticed that I'm not of English ancestry. Traditionally, Kurds don't have surnames. Mine was kindly provided to my parents by the INS. We should find out, though, if the senior Drucker is an immigrant from Germany, or if he has dual citizenship, and what his relationship is to Professor Schneider." Gretchen opened her cell phone and began making inquiries at once. Fry checked in with his team in Indianapolis, but there was no new information available. He decided to check in with Keith and warn him he was on his way. He was greeted by voice mail and a message that the phone he dialed was not connected to a network at this time. *Damn him for shutting off his phone*, Fry thought.

The meeting with the BKA was long and tedious. Gretchen managed to keep Agent Fry and his German counterparts from breaking off the heated talks, and ultimately negotiated agreement on a strategy that did not include the immediate arrest of Drucker and Zayne. It involved Fry revealing much more about his investigation than he intended. Contrary to current news reports, attacks on libraries had not been unknown before the bombing of the Kane Memorial Library. It was part of a much larger initiative that Fry had been working on for three years to track down the source of attacks on large portions of the world's information infrastructure. So far these attempts had been thwarted, but no arrests had been made and comparatively few leads to the source of the threats had been uncovered.

"The world's idea of cyber-terrorism is that teenaged hackers try to plant viruses on computer networks, or that phishing scams capture credit card information," Fry said as Gretchen translated. "The truth goes deeper. A number of cyber-attacks are cover for a larger scheme. We believed at first that the social aspects of the World Wide Web would be a positive thing, preventing government disinformation from overwhelming citizen-reporters as they delivered eyewitness accounts of political movements and even natural disasters around the world. That popular notion, however, has proven false. The social Internet is remarkably easy to manipulate."

"Who would want to do this?" asked Major Jürgen Dern, the coordinator of the German operation.

"We are not sure," Agent Fry admitted. "But we have evidence suggesting a number of news stories brought to the public through blogs and social networks have actually been planted through careful manipulation of popularity ratings and exposure through multiple networks. Take a look at this." Fry called a news story and photo up on his cell phone. The headline read, "Police turn their backs while library explodes." The photo was of two police officers looking away from the exploding pillars of the NHGA.

"It's completely specious. The officers were over a block away at the time of the explosion. The camera's telephoto lens collapsed the depth of field on the picture so it looks like they are standing right in front of the building. The story appeared in early morning editions of newspapers outside the Indianapolis area who thought they'd received newswires from Indianapolis. The story was false, but almost impossible to counter by the time legitimate channels got the facts. We believe the people responsible are computer-savvy far beyond even the typical hackers, maybe even using supercomputer technology to create a presence that appears larger than its reality."

"Why libraries?" asked the Major.

"We're still working on that, but the world over, people view libraries as being authoritative sources of information on every subject. We believe the group is gearing up to make a major attack that will discourage people from going to the most respected of these libraries, either closing them down, or simply making them appear to be too unsafe to frequent," said Agent Fry. "That would cut people off from the one source of information that they consider to be more reliable than the Internet."

Ultimately, the Major agreed that there was a credible threat. Police would be on guard in the morning when Drucker and Zayne entered the museum and would remain vigilant throughout the day. Fry had his files emailed to the BKA from his office in Washington, including a last-known photo of Keith, Frank, Madeline, and Madeline's brother Yousef. The latter had not surfaced yet after his flight from Indianapolis to Egypt. Leroy Anderson would be in Cairo in a few hours and would begin coordinating efforts with the Egyptian police.

"I NEED FOOD," Fry said flatly to Agent Holtz as they left the German police and headed toward his hotel. He had requested rooms at the Sheraton where Drucker and Zayne were staying to set up as a mobile headquarters. Two of the guards watching the librarians were contracted directly by Homeland Security. Fry wasn't sure how many the Germans had on the couple, but they could figure out their own housing. His negotiations with the Germans had been intense, but successful. It was nearly midnight and he'd been informed that Drucker and Zayne had returned to their room. He was pretty confident they would stay put until he got there, so food seemed like a good idea.

"Restaurants in Germany don't normally stay open all night," Gretchen said. "But there is a *bierstube* two blocks from here that serves food until it closes. I must ask, do you eat pork?"

"Yes," said Fry. "I'm Kurdish, but not Muslim. Zoroastrians are traditionally omnivores and drinking alcohol is considered a religious duty."

"What an interesting background you must have," she said, guiding him into the tiny pub. "I only ask because the staple of a *bierstube* is sausage and potatoes. I wanted to make sure you could eat."

"I'd be happy to have you order for me," Fry said. "All I could do is point at a picture if I saw something that looked good."

"No problem. Beer?" Fry nodded.

The sausages and *pomme frites* they were served were exactly what Fry imagined they should be. He had polished off a second beer while engaged in an animated conversation with Agent Holz—now just Gretchen to Fry—before he ever thought about Keith and Maddie.

"So I never did go back to finish college," Gretchen was saying. "From my first assignment as a summer intern, I was hooked. At that time, Homeland Security was in such chaos they didn't make a college degree a requirement. It was all about who you knew, and an intern had an immediate opening."

"I was already working in cybercrimes when they slammed the department together," Fry said. He looked at his watch. Gretchen called for the check. "As much as I want this conversation to go on all night, I have a call to make on our librarians. Here's hoping they've had enough sleep to be coherent when I get there."

"Our field quarters are next door to them…" Gretchen began. "Just in case we need more intense surveillance. I'll walk you there."

At 1:45a.m., Agent Fry stood at the door of Maddie and Keith's hotel room and knocked. Loudly.

TWELVE

KEITH WAS JOLTED AWAKE by the pounding on his door. He was momentarily disoriented. Hotel room. Mainz. Maddie. Black River. It was the Black River that he had been dreaming about. He had been swimming in it—drowning in a sea of black ink—but the promised code still eluded him. Maddie was already out of bed pulling on a hotel bathrobe. She handed one to Keith as she called out, "Just a minute!" She checked through the eye-hole and saw Agent Fry. She glanced at Keith, who was cinching up his robe, and then she opened the door and let the agent into the room as he was raising his hand to knock again. Fry stepped into the room, leaving a second person in the hall. Keith didn't quite see who it was.

"Agent Fry," Maddie said. "We expected to talk to you in the morning."

"It is either here, now, or at German Police Headquarters in the morning," Fry said flatly.

"I think I'd prefer the here and now," Keith responded. "I'm sorry we don't have anything to offer you, but we could try room service to bring us coffee."

"Coffee is on its way," Fry said. "Sorry to have awakened you. If you need a moment to collect your wits, I understand."

"I think I'm fully awake already. Keith, are you okay?"

"No. Yes, I'm fine," Keith got out. "Actually glad to be awake from my dream. I'm sure I'll be able to sleep well enough when this is over."

"Let's get right to this, then," Fry said sitting in the chair by the desk. Maddie and Keith sat on the small sofa in the room. "A terrorist is following you or tracking your movements in some way. Your proximity to two different libraries that were attacked in such a short period of time is too significant to be a coincidence, especially since there could be no other rational reason for the terrorist to target the NHGA. Logically, the next attack would have been at the Smithsonian, the Library of Congress, or the New York Public. Every move a terrorist makes is consistent with his own internal logic. The only thing that links these two targets is your presence."

"I wondered why they would choose that library," Maddie said. "But we didn't decide to visit the NHGA until the day before we arrived. How could someone follow us?"

"That's the question that makes my German counterparts want to arrest you on the spot," Fry answered. "I was inclined at first to agree, but there is a possibility that you were set up. If so, you'll be good bait. My ability to sell that idea to the German authorities is what is keeping you out of jail right now. Being bait is a dangerous occupation, of course, so if you decline there is an officer waiting outside to escort you to protective custody."

"That's a great choice," Keith said. "But unless they actually want to kill us, I don't see the danger of being bait, as you say. It seems that they have avoided killing people so far. So they are more likely to wait until we are away than to attack while we are there."

"I agree," Fry said. "But I want to firmly eliminate you as suspects, which at the moment I can't. You are planning to visit the Gutenberg Museum and Library in the morning?" Keith and Maddie nodded. "Okay, here is how it will play out. I will stay here for the rest of the night. I'm sorry to cramp you. You are welcome to go back to sleep. I would like your cell phones here on the desk so that I know that there are no changes in plans or accidental alerting of the terrorist."

"How cozy," Maddie said. Both cell phones were charging on the desk, so the demand was already satisfied.

"If you don't mind," Keith said, "before we go back to sleep I'd like to know what was in the message after the last bombing. On the phone, you said you had a message that led you to believe we were being followed, but you didn't tell us what it was." Fry opened his jacket pocket and withdrew a folded sheet of paper. Both messages had been printed on the sheet. Keith scanned the first message then read the second closely.

The seekers go to the cradle, but there is no safety there. The family extends back beyond the printed page. The Wisdom of Pharaoh is this: Flee the halls of learning and return to the land that bore you. The clay feet of this empire will not support it. It will collapse into a river of darkness. Flee the tomb of words, for only the chosen grants access to knowledge.

"It's another hopeless mishmash," Keith sighed. "What gives you the idea that it has anything to do with us?"

"I looked up your job title," Fry said. "I wasn't familiar with the term Incunabulist. The dictionary say *incunabula* means 'the cradle,' and is applied to the first fifty years of printing. Then I see that the 'seekers go to the cradle,' but the 'family extends beyond the printed page.' You were searching and continue to search in the cradle of printing. That is enough for me to speculate that it has something to do with you."

"That's silly," Maddie said. "It's no more than a coincidence."

"The Kane could be a coincidence," Fry said. "The NHGA is 800 miles away from the Kane and on the day it was bombed you happened to be there, too. That's not coincidence, whether the note existed or not. Now look. I've pulled every file on you two from your birth certificates up through your professional credentials. I know how many times you've traveled outside the country, not just this year, but in your lives. Miss Zayne, I know you are divorced from a wealthy man who owns a computer company. I know your grandfather is here in Mainz with you, Mr. Drucker. I know that you are not the type of people who would destroy libraries. But I don't know why someone with an axe to grind against libraries would follow you specifically around damaging the libraries you visit. I need your help on this or I need to take you out of circulation, so to speak."

Keith sat silently with Maddie's hand on his shoulder. He was still exhausted, but he felt he was thinking clearly. The second terrorist note included two more references to material in the manuscripts that they had uncovered. Keith was convinced that whoever had written the notes had at one time or another had access to those two manuscripts. Homeland Security could probably find out who owned and had access to those documents. But Keith could not jeopardize the sanctity of the Guild. Perhaps he could reveal enough to the Agent to help without revealing the secrets of the Guild. He would have to try.

"Agent Fry," Keith said. "I think you are right. In fact, I'm beginning to suspect we were targeted before the first explosion."

"Now we're getting somewhere. Will you explain, Dr. Drucker?"

"Please, call me Keith. We're going to be having some long conversations before this is over."

"Very well, Keith." The agent sat back expectantly, but did not offer a first name to Keith and Maddie.

"As you know, my work involves examining books and manuscripts to verify their age and authenticity," Keith began. "On the day of the Kane bombing, I was working in the Rare Books collection on a manuscript that purportedly came from a Carthusian Monastery here in Germany. It's a splendid piece—a catalog of works that had been collected and copied in the monastery over the 11th to 19th centuries." Keith paused to be sure he did not reveal too much, but making sure that he gave the agent enough to work with. "Tucked into the book was a fragment of a letter—one page—that dates back to the mid-1400s. I can give you a photograph of it. The two terrorist notes you have received have four direct references to information in those two documents: the key, the river of darkness—or in the manuscript referred to as the Black River—the Wisdom of Pharaoh, and the Tree of Knowledge. I thought they were completely unrelated at first, but now that there are four different references, I have to believe that whoever wrote the terror notes has at one time or another had access to the two documents that I was reviewing at the Kane on that day."

"You have these documents now?" Fry asked.

"No," Keith said, hedging the truth a little. They were in the basement laboratory below Rolf's house. "I can provide high resolution digital photographs, though. A collection like the one that I'm evaluating is not generally available to a wide number of people. I think that whoever is responsible for these bombings should be on the record of people who have seen or evaluated the works in the past. Probably within the past year."

"That's good. I want to see the documents, or the images and send them to the lab for analysis," Fry said. "But there is more that you need to tell me. Why did your analysis of those documents trigger the attacks? Why are they following you? And how did they know you found those particular documents they day they attacked the library." Keith had been puzzling over that piece of the puzzle himself.

"You showed us a picture from a security camera from the Kane when I was in the hospital," Keith said. "There are cameras all over the library, including in the rare books room."

"Those are pretty low resolution cameras," Fry said. "We've been working to get a better view of the picture we showed you. It would be hard to tell what document you were looking at."

"I agree, except for something that I was puzzling over as I looked at the pictures of the document," Keith said. "When we were analyzing the letter, we discovered it had been sprayed with an even coat of invisible ink. We couldn't make sense out of that." He opened his laptop and logged on. "I took pictures on the library equipment and took the memory card to download them. But when we got to my grandfather's house, he photographed the pages again on my lab camera. A few years ago I had the anti-aliasing filter taken out of my camera to increase the resolution. It turns out that it is layered with an IR filter." Keith showed two pictures side-by-side. The one taken in the library was a good quality photo in which the text was clearly readable. In the second photo, the page was dark gray with the writing scarcely visible.

"Your photo looks like it was taken without enough light," Fry said.

"The light's fine," Keith said. "The IR-reflective substance is invisible to the naked eye, but blacks out everything in the infrared spectrum. My guess is that if you examine the digital security record of the rare books room on the day I found this, the cameras that show me handling this will look like I've got a black hole in my hands."

"The security cameras in the labs are all IR sensitive," Maddie said. "It's so they can track people under low light conditions. Everything in rare books is UV filtered."

"This is important," Fry said. "I'll have the disks examined right away. Why were you keeping this document secret from me? I'd like to think you weren't intentionally withholding evidence."

"Agent Fry, there are a number of organizations in the world that keep secrets. They don't have anything to do with national security or with the well-being of any group of people," Keith began. "But they have secret rituals and arcane knowledge that is passed down and jealously guarded. I belong to one such organization that is over 500 years old. It was founded right here in Mainz—the cradle. Pieces of the rituals might be mistaken for treasure maps. This letter fragment is a missing part of the Guild's rituals. A person could assume that since it is a guarded secret, it must lead to something of great value."

"And does it?" The agent had a way of cutting straight to the chase.

"I don't know," Keith said. "We have never decoded the secrets, so no one knows what they are supposed to guard. I am working on that on behalf of the Guild." There was a long pause. Agent Fry twisted the gold ring on his finger. Keith squinted, but could not see it clearly through his one eye.

"I know something of secrets," Fry said softly, "—how to keep them and how to reveal them. I will respect your 'Guild's' need to keep its rituals secret, but am enlisting you to help on anything we find including using your Guild's secrets in your analysis if necessary. I think we will work something out. For now, copy those images for me and give me the details about the collection you were working on. I'll get my team working on a check of all those who had contact with the collection before you did."

Keith made the required copies while Maddie filled Fry in on the collection and the Carthusian catalog Keith had been working on. It was a long and relatively sleepless night.

"OKAY, HERE IS THE WAY it will go down," Fry told the couple over a room service breakfast. "The museum opens in an hour. You will enter and do your touring thing. How long do you expect to be in the museum?"

"After a tour of the main exhibits, we'll be going into the museum vaults to research the documents," Keith responded. "We won't be there for too long after getting no sleep. Maybe five or six hours."

"Only to a librarian would five or six hours in a museum seem like not too long," Fry said as he shook his head. "I'll have a man inside where he can watch you…"

"That won't work," Keith cut him off. "We will be in an area of the museum where mere mortals are not allowed. They are controlled environments deep in the museum's vaults. Your man inside won't be able to follow us."

"I don't like that," Agent Fry said. "I'm still working on trusting you. You could make a call from inside."

"Could," Keith said, "but won't. We want the terrorist caught as much as you do. You can keep our cell phones. They won't work from the vaults anyway. They are underground. You have my word we won't make any calls." Agent Fry looked expectantly up at Maddie.

"What?" she asked. "Of course you have my word, too. I don't even know how to make a call in Germany, let alone have anyone to call."

"Very well," Fry said. "Before you leave the museum this afternoon, make contact with the guard. He'll inform us and we'll be watching. You will leave the museum and return directly to this location where you will stay until we signal all clear. If he's here, we'll catch him."

"By then I'm going to need sleep anyway. We have a late dinner slated with my grandfather at Dr. Schneider's home with other colleagues," Keith said. "Between jetlag and injuries, I'm still pretty exhausted."

"Your injuries are one thing that makes me inclined to trust you," Fry said. "I have your doctor reports, by the way. If you need anything we can get it from the embassy within a couple of hours."

"I should take comfort in that?" Keith responded.

"Homeland Security takes care of its own," Fry answered.

"Actually, Keith," Maddie said. "Your painkillers are almost gone and we need more dressings for your eye."

"They'll be here when you get back," Fry said. "Do you have any questions?" Both shook their heads. "Don't try anything heroic. If you see something that is out of place, let our man know. Let's go meet him and get this started."

Thirteen

O N THE 100TH BIRTHDAY of the Gutenberg Museum, 600 years after the birth of the inventor, the museum opened a new, expanded space and exchanged the old stone façade for one of glass. A sculpture fountain in front of the building was a welcoming sight to Keith and Maddie as they approached. They had met the police contact in the hotel and he preceded them to the museum so they arrived alone. Uniformed police patrolled the central square with muzzled dogs, circling the block and the open square on which the museum was located.

"Nothing subtle about German security, is there?" Maddie asked.

"It's okay with me," Keith said. "This place is like home to me and the more secure it is the better. We wouldn't have risked as much by entering from underground."

"We could enter from underground?" Maddie asked.

"It's something that I couldn't reveal to Fry. I don't really expect to spend six hours in the few rooms of the museum, though an hour showing off the display to you is certainly in order."

"Then we are going to the vaults?" Maddie asked.

"In a matter of speaking," Keith said. "You might call it visiting the catacombs."

They made eye contact with the police officer assigned to watch the entrance and then proceeded to examine the exhibits that include three copies of the Gutenberg Bible in light-controlled rooms and ultraviolet filtering glass cases. After an hour they reached the Gutenberg workshop where a demonstration of the huge screw-press representative of 15th century printing had just been held. After the room had cleared, Keith took Maddie's hand and ducked under the rope barrier separating the area from the rest of the museum. In a moment they had slipped behind the painted scenery depicting the print shop and stood before an unmarked door. The door was unlocked and Keith and Maddie stepped through into a stairwell.

"Is this like the stairs in Rolf's home?" Maddie asked.

"Exactly," Keith answered. "One of the reasons the museum is as vibrant as it is today is because of the catacombs. In World War II, the museum was actually bombed repeatedly by Allied forces. It is really a maze down here," he continued. "It connects all the way over to Rolf's house and down several more levels." After 15 minutes of twisting through low-ceilinged tunnels, Keith opened another door and Maddie found herself facing Frank and Rolf in the lab.

"That's amazing!" she said. "You could pop up anywhere."

"Only if you happened to know that four stories under the city of Mainz there is another city," Frank said. "I was beginning to wonder if you were showing up this morning." Keith quickly related events with Agent Fry and how the square was being patrolled. Maddie added that they did not have cell phones as the agent was holding them to prevent calls to unknown parties.

"It is of no concern to us," Rolf said. "Unless you were followed into the catacombs from the museum, you are far removed from the dangers above."

"THE BLACK RIVER may mean more than the literal ink," Maddie insisted. "Maybe it simply means the line of type. The rubric could be just what rubrics have always been, the key to the message, not the message itself."

"But how do we find the message?" Rolf asked. "We do not know what kind of key it is."

"What if the rubric is actually a grille," Maddie said. "There must be some reason it was in the bound copy of the Gospels. If you lay it over the pages of the Gospel and poke holes through the nicks maybe they point to the letters that spell out Gutenberg's secret."

"Poke holes in a 500 year old printing?" Dr. Schneider exclaimed. "That's vandalism!"

"Biblio-terrorism," Keith said chuckling. "But we don't have to literally poke holes in the text. We have technology now that Gutenberg didn't even imagine then." He called up the pages on the computer screen and created a mask for the image that showed only the position of the nicks. Then he called up a high resolution image of the Bamberg Bible and laid the mask over the first page. He began reading out the letters that were below the mask. The result was gibberish.

"It seems that this could take a long time," Keith said. "If it is a grille, we don't know which page of the rubric is first, second, and third. And we don't know what page of the Bible to lay each page of the grille over. I can write a program that will capture the letters from every page of the Gospels under each page of the grille and read out the results, but it could take a long time."

"You've all spoken of Gutenberg's other book," Maddie said. "Where is the reference to that?"

"We don't have an actual reference to it," Frank said. "It's more like a legend that has been handed down through the ages in the Guild, that someday we would find his other book and then we could discover the secret."

"So we won't actually know the reference unless we read the whole letter that our fragment came from," Maddie said. "Can't we look at it?" Frank looked at her thoughtfully and then nodded his head.

"I confess, I've been thinking the same thing," he said.

"Impossible!" Dr. Schneider exclaimed. "The letter is locked in the strong box and only a third degree master can open that lock."

"Exactly what I was thinking," Frank said. "Keith, can you and Madeline set up a program to run the grille. If it takes a long time, we'd better get started. Rolf, would you join me?" The old man rolled his chair behind Frank into the next room.

Maddie pulled up a chair beside where Keith had the image up on screen and was adapting a standard application—commonly used for comparing two versions of documents for authentication purposes—to collect the data beneath the photographic masks that Keith created from the rubric. If the grille was laid over a text document it would be a fairly simple process that wouldn't take more than a couple of hours to run. But they were dealing with images of printed pages. Each time the grille hit a character, it had to identify the character from its shape. This was fairly well-tested optical character recognition, but there weren't any plug-ins for German Fraktur-style type. Added to that, there were sometimes three or four similar designs for a given character and the optical character recognition algorithms could be comparing letters for hours. When it was done, there would still be errors that only human eyes could resolve. Maddie was right. Someone needed to look at the whole manuscript and not just the fragment that had been recovered. The only person who could look at the rest of the letter was a third degree master alchemist.

"This was a brilliant idea, Maddie," Keith said. "What made you think of it?"

"I had a lot of time to think last night while you were talking to Agent Fry," she said. "I just figured that the most common form of code in the Middle Ages was sending a grille that could be placed over a known text. It seemed like it would work here. How are you feeling?"

"Running on adrenalin," Keith responded. "It's probably time to head out of the museum. And now that you mention it, my body's starting to beg for more painkillers. If I take them down here, I might collapse and go to sleep like I did on the plane. I don't want to miss something important."

"I'd wake you for it if it came up," she said seductively.

"Oh, I certainly hope so," he said kissing her. They reluctantly broke the kiss and Keith went back to the program.

"Keith, does it make any difference what order you compare the pages in?" Maddie asked.

"Not to the program," he responded. "I usually start from the front and go forward unless there is a reason to examine a particular part first. Why?"

"I was thinking that we should start with the fourth Gospel."

"Why?" he asked.

"It just struck me that if we are looking for Gutenberg's other book, we should start with the Gospel of Johannes." She looked at him as he turned to stare into her eyes. Then he swept her into another deep and passionate kiss just as Frank and Rolf came back through the door.

"Entschuligen Sie!" Rolf exclaimed when he came through the door. He glanced at Frank who chuckled to himself.

"Herr Doktor!" Keith exclaimed.

"I take it you have found the meaning of the code?" Rolf asked.

"Not yet," Keith explained. "But my beautiful, charming, and brilliant partner came up with another idea that may help make the process a little shorter."

"What is that?" Frank asked.

"Start with the Book of John."

"Set your program running and let's talk," Frank said. "We have Guild business to discuss. Maddie is a member of the Guild now, so she is welcome to listen in. But this will involve you even more than you already are."

Keith executed the program and turned to face his mentors.

"It's SO EXCITING, Keith," Maddie said in their hotel room. "A few days ago I didn't know the Guild existed, and tonight I'll be initiated as a journeyman and you will be elevated to third degree master! You'll be the first since my grandfather."

"Maddie, the Guild is over 500 years old—almost 600," Keith said. "The rituals haven't changed in all that time. When an apprentice is brought into the shelter of the Guild, it is a pretty simple ritual. You don't want to scare away the young. But Frank wants to initiate you as a journeyman. This time it is not just tasting the ink. It is literally getting it in your blood."

"They want to inject me with it?" Maddie said, genuinely horrified.

"Not exactly," Keith said. "He pulled his bathrobe down over his shoulder. "This tattoo?" he started. "It was outlined on the night of my journeyman initiation. Tonight, Frank will cut the final part of the design into it. And you will get yours."

"Yes," she said hesitantly. "It won't be something I'll regret, will it?"

"I hope not. It's not like it will be huge or obnoxious or anything like that. But it is going to put a mark on that flawless skin of yours."

"Flawless? This freckled bag that keeps my insides in?" she said. "I'm not worried about a tattoo. I can stand the pain and I want to be part of the Guild. But, I'm wondering… Could I have my grandfather's mark? The anchor and dolphin?"

"I'm sure granddad would think that was an appropriate honor."

"You'll be there for my initiation, too, won't you?" she asked. She moved toward Keith and traced the outline of his tattoo.

"I wouldn't miss it for the world," he answered. She pushed the robe further off his shoulder and in a moment it dropped to the floor.

"Maybe I should count the freckles where you are going to have the tattoo, so I'll know how many get covered with ink," Keith said pulling her toward him. Keith pulled her robe off her shoulder and caressed his lover softly. Maddie melted toward him.

"Darling?" she asked softly.

"What my love?"

"You've actually passed all the tests to become a third degree master, haven't you? This is just a formality tonight, right?"

"No." Keith sighed. "I don't know if I can pass the tests tonight."

"Of course you can!"

"Perhaps I could with two good eyes and two good hands," Keith said. "It gets harder the further you go," Keith said softly.

"Doesn't it though," she sighed.

"I mean the initiation," Keith said.

Only a dozen active members of the Guild still lived. Of those, only Frank and Rolf had seen the third degree initiation. That had been the initiation of Maddie's grandfather. Whatever the trial that was set before him, Keith knew that it would require everything he had learned and knew in order to pass it. Electronic tests and computers wouldn't help him tonight, and if he failed, the secret would remain hidden. It would be a sign that the time had not yet come.

"What do you have to do?" Maddie asked.

"I don't know what will be expected of me," Keith said. I know that it won't be easy. It's sure to involve casting metal. That is the alchemist's art. If they expect me to turn lead into gold I'm sunk."

"That's myth. You can't transmute base metals into precious." She laughed. "No. Tell me you can't."

"I've done a pretty good job with silver," Keith said nonchalantly.

"What?" Maddie asked.

"It was part of the second degree initiation," Keith said. "Of course you can't literally turn lead into silver, but I had to mix an alloy that was the same weight and density as silver using only elements that were available in Gutenberg's day. You know the atomic chart only had 14 elements on it in 1460."

"You're kidding!" Maddie said. "What did you mix?"

"I went with the traditional printer's elements," Keith said. "The alchemists of Gutenberg's day used mostly lead, tin, and antimony. By the time I took my second degree initiation, I had done volumes of research on the composition of Gutenberg's ink and type, and had done spectral analysis on half the books in the museum. So the other masters were a little surprised when I added copper to the mix. I came out with an alloy that when stamped into a coin was exactly the same weight as a coin made of pure silver from the same mold."

"That's amazing!" Maddie said. "So don't tell me you've counterfeited silver coins."

"No," Keith said, "but it wouldn't be that hard to do. All you would have to do is silver plate the slug and it would weigh and look the same as silver. How do you think they managed to start using steel cores in quarters and still have the same weight? Hardness and color are the real problems. Lead still melts at a lower temperature than silver does. A good hot hand and you could fold a fake coin in half."

"So any ideas about what you will have to make tonight?"

"I don't know," Keith said. "A missing puzzle piece, a jewelry setting, a key, a ring, or just about anything. The problem is I don't know if I can do it."

"Of course you can," Maddie reassured him. "They wouldn't even ask you to if they didn't believe in you."

"Thank you, love," Keith said. "I've had plenty of opportunity to test my alchemical skills. I know I'm capable. But with the damaged hand and eye, I'm not working with a full toolbox. You have to be able to feel and see what is happening. I don't know if I can do it like this."

"Let me see your hand," Maddie coaxed. Keith held it out to her and she began the ritual of dressing his wound, taking off the old bandages and examining the hand gently. She carefully applied the salve they had been issued at the hospital. Most of the smaller cuts had healed over and showed pale thin skin. There were still a few scabs, kept soft by the salve. Worst were the six stitches between his thumb and the center of his palm. That was where he had caught the biggest piece of glass. That cut made flexing his hand difficult and Keith had complained of numbness in his thumb.

"Maybe I can reduce the bulk of the bandage, at least," Maddie said as she began cutting gauze and tape. True to his word, Fry had left fresh dressings and Keith's prescription drugs in their room. When she was done, Keith did have more flexibility in his hand even though it felt odd. His eye was another matter, however. When Maddie removed the bandage to apply drops, Keith only saw a blurry light. At least the flashes had stopped. Maddie swabbed the eye and washed it to remove any crust that would come loose. Then she bandaged it back up.

"I'm sorry I can't do anything else about your eye, darling," she said. "I hope you can make it okay tonight."

"I hope so, too," Keith said. "I almost thought I could see a little while you were cleaning it this time. Do you know what's most important now, though?" he asked.

"That you have your health," Maddie affirmed.

"No, that I have you. You are much better than health."

"Are you saying I make you sick?"

"Love sick," Keith laughed. "If I had two eyes, I could count your freckles twice as fast. Now let's see, where was I?" He rolled over with Maddie on the bed and pointed to a freckle below her left breast. "Twenty-seven, twenty-eight, twenty-nine," he counted pointing randomly to freckles on her torso.

"Wait," Maddie said. "You counted that one twice."

"Which one?" Keith asked, shocked.

"This one just above my navel. I distinctly remember you counting that one in El Centro," Maddie laughed.

"No!" Keith exclaimed.

"Yes, I'm sure."

"Well that tears it," he pouted. "Now I'll have to start all over. One," he said kissing the tip of her nose.

"Two," she said kissing his lips.

"Three," he mumbled. Then they lost count again.

FOURTEEN

GERMAN POLICE PATROLLED the square with vicious-looking dogs. Fry approved. Drucker and Zayne had left the museum three hours ago and were escorted to their hotel. It was nearly six o'clock. The museum was closed and the staff had been led out through a rear entrance. A policeman was leading a bomb-sniffing dog up to all surfaces of the building that could be reached from the street. The dog had found nothing.

At last the inspector emerged from the building indicating there were no employees left inside. Still there was no sign of a threat. Major Dern stood with Agents Fry and Holtz near the fountain in front of the museum discussing whether the target was still under threat. The other two attacks had occurred within ten minutes after the facility closed while there were still at least a few people in the area to witness the explosion. The square had cleared as the sun set and people were mostly inside their homes, restaurants, or hotels. Dern wanted to call off the surveillance, but agreed to leave two officers on patrol for the night.

Fry turned away from the conversation toward the square after they had agreed, and told Gretchen he would go to his room to sleep and to wake him if there was any development. He wanted a meal, a shower, and a bed. Gretchen agreed to meet him in the morning. They started toward the hotel but were brought up short by a dog's bark and angry voices shouting. Fry looked up to see Madeline Zayne walking across the square in her blue wool coat with red hair flying. She angled slightly toward the museum ignoring police orders to stop. The bomb-sniffing dog that Fry had seen near the building was straining at his leash and setting up a ruckus that the other dogs on the team were quick to pick up on.

"Doctor Zayne! Stop!" Fry yelled at the woman. On hearing his voice, she changed course and headed directly toward Fry and the museum. Something was very wrong. *That's not Zayne,* Fry thought as the officer released the dog. She was a few yards away when the dog brought her down. The dog's master was moving in with an automatic weapon drawn, shouting orders at the woman. Fry could see a device in her hand and sprinted toward her, yelling at the officer to back off. He could see the woman's face as she turned and smiled at him past the dog. Without stopping, Fry bowled the dog over off the terrorist and rolled to the feet of the officer as the explosion rocked the Platz and knocked the officer off his feet onto Fry. Shards of paving stones pelted the two of them. Forty feet away, Gretchen was being lifted to her feet by the Major as officers rushed to the scene.

Unrecognizable body fragments followed the rubble to the ground and Fry could see in his mind the grim determination of the woman as she smiled at him and raised the trigger for the explosives she was wearing. He knew her and in the aftermath of the explosion he could see the red wig askew and her blonde hair showing beneath it. He knew exactly where he had seen her. He was struggling for his phone as the officer on top of him struggled to comfort his whimpering dog next to them. Sirens began to blare and an ambulance arrived in moments. The police officer and dog had taken more of the blast's impact than Fry, but were both alive. The woman was dead—all for the sake of a small hole in the pavement.

"Danke. Danke," repeated the officer as he cradled the wounded animal in his arms. He looked at Fry through a sheet of blood that ran from a cut above his eye and repeated again, "Danke."

This was serious. In America, the bombs had been planted and set off from a distance. Fry had allowed himself to believe this group would not send suicide carriers to deliver a bomb for such small stakes; but that a suicide bomber would be the same person who had orchestrated the other explosions was unfathomable. He was on his cell phone by the time Gretchen reached him.

"Hu," Fry barked into the phone. "What's the status on locating the woman in the security footage of the Kane Memorial Library?"

"We have a name," Hu responded, "but it doesn't check out. The student ID she used to check books out was stolen."

"I need the footage that shows her leaving the library ahead of Drucker. We need a positive ID on both her and the boy she was with," Fry said. "Don't worry about trying to find her, she's here. We just need to identify the remains."

Fry replayed the security tapes in his mind. A young woman and her apparent boyfriend leaving the library ahead of Druker. They were out of the picture when the explosion went off, but Drucker had said they were fumbling for keys as they juggled the books. There would be no rest tonight as they tried to identify the body and waited for the inevitable message claiming credit for the bombing.

AGENT FRY SHOWED UP at Keith and Maddie's room an hour before they were scheduled to join Frank and Rolf for dinner. They were shocked at the news. When they heard the sirens converging on the Platz they tried to go see what was going on, but the guard stationed in their hall asked them politely but firmly to stay in their room. Fry interrogated them about their activities during the day. Keith said he had been invited to a Museum laboratory in the lower levels to examine some recent acquisitions.

"I need to account for everyone," Fry said. "Were your grandfather and Dr. Schneider with you?"

"Yes. They were there before we arrived," Keith said. Agent Fry looked at him, scowling and absently twisting the ring on his finger.

This time Keith was near enough that he could see the symbol on the ring. Fry turned to Maddie.

"Ms. Zayne, when is the last time you saw your brother?" he asked.

"Two days after the explosion at the Kane Library," Maddie said. "I talk to him on a regular basis and after the explosion he became very protective."

"Was he in town at the time of the blast." Fry asked.

"He said he flew in from Japan," Maddie said. "He's kind of a free spirit and doesn't really call anywhere home. He spends a lot of time in Iran. He has dual citizenship."

"Did you tell your brother you were coming to Mainz?"

"Not precisely. I called him from the San Diego airport to let him know that Keith and I were doing some family research and then flying to Germany. I didn't say Mainz in particular. You can't think my brother is involved in this can you?"

"We believe the terrorists are getting their information about your movements from someone. So far the only people who have come up that have had contact with you and knew where you were going are your brother and the senior Mr. Drucker," Fry said. He rubbed his eyes. "Do you know where your brother is now?"

"No. He said he was going to resume his trip the last time I talked to him, so I assumed that meant Japan." Maddie shook her head. "He's a little paranoid, but he's not the kind of guy who would bomb buildings."

"I'd like you to take another look at this photograph," Fry said. "Please search your memory." He pulled a photo from his briefcase and handed it to the two.

"No," Maddie said. "Isn't this the photo you showed us in the hospital? There just isn't enough detail to recognize her."

"Yes," Fry said. "It is from the security camera."

"I'm in the background," Keith said. "I don't recognize her from my class if that is what you are thinking."

"This young woman just blew herself up in front of the Gutenberg Museum, half an hour after it closed tonight."

"My god," Maddie whispered.

"Keep me informed if you have any strange contacts, see anyone following you, or think of anything that might be useful in preventing more attacks. And let me know if you're planning to visit any more libraries on your trip."

"Can we continue with our plans for dinner and the evening?"

"Of course. Oh, and here are your cell phones. Call me if anything develops." Agent Fry left the room.

After a few minutes, Keith and Maddie left to join the Guild ceremony. There was no longer an officer in their hall.

"It seems we're no longer under suspicion," Maddie said.

"That, or we're no longer considered worth protecting," Keith answered thoughtfully.

FIFTEEN

"THERE'S NOTHING TO be nervous about," Keith reassured Maddie. He was sweating in anticipation of his own coming ordeal and the bandage on his eye felt wet and clammy. Nonetheless, he was doing his best to project calm to Maddie. Her part of the initiation was well-rehearsed. She knew what was expected and was prepared with the answers to the questions that she would be asked. She had even joked that Frank would have it easy when it came to doing her tattoo. All he had to do was connect the dots.

Keith was unsure about taking on the third degree initiation. Frank had flatly refused to do it when Keith suggested he was the right one. He insisted that he had turned the opportunity down fifty years ago and his decision still stood. He was too old to take it on. Rolf, the only other Second Degree Master simply said he wasn't able to work with the metals from his wheelchair. It had to be Keith or they lock the manuscript fragment and rubric up and wait for the next generation—if there was one.

Now, Keith and Maddie stood in an antechamber somewhere under the museum, but deeper than they had been earlier in the day. As they made their way down the stairs from Dr. Schneider's house and through the lab, Keith noticed that his computer program had quit running. There was no chance to check it, however, as they continued down into the catacombs. Once in the antechamber, they were dressed in black robes, over which they wore incongruous leather aprons.

"You know, an apron will not make me a cook," Maddie laughed. "Is this supposed to be your name or Frank's on my apron? Teufel des Drucker. What does it mean?"

"Printer's devil," Keith answered. "Our tradition doesn't really have apprentices, even though that's how we refer to them. The entry-level position in a print shop is printer's devil. They run errands, check type, haul lead, and pull the handle on the big press."

"Your name would be Printer, wouldn't it?" she grinned.

"Obviously it wasn't Americanized," Keith laughed. His own apron was adorned with the twin shields that he bore on his shoulder. Their conversation was cut short by the arrival of a hooded figure opening the door in front of them. He beckoned them forward.

"It is time to begin," the figure said. Keith recognized the voice of their driver Günther from the day before.

"Master of Arms of the Alchemists," Keith intoned formally. I wish to present this printer's devil for initiation as a journeyman in the Worshipful Society of Typefounders and Alchemists."

"Printer's devil," said the Master of Arms turning to Maddie, "do you agree to be bound to your master, to bear the mark he chooses for you, and to learn all things that he may teach you, no matter the cost, no matter the hardship?"

"Master of Arms," Maddie returned, bowing to the hooded figure. "I freely bind myself to my master as his journeyman in all things alchemical and will learn all he may see fit to teach me."

"Follow me to the chamber of mysteries," said the Master of Arms. Keith and Maddie followed him into a world that had not changed in 500 years. The descent was steep, narrow, and unlit. Maddie put her hand on the Master of Arms' shoulder and Keith laid his hand lightly on her shoulder as they descended. At the foot of the stairs, the Master of Arms opened a door into a candlelit room that seemed glaringly bright after the depth of darkness through which they had just passed. Seven robed and hooded figures awaited them in the chamber.

"Teufel des Drucker," said the man in the center. Keith immediately recognized Frank's voice and hoped Maddie did as well. "The Worshipful Society of Typefounders and Alchemists has existed uninterrupted for 500 years. We have not taken a new member in nearly twenty," he continued and then chuckled a little. "Forgive us if we are a little rusty on the formalities." Keith still had his hand resting lightly on Maddie's shoulder and could feel her relax as Frank spoke. She may have said that she was not worried about the midnight ritual, but just the passage through the dark was enough to bring on excited tension.

"There was once a celebration held each year called a Wayzgoose," Frank continued. "It was a feast held in August hosted by the printers for their staff. It marked the beginning of the season of working by candlelight. After the festivities, the separate masters of the town came together for more solemn rites. It was the one time of year when new apprentices were given their oath and the more experienced printer's devils were elevated to journeyman. Ultimately it was where journeymen were raised to the level of master. In each of these instances, however, there was more than a simple acknowledgement of the level of skill the craftsman had acquired. There was also the initiation into the next level of the mysteries of alchemy—for we have protected those mysteries in the face of religion, science, and society for half a millennium. When you are initiated, you will be given some of those secrets, and we charge you with their protection. Do you, Madeline Beatrice Wadsworth Zayne, swear to preserve and protect the secrets of the Worshipful Society of Typefounders and Alchemists?"

"I so swear," answered Madeline. Keith led her forward half the distance to his grandfather and they stopped again. This time Rolf asked the question of Maddie.

"Do you, Madeline Beatrice Wadsworth Zayne, swear to learn from your master and his masters all they can teach you, to practice diligently, and in full course to come to the mastery of the art?"

"I so swear," answered Madeline again. Keith led her forward until she was directly in front of Frank. He whispered to her to kneel. She did and the others in the room closed the circle around her. Keith pulled the hood on his robe up and stepped in front of Maddie. As the third second degree master in the room, he also had a part in this ritual.

"Do you, Madeline Beatrice Wadsworth Zayne, swear to diligently seek others who may learn to be adept in the art, to bring them into this circle as you have been brought, and to teach them so that the secrets of this society do not die; and if none can be found to share in this ritual, do you swear that it will die with you, having been true to your vows until your last breath?"

"I so swear," Maddie answered. Her voice broke as she answered. As anachronistic as the ritual was, it always elicited this response in those who took the oaths. They seemed suddenly to realize what they were being entrusted with, even if they had not yet learned the secrets. Keith thought of his own initiation and of the fact that in all these years, Maddie was the only one he had brought before the Guild for initiation. Had he been diligent about finding others? If they did not fulfill this part of their oaths, the society might truly die with them. No matter how absurd it may seem, there is something precious about every bit of human knowledge, every story that makes up the human race. They really couldn't let it die.

"You have agreed to bear the mark the Guild has chosen for you," Frank said. "The marks of the Guild are the original printer's marks, sometimes altered or enhanced with characteristics that embody the personality of the initiate. The first to bear it was Peter Schoeffer. Johannes Gutenberg, as the first master of the Guild, never used a printer's mark on any of his works. After the fifteenth century, the marks became so complex that they could not be effectively branded or tattooed, so a library of basic shapes was created that start the marking. From there, at each successive initiation, the mark is filled in and built upon. They have become less a printer's mark than a sign of inheritance or heritage that stretches back uninterrupted to the first printers."

This was lore of the Guild, Keith knew. There was no scholarly evidence of this origin of printer's marks, but the documents in the Guild archive went back centuries. This was lore that would never see the light of day as far as scholars were concerned.

"Your first task as a journeyman will be to learn and memorize the catalog of printers' marks and to bear the one the Guild has chose on your own body. Are you prepared to accept the mark your master has chosen?" Frank asked.

"I am," Maddie said quietly. She knelt and reached to her left shoulder to pull the robe away from the shoulder blade. Frank knelt behind her and swabbed the area with alcohol before dipping the special stylus in ink and carefully drawing the small shape on her shoulder blade. The tattooing process was done with scratches of the sharp stylus packed with ink rather than with needles.

When Frank had finished the simple drawing on her shoulder, the other masters moved around behind her to look at his work. There were murmured words of assent among them. Keith pulled her robe back up over her shoulder and lifted her to a standing position. He gently kissed each of her cheeks and then moved aside as each of the masters and journeymen greeted her in the same way, some saying a welcome in English and others in German. Last of all, Frank stood before her again. After kissing each of her cheeks, he looked deeply into her eyes.

"If you were my own daughter," he said, "you could not be more a part of my family than you are tonight."

"I am so honored to be included in your family," Maddie said, "and to include you in mine."

AFTER MADDIE'S INITIATION, the atmosphere changed. There was a bit of informal time when everyone gathered for coffee from a thermos and the aptly named *butterkeks*, German butter cookies. Keith introduced Maddie to each of the men and one woman as they pushed back their cowls. As they were introduced, each told her a little of his or her own story. Rolf and Frank were the oldest, Maddie and Keith were the youngest. Günther, who had acted as the Master of Arms, was about the same age as Keith and had been a good friend when he studied in Germany, though he had never progressed past his Journeyman status.

Keith kissed Maddie lightly on the cheek. "See you when this is over," he smiled. "Don't wait up."

"I love you," she whispered back.

He moved to a far corner of the room and pulled his cowl over his head. Three of the Guild had busied themselves preparing what looked like a cross between a religious altar and the print shop upstairs. As the acolytes worked to set up the space, they moved kerosene lanterns to eaither side of the worktable. Frank led Maddie and Günther over to the setup to explain what they were seeing.

"We are, in fact, in a catacomb," Frank began. "It was not an uncommon practice in Europe to empty the old sections of cemeteries as space became more precious and to move the bones into the lowest sections of the tunnels that had been used for extracting stone for building. Günther, you've seen this in previous rituals and meetings of the Guild, but it might be new to you, Maddie."

"I've seen similar things in Italy and in Paris," Maddie said. "It always amazes me to see how beautiful piles of human bones can be."

"Those who moved the bones did so with reverence," Frank said. "The people who once lived in Mainz over the centuries became loving bits of artwork in the catacombs." He pointed to the niche behind the altar/worktable. "In this niche rests a chest that was locked by Johannes Gutenberg. The test of a third degree Master is to unlock the chest. Normally this ceremony would only be seen by second degree Masters," Frank stated sadly, "but there are only three of us, including Keith, and we have decided that our society is too small to strictly abide by that tradition. Only Rolf and I, among the members of the Guild, have ever observed this ritual, and only Errol Wadsworth—your grandfather, Maddie—among the living has ever completed the task. We will ask you to stand quietly in the shadows during Keith's initiation and no matter what you see, do not disturb your brothers. And, if you are so inclined, pray that Keith is successful in completing his task."

When Maddie and Günther had retreated to the shadows the remaining Guild members led Keith to the center of the chamber. Rolf wheeled himself to the front and turned to address Keith.

Sixteen

" **D**O YOU SOLEMNLY RENEW the oaths you took at your initiation and at your ascension to the first and second degrees of mastery?" Rolf asked. Keith answered with the required phrase and was led forward to kneel before the old man on the stone floor. The remainder of the ritual took place in an archaic German dialect with words that were over 500 years old. Keith was asked if he was worthy to ascend to the highest level of mastery and responded that if God willed he would achieve this degree

Keith stood and was led directly in front of the altar where he knelt again.

With Frank on one side of him and Rolf on the other, Keith was presented with the elements. The ritual was reminiscent of a Catholic Mass, and if the Guild's lore was correct, Archbishop Dieter von Isenberg had been the first to administer this sacrament to the masters of the Guild, which at the time had numbered only Johannes Gutenberg and Peter Schoeffer. After the ritual blessing of the elements, Frank dipped a tiny fragment of parchment in a dish of printer's ink held by Rolf. This he placed on Keith's tongue. Keith swallowed and his mouth felt bitter with a strong metallic aftertaste of the ink. Half the ink's ingredients were toxic by all current standards, but 500 years ago Newton was drinking straight mercury as a health tonic, so Keith figured he would survive a little lead, antimony, lampblack, and boiled linseed oil. Nonetheless, his stomach fought to keep its contents down.

"The sacred elements of alchemy are blended together in precise measure to create a durable new element that will withstand the pressure of a printing press. We call these hardened metals type," Frank said. "But if the type is damaged and is no longer able to fulfill its purpose, it is cast back into the melting pot where it separates into its native elements."

"May God so separate my body and soul if I am found unworthy for my task," Keith responded. These were the words that gave the ritual its greatest power. Keith had committed himself to attaining the third degree no matter the cost. Now he would be given the task that might cost him more than the eye he struggled to compensate for tonight. The toll could be both mental and physical.

He was given a written set of instructions and examined the table before him. Frank and Rolf moved back to join the other members of the Guild against the wall with cowls pulled over their heads so that they all but disappeared against the bones that surrounded them. Keith felt alone in the room.

"Is there anything lacking on this table that you need to complete your task?" Frank asked. Before Keith, hot coals burned in a brazier. It was positioned just a few inches in front of the secret chest of Gutenberg that rested in the niche. According to the instructions, it was not to be moved during the ritual. Additional coal was in a basket at his side, as was a small bellows. On the table were various metals, a scale, crucibles for heating and mixing the metals, and a mold.

"All that is needed is here," Keith responded formally. "I will assay the task."

Keith had been honest with Maddie when he told her about creating an alloy with the same specific density as silver. But the task that was before him was far more sensitive than the typecaster's art. Gutenberg's secret alloy for lead type contained not only lead, but also tin and antimony. Primitive experiments in pouring hot metal type left gaps in the printing from some letters being smaller than others due to shrinkage while cooling. Unlike most elements, the highly toxic antimony has the property of expanding as it cools from molten to solid, not unlike water turning to ice. Its melting point is over 600°. Most people equated softness with a low melting point for metals, but the fact was that the melting point of lead was nearly 100° higher than that of tin. Like mixing silica with soda to make glass, mixing the three metals together changed the melting point of all three. The lead kept the type metal from being too brittle, while the tin made it more durable so it could withstand the pressure of the press without deteriorating. But antimony, expanding while the other elements contracted, provided the essential ingredient of dimensional stability so that each character of type was the exact same height. In front of Keith were other metal powders as well, including iron, copper, and zinc. Nothing in the instructions indicated what combination of elements he should use or how much of each. Keith had to determine the formula to fit the task he was given.

The test was to mix a perfectly dimensionally stable alloy, melt it, and forge it at exactly the right moment—all with the most primitive tools and measuring devices.

Nothing, of course, was as easy as it seemed. Metal type was exactly 23.33 millimeters or 0.9186 inches in height, known universally as "type-high." Its size was measured in points, or approximately seventy-seconds of an inch and was as small as 9 or 10 points for most printing work. At that dimension, tiny dimensional imperfections might not be noticed as ink would make up the difference. The mold Keith had in front of him was easily five times that size, both in length and girth. The increased volume of the larger mold left less room for error and the conclusion of the task required that the result be stronger than lead type.

Keith could measure the elements all he wanted, but the real alchemy would happen only if he felt the proper proportions. He had to simply *know* when the brazier was the right temperature as he pumped the hand bellows gently across the coals. He had to blend the metals at the correct moment and stir them to make the alloy uniform. And he had to make enough of the mixture to fill the mold. Sweat was running down Keith's face as he shrugged his arms out of the robe, which dropped, leaving him bare from the waist up, the bruises on his back still evident in the dim light. He reached across the brazier to add lead powder to the crucible and a stray thread from the bandage on his left hand touched the coals and flashed in flame. The fire-point for cotton is only 400° and Keith's brazier was well over 600° already. For a moment it looked like his hand was on fire as he stripped the bandage off the injured hand and heard an involuntary gasp from Maddie in the shadows. He shook his head, trying to focus his one eye on the scale. It wasn't correct. Keith lifted the beaker, felt its weight, and then added another half-scoop of antimony. He could not see the blue tinge that he expected with his one good eye. Seeing the colors of the metals as they heated—even the color of the coals—was critical to completing the task.

In frustration, Keith ripped the patch off his left eye and rubbed it softly. This time he heard both Frank and Maddie catch their breath as he struggled to see through the film across his eye. He reached into the bucket of water next to him and scrubbed his eye with it. Then he looked again. It wasn't perfect, but he had better depth perception than he'd had before and he could see the color. He could at least reach for the elements or the crucible and know his hand was in the right place. He reached into the brazier with tongs and grasped the crucible, swirling the metals together in the pot and then quickly returning it to the coals so it would not cool prematurely. The volume of lead he was making was not unlike the amount that would be used to pour an average alphabet of lowercase letters, but it felt much heavier to Keith.

Every muscle in his neck and shoulders ached with tension as he lifted the crucible from the coals and poured the mixture into the mold. With the mold filled, Keith lowered the crucible and plunged the mold into the bucket of water, releasing the mechanism.

Into the water floated a key.

The third degree master is able to unlock the secrets of the Guild, Keith thought. He had not expected the interpretation to be so literal.

If his formula was correct and he had mixed the elements in the exact proportions and poured them into the mold at exactly the right moment, the key would be the perfect size and shape of the mold. If he had erred in his judgment and the metal had not retained its dimensional stability from molten to solid, the key would not open the lock on the chest. The alloy, though stronger than lead type, was not so durable as iron, so it would not take any extra degree of twisting in the lock without bending or breaking. It had to fit perfectly.

He plunged his arm into the water up to the elbow and clasped the key in his hand. This act, too, was carefully timed. A moment too soon and the key would still be hot enough to scar his hand. He felt the living metal with his flesh and drew it out of the bucket.

Keith read from the instructions again. "Each third degree master must forge his own key to the lock. At his death, the key is to be broken and melted. The key to the lock does not exist unless there is a master to wield it."

There was still the final proof, however, and Keith began sweating anew as he read the instructions. He placed the crucible in which he had melted lead back into the coals, refilled it, and used the bellows to heat the fire. Lead melts at 621° Fahrenheit. Keith still bore the scar on his stomach where a streamer of molten lead from a jammed Linotype machine had hit him in the stomach from 20 feet away. But the instructions were very clear. It was the final test. He had to reach across the crucible of molten lead in order to reach the lock. He would have seconds in which to turn the key in the lock before the heat would become unbearable on his arm and he would have to withdraw or suffer burns over his entire forearm. If the key did not work at the first try, there would be no time to try again. Keith blew the bellows on the coals, and added more lead filings to melt. He examined the key carefully to be sure there was no excess metal at the seams in the mold. Satisfied that the edges were undetectable and that the metal in the crucible was molten, he closed his eyes for a moment, took a deep breath and stretched out his hand.

There was a collective intake of breath in the chamber as Keith reached across the brazier and inserted the key in the lock. What was left of the hair on his arm singed away in an instant and Keith could feel the pain growing as he struggled to turn the key. Tears sprang to his eyes as he turned. It caught and stopped, then gently slid past the catch-point to release the mechanism. The lock popped open and the chains that bound the chest fell to the sides. He pulled the key from the lock and plunged his arm back down into the pail of water, craving relief from the burns up his arm.

Frank moved up behind Keith. Marya, a first degree master, quickly applied salve to Keith's burned arm while two of the men brought candles close to Keith so Frank could see. Keith felt the cold swab of alcohol against the bare skin of his shoulder blade where his tattoo had been started with just an outline twenty years ago. Twice since then he had endured the cutting of the stylus into his skin as Frank applied more ink to the tattoo. Tonight would be the last time he would be marked in this way and he would know the final piece to the design begun at his first initiation. He bore the twin shields of Schoeffer and Fust, one filled with the traditional tools of the trade and the other still awaiting the final pieces. Keith would scarcely feel the final images being drawn in his current state and he would not see or be told what they were.

When Frank had finished the other Guild members looked at the artwork with approval. Even Maddie and Günther were brought forward so they could see the last engraving on Keith's skin. Frank started it, but in an instant the entire room was applauding. Keith Drucker was a Third Degree Master Alchemist. Maddie rushed to him and began to examine his eye and his arm. A small amount of blood trickled from his eye like a tear, but Keith insisted that he could see. His arm was another matter. The skin was red and had already blistered in spots. Marya applied more of the salve.

"Burns are the most common injuries in a typefoundry," Frank explained as Maddie watched and comforted Keith. When she asked for bandages, however, Marya said that the burn needed open air. Gauze would only stick to it and make it worse.

Keith was shaking and was still clasping the key in his hand. He looked at the unclasped chest and then appealed silently to his grandfather. Frank directed the brazier and other implements to be removed and clean towels were brought to the table. Then the chest was lifted from its alcove and set on the table. Battery-operated lights replaced the lanterns around the table and when Keith had equipped himself with the other tools of his trade—gloves, magnifying glass, and tweezers to lift fragile pages with—Frank directed everyone else to leave.

"Aren't we staying to see the documents?" Maddie asked.

"The third degree master is the only one allowed in the room when the chest is opened," Frank said. "He will decide what, if anything, in the chest we need to see or hear about." He ushered Maddie out the door. Frank glanced back through the door at his grandson, still motionless in front of the chest, and then closed the door.

SEVENTEEN

"BEFORE YOU EVEN ASK, she's fine," Derek said into the phone. He knew Yousef would be calling when his plane landed and that his first question would be about Maddie's safety. "She's safe and sitting in her hotel room. How about you? Did you have any trouble?"

"I don't know," Yousef said. "It was too easy. What if they are following me? It always makes me nervous to travel with my Iranian passport. They wanted to know why I didn't have any luggage."

"Relax. There's no need to worry."

"Someone must be looking for me. They were at Sophie's apartment before I left. I know." Yousef was breathing heavily. If he wasn't being followed, it was a miracle. He inspired suspicion.

"You *thought* they were at Sophie's before you left, Joey," Derek said. "You *thought* there was a bomb. But nothing happened, right?"

"I know someone was there," Yousef answered.

"Now look," Derek calmed him. "Have you picked up the package I left you?"

"I came to a quiet place to call before I caught a taxi," Yousef said. "I didn't want to make a call where anyone might hear me."

"That's very smart of you, Joey," Derek continued to soothe and encourage him. "But you don't have anything to worry about now. You can check into your hotel, pick up the package, and deliver it to my associates. It's time to throw a monkey wrench into the works. We'll have a little diversion in Alexandria and they'll have to go investigate it while we get to the real treasure. It's close now, Joey. This is what you wanted all along, isn't it? You wanted to find the treasure your father died searching for. It's all going according to plan. I'll send you the coordinates soon as they move and you can meet us."

"You… You're sure she's all right?" Yousef asked.

"Absolutely positive. Don't believe what you read in the papers either. I'm seeding the news the way I want it heard. Now go make the delivery and then get some sleep. You've been traveling a long way. You must be exhausted."

Derek disconnected and dropped his chin to his chest to stretch his neck. Yousef was sometimes a pain in the ass, but he'd brought some of Derek's greatest treasures to him, including his sister; but it was going to be hard to tell him about Sophie. *I should be feeling relieved,* Derek thought. *She's gone.* But the sudden feeling of emptiness dragged at him. He didn't realize how much he had come to depend on her to anchor him. *How could she be so stupid?* The manipulative little whore now had her brains spattered all over Mainz. *Well, that couldn't make much of a mess.* Blowing herself up wasn't in the plan. He'd told her no one was to get hurt. Why would she do this?

He watched the video feed of the event again. The cameras had been hidden the day before, far enough from the museum not to draw attention. But Sophie had not been able to get near enough to the museum/library to set charges. The Germans had buttoned up the area tightly. Sophie had steamed when Derek suggested they set off the decoy in Alexandria. Once she had her head around an idea, nothing would shake it loose. She insisted that he monitor the feed and see how clever she would be about succeeding.

He should have known something was wrong when she kissed him. There was something more extreme in the passion of that kiss than he had experienced from her before. She had used her kisses and her seduction to control him for years, but this was different. *She was kissing me goodbye.*

At almost any other time of his life, Derek would have welcomed it, but now that bit of initiative on her part could cost him. Joey liked her. Maybe even loved her. She had carefully explained to Derek how important it would be to keep Joey in line and how she intended to go about it. Derek couldn't believe she'd blown herself up. He watched the recording from the remote camera they planted yesterday. It made him sick. *Crap!*

Derek had seeded his first news stories before the dust from the explosion had settled. Now it was time to send the messages claiming credit. His lip quivered ever so slightly as he hammered out the words. If Sophie was going to raise the stakes, so was he.

If the books are in accordance with the Tree of Knowledge, they are superfluous, for the Gospel more than suffices. If they contain matter that is not in accordance with Holy Writ, we need no key to their heresies and false prophets. Therefore, burn them all and there will be a great conflagration.

Derek smiled at his deliberate twisting of the words. Someone would figure it out. But they would be too late. It was time to begin the next phase of the plan.

For Sophie.

Eighteen

KEITH SAT ALONE in the lab beneath Rolf's house and wolfed down the sandwiches and coffee that had been left for him. Tradition said that the third degree master could have whatever time alone that it took for him to study the contents of the chest; but it did not dictate that he had to starve while doing so. He pushed away from his meal and returned to photographing the documents. He would need to refer to these in order to put the pieces together, but everything had to be locked securely back in the chest before he left. Pieces were beginning to fall into place.

Maddie had been right when suggesting that he start with the Gospel of John when applying the rubric to the printed pages. When the correct grille was lined up over the first page of this Gospel, the first twenty marks spelled out the perfect beginning. "*In principio erat Verbu.*" In the beginning was the Word. The combination of the next several letters confused Keith until he realized that the text he was reading had switched from Latin to German. Spaces between words were not marked, so he had to divide the letters into sensible words and sentences. It was made more difficult by the fact that most of the vowels had been omitted.

"Jeder Wort man schriebt ist unter den Hierothesion konserviert…"

Every word man has written is preserved beneath the Hierothesion, where gods and men commune. Stand beside the king and follow the symbols of initiation to the water's edge. There you will find the path to enlightenment. Fierce protectors—the fire of the desert—guard the word. Their religion is salvation of the word. In their temple, I learned the art of the book. Tutored by the Wisdom of Ptolemy, I made my greatest alchemical work. Ptolemy created the Protectors to guard his knowledge. This secret must remain hidden until the world is ready to learn.

Keith had an advantage that no other third degree master had before him—the Internet. He called up his search engine and entered the term *Hierothesion*. The word meant nothing by itself. If it was Greek, "hiero" would refer to something sacred. The only relevant Greek terms that included the second half of the word, however, referred to various mountains. Finding one sacred mountain in the world, even in Gutenberg's world, could take years. What the Internet search returned, however, was unbelievable. Only half a dozen websites came up on the search, and they all pointed to Nemrud Dagi in Southeastern Turkey—the burial tumulus of Antiochus I of the last century BC kingdom of Kommagene. The tumulus burial place was referred to as the *Hierothesion*.

"Antiochus' tomb is concealed somewhere inside the 165-foot high man-made burial mound, with its spectacular terraces on three sides.

"On either side of the east terrace stand reliefs of the King's ancestors, framing 20-foot tall figures of the gods facing the main altar. These include, in addition to eagles and lions, Zeus, Ares, Apollo, and Tyche, as well as Antiochus himself."

Stand beside the king, Keith thought. He would know when he got there. It was only one of the pieces of the puzzle that was included in ritual.

The manuscript page they had brought with them from the Kane Memorial Library was the sixth of seven pages and must have been removed by a third degree master sometime in the past. It gave the clue to what they were looking for. The encoded rubric told where. One was really no more than an interesting artifact without the other. Keith had placed the missing page back with the others and added to the collection the twelve pages of rubric that served as a grille.

These pieces could get him into a lot of trouble. Mount Nemrut was a national monument in Turkey. He could scarcely drop in and start digging. Besides, according to the archaeological website, digging in the tumulus had been tried in the 60s with disastrous results and was banned to preserve the monument. He really knew nothing about dealing with the Turkish government.

But he did have a key. Keith opened the Carthusian manuscript to the title page and laid the key on the page. The business end of the key looked like any other skeleton-type key fitted to a custom lock. He supposed that a good lock-picker could open the lock on Gutenberg's chest without too much problem. But the decorative shank of the key was surmounted by a cypher 4 cross, identical to the coat of arms drawn on the title page of the monastery catalogue. All that was missing was the motto "Guardians of the Word." Keith knew now what he would have to do.

He locked the chest and went to the lab. He copied all his files to a memory card and then erased them from the lab computer. He could not simply destroy the disk, but he used a downloadable utility to write all blank sectors of the disk to zeros. A computer forensics expert might be able to recover the information, but the Guild would never engage an outsider to examine their secrets. If Keith failed, it would take the next third degree master to unlock the chest and the secrets of the Guild.

Finally, Keith removed one of his shoelaces and threaded it through the opening of the loop at the end of the key he had forged. *I'll get a new shoelace at the airport*, he thought. He tied the lace around his neck and buttoned his shirt. Now he needed to set things in motion.

"LET'S TALK ABOUT the explosion last night," Fry said. "You believe there is no way they could have tracked you."

"Anyone with your resources could track us. It's not like we've been hiding," Keith said. Agent Fry sat back in the chair in his room at the Sheraton in Mainz. Keith sat on the sofa facing him. Agent Holtz sat quietly nearby, observing the exchange. Either the room had been made up before he got there this morning, or the Homeland Security agent had not slept in his bed. Either way, it looked much like any other hotel room in the world except for the remains of the agent's breakfast on his desk.

"There are more direct means of tracking you," Fry said.

"Only my grandfather and Maddie knew for sure where we were going," Keith said. "You can't think that either of them would lead a terrorist around." Keith shifted uncomfortably on the sofa. His arm still hurt from the burns, even after additional applications of the soothing salve. He had re-bandaged his eye after the ordeal last night, but he had reduced the covering on his left hand to a gauze pad and cotton glove from the stock of document handling gloves in the underground laboratory. Any move he caught in his peripheral vision caused him to turn his head to see. Agent Holtz kept changing positions, pulling his attention away from Agent Fry. He had the feeling it made him look shifty.

"Maybe not intentionally," Fry said. "Your girlfriend's brother, however, is another matter."

"We've never met."

"She talks to him, and I suspect that he has the code to the tracking software in her cell phone," Fry responded.

"A GPS?"

"We weren't idle when I kept your cell phones," Fry said. "There is commercially available software that can be installed on a cell phone that will inform a computer where the phone is. It's commonly used for tracking down lost cell phones or for parents keeping track of their kids. She may be unaware that the software is on her phone." The agent looked at Keith while he considered his next phrase. "Or she may not."

"Maddie is not aiding a terrorist."

"You need to read the morning newspaper," Fry said. Keith was puzzled, but took the offered paper from Agent Fry.

"Do you need a translator?" Agent Holtz asked.

"No, I read German," Keith responded automatically.

"Of course."

Keith scanned down the article with mounting disbelief.

Police Kill Passerby at Historic Museum

Over-zealous police guarding the Gutenberg Museum in Mainz against unspecified threats shot and fatally wounded a passerby in the city's main square. The woman, believed to have been an American tourist who didn't speak German, failed to heed police warnings to stop. Police dogs attacked the woman and when she struggled, an officer shot her. The woman died on the scene.

An eye-witness who chose to remain anonymous for fear of reprisal, nonetheless took photographs of the scene as it happened. "They just shot her," he said. "She didn't do anything."

Police have declined to comment on the incident, having released only a terse statement indicating that a suspected terrorist was killed in an explosion in the Mainz city square.

Independent sources indicate that the woman may have been American scholar Madeline Zayne, known to have been touring Mainz on her spring break. Dr. Zayne is Director of the Whitfield Rare Books Room at the Kane Memorial Library, which was attacked by unidentified terrorists less than a week ago. Associates say that Dr. Zayne was an outspoken critic of government censorship and regulation of libraries. Sources have been unable to reach Dr. Zayne since the incident.

KEITH REACHED for his cellphone. He had not called Maddie since he came up from the catacombs. Fry cut him off.

"She's fine. She went out for coffee this morning and stopped at a pharmacy. She's no doubt waiting to hear from you, but you can call her later."

"This is incredible," Keith said in disbelief. "First that the world knows she is here and second that there is a news story that is so completely wrong. The police didn't kill the terrorist, did they?"

"No," Fry said. "I was there, in fact, I'm in one of the photos. These pictures are carefully selected frames taken from a video feed. They imply, but they don't actually show what was happening. But what they indicate is that you are squarely in the center of what these people want. Before I give you the help you say you need, I want you to look at the newest note claiming credit for the bombings. They've upped the ante by using a suicide bomber. That leads me to believe there are a lot more of them than we originally thought. A group that only has one or two fanatics in it doesn't waste them on suicide bombings." Fry handed Keith a printout of the note. Keith read and re-read the note then shook his head.

"It's another mish-mash. They're playing with you."

"What do you mean?"

"Someone found a reference to a questionable historical quote and then changed specific items in it to relate to what we are doing," Keith said. "Around 635, the Moslem general Amrou conquered Egypt. The last place to fall was Alexandria. According to the story, Amrou asked Caliph Omar what to do with the books in the great library. Omar's verdict was that if the books in the library agreed with the Prophet, then they were superfluous. If they did not agree, then they were unnecessary. So he commanded that they all be burned. The scrolls were said to have fueled the baths of Alexandria for six months." Keith shook his head again.

"I thought Caesar burned the Library of Alexandria," Fry said.

"An equally unlikely story," Keith said. "The Library was reportedly burned three different times, so while there may have been fires, it is unlikely that it was ever destroyed—least of all by the Moslems.

This story was disproved in the 18th century as being the writing of a Christian monk of the 900s who was demonizing Islam. But it keeps cropping up in different eras. This is the same story, but is now applied to the Tree of Knowledge and the Gospels. We've seen that reference in the other notes. Now he's looking for a legend to justify his work."

Agent Fry nodded as he processed Keith's information.

"There is one other thing you should know," Keith said when it appeared the agent would not speak again. Fry looked up at him questioningly. "Gutenberg believed he had found—or was shown—a remnant of the legacy of Ptolemy Soter, the founder of the Library of Alexandria. It could be the entire hidden library."

"Tell me," Fry commanded. Keith looked uncomfortably at Agent Holtz. What he had to say was for Fry only. Fry seemed to understand and finally asked the other agent to leave them alone for a while.

"AND EXACTLY WHY are you telling me all this now?" Fry asked when Keith had told his story. Keith had to admit to himself that it seemed strange to have sought out the agent after what he had learned last night, but he was convinced that it was the right thing to do. He pulled the key from his beneath his shirt and held it in front of Agent Fry. The agent did not touch it.

"It looks like a bent cross," the agent said at last.

"The design is cataloged as an old printer's mark," Keith said. "It was first used by Conrad Humery after Gutenberg's death. Humery didn't really print much on his own, so there are only references in the early writings of the Guild from when they standardized the basic marks. There's no reference as to its meaning, although it is listed as the parent mark of any number of broken and multi-arm cross designs. But this symbol is faceted." Keith rotated the key in his fingers until the side view was visible to the agent. It occurred to me that this symbol is the same as the one on the ring that you constantly twist when you are concentrating." Agent Fry involuntarily twisted the ring on his finger, showing a simple version of the symbol engraved against a black field.

159

"If I am wrong and you just picked that up because you need a worry stone, then there's really no reason for you to be involved further."

"Guardians," the Agent remarked. "The missing piece."

"I don't really believe in coincidences," Keith said. "Why would my 600-year-old guild include a symbol that you happen to wear on a ring?"

"It appears our societies are linked," Fry said.

"But what does it mean?"

"That's where this is going to be very disappointing for both of us," Fry said. "We don't know the meaning. The symbols have been passed down from generation to generation in certain Kurdish families as part of a coming of age ritual. The ritual is taught in steps. There was considerable disruption in the line of descent generations ago when the Turks tried to cleanse the land of all Kurds, and not all the steps were taught. The why's have long-since vanished. The only things we retain are the steps of the rituals that we know and the name Guardians of the Word."

"Wait," Keith said. He recalled details of the manuscripts he had been studying. "Not a hundred miles from here there was a monastery that was abandoned about 150 years ago. It was a Carthusian monastery devoted to silence and copying books. In the front of their catalog of manuscripts this symbol was accompanied by the inscription 'Guardians of the Word.'"

"And you don't believe in coincidences," Fry concluded. "You'd make a good Homeland Security agent if you decide you need a new career."

"Here's what I think," Keith said, ignoring the comment. "I have the clues that lead to a precious manuscript, or perhaps several—a cache of ancient knowledge, if you will. You are a guardian of the word, and pretty good at it from what I've seen the past week or two. If terrorists are somehow tracking us with the intent of destroying this cache, then maybe you should go where we are going," Keith answered.

"Why go at all?" Fry asked. "Sometimes the best way to protect something is by simply keeping it secret. If part of your intention is to protect this manuscript—or collection of books, whatever—then it seems like the sensible thing to do is keep the secret and just not lead them to it. They don't know where to go unless they follow you." Keith nodded. He'd asked himself the same question. Why race to discover the treasure first if the enemy is using you to find it? The evidence Keith had uncovered last night showed that this was not a new battle, but one that had been going on for centuries. There was only one way to end it that he could see, and that was to bring the manuscript to light.

"Keeping things secret is always a temporary solution. The right way to protect the documents is to make them public. Put them where the world can protect them. The Guild has protected the secret of this location for 500 years by keeping the pieces apart. But now they've come together. It would have come to light eventually because we have tools for finding things that Gutenberg never dreamed of. But it's not just a function of being in a global community tied together by the Internet. Movable type was being used in China, Korea, and India at the same time Gutenberg was revolutionizing the book-making world in Europe. Nothing ever happens in isolation." Keith paused and shook his head before he could lecture the agent any more. "In short, if I've discovered the secret, someone else has discovered it—or soon will."

"So why not just tell me where it is and I'll send in some people to guard it?" Agent Fry asked.

"You know it can't work that way," Keith said. "I don't have the location. I have a path to follow, just like you have a series of steps. I know how to read the signs."

"And these signs say to start in Istanbul," Fry said. "That's not exactly the easiest place in the world for us to protect you. The Turkish government is friendly to the United States, but they have their own way of doing things."

"Not exactly Istanbul. It's in a remote part of southeastern Turkey." Fry's head came up and once again he twisted the ring on his finger.

"If we disappear, I'd at least like the U.S. government to know where to start looking." Keith stifled a yawn in spite of himself. He had been up all night reading the documents in the locked box and then working on the computer program that analyzed the grille and the four Gospels of the Bamberg Bible.

"That makes it interesting," the Agent said at last. "I'll give you what help I can, but Turkey is way outside the bounds for Homeland Security. Even if there is no cache of documents or ancient bond of brothers or secret handshake, I want to bring whoever is responsible for these bombings down hard and I'll try to get as much cooperation as possible. But there are conditions."

"Of course," Keith said.

"First, I'll have a driver meet you who will advise me of your progress. That doesn't make him a confidant, though. I want you, and you alone, to carry this," Fry said. He rummaged in his briefcase and for a moment Keith was afraid he would be asked to carry a gun. What Fry emerged with, however, was a cell phone. "This is a global satellite phone. Your current cell phone won't do you much good simply because there aren't that many cell towers in southeastern Turkey. This phone also has a GPS chip in it that will let you determine your exact position if you need directions, and will also give me a bearing on where you are. I will track the phone."

"Fair enough," Keith responded. "That gives me some security."

"Don't feel too secure," Fry said. "It's a dangerous area. Just because I know where your phone is doesn't mean I can get to you. But there's more."

"I somehow expected there would be," Keith responded. But when Fry told him what he wanted, Keith was reluctant. He couldn't bear the thought that any of the people close to him could be passing information that would harm books in any way. But before he had left the agent's hotel room, Fry had extracted Keith's promise and they had made the necessary plans.

"I have a low tolerance for betrayal," Fry said as Keith was leaving. "Don't think anyone will mess with me and not pay dearly for it."

"I understand," Keith said.

NINETEEN

K EITH DID NOT RETURN directly to the hotel. They had several hours before departure and he didn't want to risk giving away too much before it was time. He headed back to the lab, but before descending he called Maddie.

"Are you OK?" she asked immediately. "Are you on your way here?"

"I'm fine. And thank you for leaving sandwiches for me in the lab. I just came up to make flight arrangements and call to tell you we're leaving. I'll be there in about two hours."

"Where are we going?" she asked.

"Back to where it all started," he said. "The Library of Alexandria. I'll let Granddad know. He's going, too."

"Keith, you can't imagine how much I miss you. Please hurry, darling," Maddie said to him.

"I'll be there soon," he assured her. As much as it pained him to deceive Maddie, the call to his grandfather was even more stressful.

"The newspapers are full of this rubbish. Has Madeline seen it?"

"No, and fortunately she doesn't read German," Keith answered.

"Even in German she would recognize her own name. And there are English language newspapers here."

"Right now she's in her room waiting for me. I need to finish getting our tickets and then I'll meet you at the hotel," Keith said. "You'll finally get to see the Library of Alexandria! I'm sorry Maddie and I will be headed a different direction."

"Keith, you can't just run off looking for buried treasure," Frank said. "That's what happened to Errol fifty years ago. He came up out of that chamber and left. He never came back to us."

"Granddad, Errol didn't have all the pieces," Keith assured his grandfather. "I do. I have to put an end to this."

"I hope you know what you're doing, son," Frank said.

"It will be okay, Granddad," Keith said.

MADDIE AND FRANK were waiting in the hotel lobby when he arrived and Günther was parked at the curb to take them to the airport. Keith gave Frank his ticket, but took Maddie's passport to hand to the guard at security who waved the two through quickly. They were in a small wing of the terminal and Maddie could see flights posted to all parts of the Arab world: Dubai, Lebanon, Istanbul, Cairo and Kuwait. They sat down in a waiting area and Keith commented that they had a few minutes.

"Maddie, there is one other thing that we have to do. I'm sorry about this."

"What?" she asked, looking terrified. "You aren't leaving me."

"No, but we are leaving our phones."

"I don't get it."

"Someone has been tracking us. The most likely means is through our phones. Please give Frank your cell phone. He'll dispose of it." Keith reached in his pocket and pulled out the phone he had carried from the U.S. and gave it to his grandfather. Maddie shrugged and pulled her phone out as well. Frank smiled at her.

Keith embraced his grandfather and whispered in the old man's ear. "Do you have it?"

"Just like you asked for," Frank answered. He handed his grandson a small brown envelope.

"You approve?"

"Of course! Now go in peace, Son," the old man said. He quickly embraced Maddie and then turned to board the plane.

Keith grabbed a confused Maddie's hand and dragged her away from the gate.

"Hurry, we'll miss our flight," he said as he led her toward the flight boarding for Istanbul.

"I thought we were going to Egypt," Maddie said following Keith and glancing back toward Frank as he disappeared down the jetway for the flight to Cairo.

"Granddad is going to Egypt," Keith said. "We're going to Turkey. I'm sorry I couldn't say anything earlier, but it's necessary that the two of us do this alone. I couldn't bring Granddad along. It would be too strenuous for him. Besies, he's always wanted to visit Alexandria."

When they were seated and the plane was taxiing onto the runway, Maddie turned and glared at Keith.

"Tell me what is going on," she demanded. "You said the Library of Alexandria…"

"…is no longer in Egypt," Keith finished. "Or at least what remains of it. Granddad is going to visit the new library in Alexandria, Egypt. But according to the details in the rubric and the rest of the Gutenberg letter, principal pieces of the library were removed before the time of Caesar and ultimately made their way to Southeastern Turkey. We're on our way to find the remnants of the original Library."

"Keith, that's incredible!" Maddie exclaimed, quickly forgetting that she was angry with him. "It was a map?"

"In a manner of speaking. It wasn't a drawing, but a set of instructions on how to find the manuscripts and how to recover them."

"Why Turkey?" she asked. "And how would Gutenberg have known about it?"

"According to the letter in Gutenberg's chest," Keith said, "in the years before he came to Mainz to start his printing operation, he was guided by a monk on a pilgrimage to a secret location. It was just before the fall of Constantinople to the Saracens. He was shown secrets of alchemy and received an initiation into arts of transmutation that he had never dreamed possible. It was on that trip that he discovered how to make lead type. When he returned to Germany, he set up his print shop in Mainz and sought out investment to print the Bible. He lost the print shop because of his continued experiments in alchemy and dedicated his life to preserving the location of this remnant of Alexandria so that one day a descendant of the Guild would be able to find what he had found."

"So are you telling me that Gutenberg discovered the Philosopher's Stone or something? That's very Harry Potter of him," Maddie joked. "Is he supposed to still be living somewhere in Turkey?"

"Maddie," he said seriously, "the manuscript he refers to is called 'The Secret Wisdom of Ptolemy Soter.' It's the same book listed in the catalogue of manuscripts at St. Luke's. Gutenberg was told that it was written in Ptolemy's own hand."

"*The* Ptolemy who founded the Library of Alexandria? It must be sealed in an airtight container or have been copied multiple times if it still exists. Even for Gutenberg to have read it 500 years ago would have jeopardized its integrity."

"That may be why it was brought to the monastery for copying. And to preserve the secrecy, why the ink was laced with cyanide."

"They killed the monks?"

"It seems more likely that it was a mass suicide. Those monks called themselves The Guardians of the Word."

Maddie quickly shifted her thinking toward document preservation, listing the things they would need in order to recover the document and protect it if they should find it. The more Keith talked to her, the more excited he became. This was his Maddie and they were in love—with each other and with books.

WHEN THE PLANE touched down, Maddie immediately wanted to locate the specialized equipment they would need before they started out again, but after they had cleared customs, Keith guided her straight through the narrow passage from the International Terminal to the Domestic Terminal.

"Where to now?" Maddie asked.

"Adana," Keith said. "It would take us a couple of days to drive all the way across Turkey, and it's not particularly safe."

"Where is this place?" she asked.

"In the cradle of civilization."

Their flight was boarding when they reached the gate and it was after midnight when the plane was finally airborne. Keith and Maddie collapsed together in their seats, too tense to sleep. It was only an hour and a half flight from Istanbul to Adana and the plane bounced roughly on landing, feeling like it was running over a rutted cow path as they taxied near the terminal. They walked down the stairs that had been wheeled out on the tarmac and were jolted by the brisk wind that blew across them. Maddie pulled her coat closely around her and Keith pulled the collar of his sports jacket up around his ears. He would have to do something about this. If he made the trip out into the desert with no better protection than what he had on he would freeze before he uncovered the clues he needed. And he was reminded that he had not yet replaced his shoelace when he tripped and slipped out of the shoe on the tarmac.

Inside the terminal, people scattered rapidly through a limited barrier between secure and non-secure areas. As they passed through the turnstile, Keith spotted a man standing nearby with a sign that said "Herr Drucker."

"What? No Doktor?" Maddie smirked as Keith waved to the man.

"I didn't have time for formalities when I made reservations," Keith said. "Guten Morgen," Keith said to the man with the sign. "Do you speak English? *Sprechen Sie Deutsch?*"

"*Parlate Italiano?*" Maddie added helpfully.

"Thank you, I speak English," the man said. "May I take you to your hotel, Herr Drucker?"

"Yes, that would be great," Keith said. "We could use some more sleep and then we have shopping to do before we can leave tomorrow."

"We have many very good shopping in Adana," the driver said as he led them to his car. Whatever Keith had expected, it was not the beat up Land Rover that they climbed into. "What Hotel?"

"Seyhan Hotel," Keith answered.

"It is too bad you will not be staying longer, then," the driver answered as he sped away from the airport.

They understood the response half an hour later when they arrived at the luxury hotel in the heart of the city. They were escorted to a suite on an upper floor overlooking the River Seyhan. Keith flopped down on the sofa, almost too exhausted to move, but quickly shifted his position to ease the pressure on the fresh tattoo. He had let his eyes drift closed when Maddie called from the bathroom.

"Darling, you simply must come in here and see this view," she called. He could hear water running and assumed she was in the shower. Well, that was a view he could stir himself to see.

When he walked into the spacious bathroom, however, the sight was even better than he had anticipated. The room was marble with elegant fixtures. Three steps led up to a huge tub into which steaming hot water was running. Behind the tub windows stretched across the entire wall from floor to ceiling, giving one the impression of being outdoors overlooking the lights of the city. Against this panorama, Maddie was silhouetted. She stepped away from the window into the light as she ascended the steps to the tub. Keith wanted his other eye now more desperately than he had in the chamber in Mainz and pulled the bandage away from his face as he approached the tub.

"You should take your clothes off before you join me in the water," Maddie said smiling at him. Keith was mesmerized and shed his clothes as he approached the tub, leaving them strewn on the floor. He pulled the glove and gauze from his hand as well and stepped into the steamy water with his lover. Both of them winced slightly as their fresh tattoos submerged.

"I feel like we haven't really been together since the damn explosion at the library," Maddie said. "I mean the first one. I missed you last night."

"I missed you, too," Keith said. The feeling of having her pour hot water over his aching body was heavenly. He allowed himself to succumb to her ministrations as she washed him and examined his wounds. Then he returned the service, abandoning the wash cloth and using just his hands as he stroked and explored her skin.

"If you start counting, I'll drown you," Maddie said laughing.

"I was just checking to make sure Granddad connected the right dots," Keith said softly. "He is really an incredible artist."

"I looked in the mirror," Maddie said, "but it's hard to see."

"They aren't intended for you to see. That's why they are on our backs. They are intended for you to feel. I've seen a couple that were pretty ghastly. Rolf's master had palsy when he was initiated and you can hardly tell what the tattoo was supposed to be. But Rolf can describe it in every detail as if it were Rembrandt masterpiece."

"And you?" Maddie asked.

"I have the shields of Schoeffer and Fust, the oldest printer's mark in existence," Keith said.

"And now you have this as well," she said lifting the key. "It's beautiful. If you get tired of turning lead into gold you could always go into making jewelry."

"Now we both have jewelry around our necks," he said, touching the photo locket of her parents that she always wore. "And we both have tattoos. We could be Keitheline." Maddie giggled and lay back against Keith in the luxurious bath.

"I could feel the anchor taking shape. I started thinking that anyone who saw it would think I was a sailor. Then the way the dolphin sweeps around it... I could see the image burst in front of my eyes. I just wanted to look to see if it was as beautiful as I imagined."

"It is," Keith said softly, kissing her neck. "And you are more beautiful than I ever imagined." He kissed her and stroked her skin, then looked her in the eyes. "This water is so comfortable and relaxing that I may go to sleep and drown. Let's get out and go to bed."

TWENTY

FRY CONFIRMED THAT Keith and Maddie had arrived in Turkey as he was being driven to the Wiesbaden Army Airfield not far from Mainz. He could move much more quickly than the two librarians by flying directly from Wiesbaden to Incirlik Air Base near Adana. He would join the two in the morning with the driver he sent to meet them. For the first time since he'd become involved in this mess, Agent Fry felt he was in control and one step ahead of the game. In sparsely populated southeastern Turkey, it would be easier to spot trouble before it was on top of him. He had contacts—relatives—in this region who would provide cover for the expedition. Having Kurdish parents might finally prove an advantage.

He twisted the cypher ring on his finger and contemplated the other angles of this case. His first task was the security of the United States. He would stop this terrorist threat once and for all. But beyond that, Keith had hooked him with the connection between the Guardians and the typesetters' guild. How deep did that connection go?

Fry's initiation had been little more than learning the pattern of an elaborate dance and the chanted instructions that went with it. To his knowledge, that information was not written down anyplace. His father's Kurdish tribe passed the information from generation to generation through the coming of age ritual. Somewhere, Fry knew those steps would cross paths with the rituals of Keith's guild. He was determined to find out where.

He had spent the day in the Gretchen's company working with a German forensics team attempting to identify the remains of the suicide bomber. He was sure she was the same as the girl in the security tapes of the Kane Memorial Library and now his team in Washington was comparing all available footage from the Indianapolis attack as well to see if she showed up anyplace. The student ID used to check out books on the day of the first library attack was stolen. There was no ID on the suicide bomber. Identifying her would simply take time.

Police had also located the camera used to film the attack, located on a rooftop across the platz from the explosion. It was set to broadcast on a closed channel, but there was nothing that indicated who had received the broadcast. The camera had been wiped of prints. Trying to trace its origin could take weeks Fry didn't have.

Gretchen slept a few hours during the night while Fry was online with his office and on the phone with his cousins in Turkey. He spoke quietly as she slept stretched out on his bed. Her presence was distracting, but Fry had not permitted himself to lose focus or to collapse beside her. The security camera disks from the Kane Library confirmed Drucker's suspicion that the document was recognizable from the IR camera. Fry sent a computer expert to the library to search for traces of an external hack into the library system. Another agent was questioning the man who monitored the security cameras during the day.

The downside of leaving for Turkey was that he had no need of a German translator there and therefore no official need for Agent Holtz. Fry liked working with Holtz and could see possibilities beyond the office. She had certainly left the door open for him to contact her "anytime" he was in or near Germany. Fry had already decided that he would be in or near Germany sometime in the near future. His encounter with her left him a little more understanding of Keith's inability to suspect Madeline Zayne of anything. Nonetheless, time would tell if Zayne was an active or passive participant.

Fry's phone rang as he was boarding the U28 utility plane.

"Rob. Change of plans," his chief barked into the phone. "We have a hit in Alexandria, Egypt. It looks like you were right about the phone being tracked. Leroy Anderson went in with pri-zero clearance according to plan. The Egyptian Al-Mukhabarat Al-'Ammah have been remarkably responsive and cooperative since we brought them the intel. They've confiscated the phones and have asked the old man to remain in his hotel room as their guest. Anderson checked in on him and he's fine. Three suspects carrying explosives near the new Library of Alexandria were arrested. The Egyptians haven't been cooperative about letting Anderson in on the interrogations, though. We need someone in there who speaks their language. I want you in Alexandria stat."

"Not all the Mideast speaks the same language, Chief," Fry shot back. This was going to delay his rendezvous with Drucker and Zayne. *If the terrorists are following Zayne's phone location, the two scholars should be safe for the time being,* Fry thought. He knew that the local bombers would only be foot soldiers, but perhaps they could lead him to the money behind these attacks. It was probably good that Anderson wasn't allowed in the interrogations. The Egyptians might be using techniques that Homeland Security wouldn't approve. "Do we know the location of Zayne's half-brother?" Fry asked.

"Negative on that," the Chief responded. "We're comparing all the records of flights landing in Egypt with those taking off after the bombing. That should give us a short-list of possible suspects, but it will still be a few thousand possibilities to sift through. We're giving top priority to those who flew from the U.S. and those who leave for the U.S., Iran, or Turkey. If he's using a false passport we'll find it, but it will take time. Manpower is a problem, as usual."

"I'm just about to board. Can you get a message to command that we need to reroute?"

"It's already done. I just wanted to let you know you'll be landing at Cairo West instead of Incirlik," the chief said. "A helicopter will take you from Cairo to Alexandria. Nail these fuckers, Rob."

"You've got it, Chief." Fry boarded the plane and fastened his seat-belt as the plane taxied to the runway and was off the ground in three minutes.

TWENTY-ONE

KEITH AND MADDIE were awake before 8:00 in the morning. It was only an hour time change, but they had slept little the night before. Unfortunately, their stay in the luxury hotel was to be short. Keith called the driver and gave instructions.

"We'll be ready to depart at 9:30. We need a store that sells mountain gear and cold weather clothing. Can you be ready?" He waited while the driver gave him instructions and then hung up.

"Cold weather clothes and mountain gear?" Maddie asked. "Adana is beautiful and balmy. Where are we going?"

"Northeast into the mountains," Keith answered, "and our driver is impatient to get started. He says he only wants to drive during daylight hours and it's at least five hours to our next stop."

"Can't we stay here another day?" Maddie asked.

"No, but I have a nice hotel reserved for us tonight," Keith said. "Maybe we can stop here on our way home."

"What did you tell the man at the desk last night that got us this incredible suite?" Maddie asked. "Are you suddenly made of money?"

"No," Keith answered. "I told him we were newlyweds on our honeymoon and could only spend one night here. He did the rest."

"I like that," Maddie said, tying her robe and opening her suitcase. She tossed the remaining items from her planned trip to Jamaica onto a chair then pulled out wool slacks and a shirt. "I miss having my cell phone. It's how I check the time."

"You can use mine if you need to make a call," Keith said. "It's a satellite phone and where we're going there isn't much cell coverage."

"Why did you send our phones to Cairo?" Maddie asked.

"For the same reason I sent Granddad to Cairo," he said carefully. "The terrorists have been tracking us through some means. It could have been your calls to your brother. It could have been someone inside the Guild. I'm sorry to say, it could have been Granddad. Or maybe they just were tracking our phones. In any case, I had to get rid of anything that might give our location away."

"You didn't dump me," Maddie said flatly. "I haven't called anyone since we left the country. I don't even know who I'd call."

"Maddie," Keith said softly, "your brother was in Indianapolis when the bomb went off there. We'd just left. And he knew we were coming to Mainz." Maddie was silent—near defiance. A tear trickled from one eye down her cheek.

"Joey is a good kid," she said, shaking slightly. "He wouldn't do anything like that. He's always afraid someone is chasing him. Maybe he thinks 'they' are after me now. Keith, do you think we—I—would do anything to hurt you or a library? Joey read every issue of *The Printer's Devil*, just like I did. He should be in the Guild. How could you think that of him? How could you believe I would…?" The tears flowed freely with the outburst. Her sobs became so violent that she pushed Keith away and rushed to the bathroom. Keith could hear her throwing up. He went to her and wiped her face with a cloth and warm water. He sat down on the marble floor with her and held her in his arms.

"I wasn't accusing you of anything," Keith said. "We promised to be honest with each other. Ditching our phones and keeping our destination secret was a condition for getting Agent Fry's help."

Both Keith and Maddie were drained by the sudden outpouring of emotion. They sat on the cool tile of the bathroom and held each other. When Maddie spoke, it was scarcely above a whisper.

"I didn't know my dad was hunting for a hidden treasure at the time. He never told me about it before he died. Aunt Virginia told Joey and me the story just before I left home for college," she said. "I was born near Cairo during the Egypt-Israeli 7-Day War. My mother was killed in an air raid. Aunt Virginia raised me, but Dad went back to the Middle East—first Iraq and then Iran. That's where he met and married Lily. He brought her back to the U.S. where Yousef—Joey—was born. He parked them with Aunt Virginia, too. But Dad went back to Iran. He was in the far north of Iran during the revolution in 1980 and was killed as a decadent western infidel. With the hostage situation in Tehran, no one officially even recognized he was missing. Lily's cousins brought word when they escaped."

"And you didn't find any of this out until you went to college?" Keith asked gently, petting her hair and holding her close.

"I knew the basics, but not the why," Maddie responded. "Dad was following some kind of clues he'd found, but Virginia didn't know what they were. I asked Errol, but all he would say was that it wasn't Dad's to find and I should never think of it again. As Joey reached his teens, though, he became more and more convinced Dad was killed because of the treasure, not because of the revolution. 'They' were coming to get us next."

"I hate to even suggest this," Keith said, "but do you suppose your father and brother were trying to follow the clues in the Gutenberg manuscript we found?"

"How could they do that?" Maddie asked.

"The page of Guild ritual we found in that manuscript could only have been removed by a third degree master. Errol was the last person before me to undertake the ritual. Of course," Keith hastened to add before Maddie could respond, "the page could have been removed a hundred years ago. We wouldn't know without asking your grandfather. But something Frank said has been puzzling me ever since I examined the documents. He said that Errol just disappeared from the Guild after his elevation."

"Even if he had it—and I'm not denying the possibility—how could Joey have it and hide it in a manuscript for you to find? That would require a degree of cleverness and manipulation that is beyond Joey. It sounds more like Derek."

"Who?"

"You remember—my ex."

"Oh yes," Keith said. "The one I never got to thank for my hospital stay. Why do you say it's more like him?"

"He always has a scheme of some sort going on. I wouldn't be surprised if he took up with Joey at Princeton just to get an introduction to me," Maddie confessed. "The difference between his schemes and others you might have heard of is that his schemes always seem to work. He's incredibly wealthy as a result."

"And you think he might have used Joey to get to you?"

"I'm sure I'm flattering myself," Maddie laughed. "Derek never seems to do anything without a reason. He and Joey started hanging out together when Joey was a freshman and Derek was a junior. Derek sponsored him for fraternity membership. I was finishing my Master's and was ready to start my PhD and had pushed for Joey to join me at Princeton. Pretty soon, it was the three of us hanging out in our free time. At first I thought Derek was just being polite to me for Joey's sake. He was always kind and generous. Had a great sense of humor. And he seemed to have a soothing effect on Joey. Joey was fluent in Farsi and English before college and picked up three more languages in school. He has a real gift and Derek encouraged him all the way. When he asked me to marry him, it seemed like a fairytale come true."

"What happened?"

"When Derek's father died, he was named the executor of the estate instead of his older brother or sister. That also put him at the head of his father's computer company. They make custom super-computers. All of a sudden, Derek was gone all the time. I never knew where he was, but he kept piling up more and more money. He bought his siblings out of their share of the estate and hasn't spoken to them since."

"And...?"

"And one day I went to see him at the office. I'd just received confirmation that I'd been named to the staff at the Kane Memorial Library. I wanted to celebrate. Instead, I found him with his "assistant" in a position that left nothing to the imagination. Come to find out, he'd been sleeping with her ever since he took over the company. I was crushed, bitter, angry, betrayed, vengeful, spiteful, and generally rude. It was one of the fastest divorces in history."

"You lived in a community property state. Are you saying that you are fabulously wealthy and I didn't know it?" Keith asked.

"Pre-nup. I got to keep the name of Zayne, since it was on my PhD and I had already built a professional reputation with it. I got a $250,000 trust fund. And I got to say goodbye."

"But Joey stayed friends with him?"

"I could scarcely tell Joey he had to quit his best friendship, but I put a lot of pressure on Derek. It wasn't Joey's fault. It was right after the divorce that he gave me this locket with the pictures of my mother and father in it. He said we'd both lost loved ones and that he was sorry my marriage didn't work out. The locket would be a reminder that they were still in my heart," Maddie said.

"May I see the pictures?"

"No. Joey didn't want me to ever have to take it off, so we went together to a jeweler and had it soldered shut. I've never taken it off," Maddie said. They sat in silence for a few moments. Then Keith straightened himself.

"I'm afraid we have to go," he said. "Our driver was insistent about leaving the city before noon and we have a lot of shopping to do."

"Where are we going? You have to tell me, Keith."

"I've tried to tell you everything that I was free to reveal and not break my oath to the Guild," he answered. "Granddad and Rolf weren't pleased that I was bringing you with me, but I insisted that it was the privilege of the third degree to choose my companions. That wasn't exactly true. But since we've come this far, I'm ready to go all the way. We're headed to Nemrud Dagi, about 250 kilometers north-east of here," he said. "I don't know exactly where from there because there are stages of the puzzle that I have to solve when I see them. Somewhere beneath the tumulus, King Antiochus and the Ptolemy treasure are buried. No one has ever found a way in as far as we know. But Gutenberg saw it. He left the clues."

"Let's leave, Keith," Maddie said, suddenly shaking again. "Let's not go there. Let's fly back to the U.S. and forget we ever heard anything about this treasure. It scares me, and what it does to us scares me. I always thought Joey's treasure-hunt was silly. Now here I am, maybe looking for the same treasure that my brother is and my father did. I'm getting as paranoid as my brother. I don't want anything to happen to us."

"The time has come, Maddie," Keith said. "The treasure needs to come to light. I might be able to find the damn thing, but if it is a manuscript or collection of manuscripts, no one could care for it like you could. And there might be more."

"I'm frightened, Keith," Maddie said.

"We're safe. It's not worth getting sick over again," Keith soothed.

"I didn't get sick because we were fighting exactly," Maddie said. "I'm pregnant."

TWENTY-TWO

WHEN THEY REACHED the car with their bags, they discovered it was not the same driver who met them at the airport. Keith looked at the car to be sure it was the same one, with his name on a hand-lettered sign in the window that said "Drucker."

"I am sorry, sir," the man at the car answered Keith's inquiry. "Hasad had a family emergency and asked me to take over for him. You need equipment and we must hurry. It gets dark early and I do not wish to be on the road after sundown. This is not safe country."

"What do you mean?" Maddie asked.

"The PKK, Kurdish resistance, has been pushing west from its normal territory," the driver answered. "It is safer not to be on the roads after dark." Relieved that the driver seemed to be taking their safety seriously, Keith held out his hand.

"I'm Keith Drucker," he said. "This is Dr. Zayne."

"I am honored, Mr. Drucker," the driver said without looking at Maddie. "I am Najat. Now, we must hurry."

At a mountaineering store in a local shopping plaza, Keith and Maddie bought boots, heavy parkas, gloves, and winter clothes. Keith added an ice axe and binoculars to his kit along with maps and basic camping gear. Maddie was responsible for figuring out how to pack and preserve the documents they might find with a minimum of equipment. To Keith's surprise, she asked the driver stop at a grocery store. Keith had to repeat the request before the driver responded. Maddie bought black plastic garbage bags, cellophane wrap, drinking straws, and packing tape.

"I don't have time to get archival supplies," Maddie said. "I have a knife to cut the bags into sheets if I need something bigger than the plastic wrap. Otherwise, we wrap the document in cellophane, put it in a plastic bag, and tape it shut. Just before it's fully sealed, we insert a straw to suck out all the air from the package we can and then seal it shut. It's as close to vacuum packing as I can get with no real equipment."

"Brilliant," Keith agreed. "It just gives me the willies to put an ancient document in a garbage bag. We'd better get back in the car before the driver decides to leave without us."

The ride in the back of the Land Rover was a quiet one and the driver drove with an intensity and speed that kept the two clinging to each other for security. Even at his breakneck speed, it took more than five hours to navigate the narrow roads. Soon after dusk, they arrived in Adiyaman, a small town more used to tourists in the summer than in the early spring.

They went directly to a hotel in the center of town and unpacked the car.

"We leave at first light in the morning," the driver said. "You may have a long walk because the roads are not cleared that high up. Too much snow to safely drive. I will give you a map to the village of Kiran. There is only a footpath, but I will meet you there when you return." Then the driver left them and went to his room.

KEITH LOOKED AT the cell phone Fry had given him, thinking that he should check in with the Agent, but the phone was dead. "The satellite connection must use an incredible amount of battery. I charged this before we left the hotel and it's dead already. I'll have to plug it in again tonight," Keith said. "I think I'll keep it off until we need it so we save the battery."

The room did not compare to the palatial suite in Adana. But the bed was comfortable and, after a quick dinner, they made good use of it.

"I don't think I know how to make love to a pregnant woman," Keith whispered.

"You seem to be doing all right," Maddie whispered back.

"When did you find out?"

"While you were in the Guild vault the morning after the ritual. I'm pretty late, so I went out and got a test strip. That was a good trick for me with my limited German. I wanted to tell you right away, but there was so much going on. We had to pack and then fly and we were so exhausted in Adana. I just couldn't find the right time to tell you until we were ready to leave."

"I love you, Maddie, and I couldn't be happier. Maybe you should stay here in Adiyaman tomorrow instead of climbing up to summit."

"You've got to be kidding, dear man," she said, laughing. "I am not letting my daughter's father out of my sight!"

"Oh, you're already sure it's a girl?" Keith asked. "Well, she'd better have freckles."

MORNING'S FIRST LIGHT came before they were ready for it and they met their driver waiting with the car warming at the entrance of the hotel.

"Nemrud Dagi is 100 kilometers north of here," the driver said as he pulled out. Keith and Maddie had packed all their belongings in two backpacks and were dressed for the chill morning air. "It is over 2,100 meters tall. That's about 7,000 feet. Here we are only at about 700 meters. It is always windy at the summit, so it will be much colder. I'll drive as high as I can, but you will have to walk a kilometer at least."

"We have cold-weather gear if we're forced to stay out at night," Keith said.

"Try to get down to Kiran on the west side. It is three kilometers below the summit and a straight walk. I'll meet you there," the driver responded. "Archaeologist's tents have showed up thirty kilometers from their campsites. Most of them were empty when they landed."

Keith and Maddie got the point. As popular as this site was as a tourist destination and archaeological dig in the summer, it was not often visited before May. When the Land Rover finally coasted to a stop after more than two hours, Keith and Maddie could see the crest ahead of them, but snow and mud blocked what passed for a road.

"We'll be down by nightfall," Keith said, and they set off.

TWENTY-THREE

THEY COULDN'T TALK much on the ascent. It wasn't steep, but it was slippery. Their gloved hands felt strange when they held them. They kept their heads down and trudged along.

Keith nearly stumbled into a massive stone head before they realized they had reached the terrace where the gods sat with men.

"Oh my…" Maddie began. "This is amazing. This head is taller than we are!"

"It's *only* the head," he said pointing. Beyond him on a platform above the terrace were the remains of five thrones with seated figures. If the heads were attached they would rise more than twenty feet above the platform, dwarfing everyone and everything else.

"In all of the classical sites that I can think of, there are only standing gods. These are all seated. I thought that was a convention that originated in the Renaissance."

"There aren't many websites that talk about this site and most of them have copied and pasted from the same source as far as I could tell," Keith said. "I didn't have time for extensive research, but I remember reading that when Antiochus was asked why the gods were seated, he responded that this was their home and there was no reason for them to stand."

"It's like being in the living room of the gods. What is this style?"

"A bit of a cross between Hellenic and Persian. Antiochus's mother was descended from Alexander the Great. His father from the Persian emperor Darius," Keith explained. "It's the only place recorded where the two are equated and pictured as one."

"Who is the big one in the middle? Zeus?"

"Yes. It starts with Antiochus, then the goddess Kommagene or Tyche. On the other side of Zeus are Apollo and Hermes. They all have Persian names as well. Antiochus claimed not only kinship but complete equality with the gods and instead of being called King Antiochus he was called Theos, or God Antiochus."

"That's an ego for you," Maddie said. Keith turned in a slow circle to look out over the valley below.

"Look. That must be the village where Najat wants us to meet him." It was scarcely a dozen houses clustered together beneath them.

"At least it doesn't look too far away," Maddie said. "I hope *he* can get there. I don't think he likes me much, though."

"He's a chauvinist," Keith agreed.

"Well, where do we start?"

"There." Keith pointed.

She turned and looked up at the statues. Behind them rose the tumulus, 150 feet in the air and nearly 200 yards across. It was made of loose gravel. No one had ever found the burial chamber of the King.

"We have to climb that?"

"No. But on the other side is another terrace, pretty much the same as this one," Keith said. "Gutenberg's instructions were clear. The clues are on that side. According to the site map, there is a processional path that circles the tumulus."

It took another half an hour for them to move to the eastern terrace on the narrow track around the huge mound of gravel. It was muddy and slippery with patches of ice. What they found on the eastern terrace mimicked the western with the seated gods surrounding a level area where worshipers participated in various festivals.

"Antiochus decreed that his birth and his ascension would be cele-brated every month," Keith told her. "So on the tenth and seventeenth of every month there were parades and feasts on each of the terraces."

"Where's the entrance?" Maddie asked.

"That's the problem."

"Don't tell me we have to look around for an entrance that archae-ologists haven't found in fifty years of digging!" she said.

"Well, we have clues the archaeologists haven't had," he answered. "First I'm to stand beside the king."

"Look, there are all kinds of kings and gods and what-have-you around here," Maddie said. "Can we be any more specific?"

"Well, let's start with Antiochus," Keith said. "He was King of the Kommagene. Then we'll try Zeus, King of the gods."

"So what then?"

"I need to follow the symbols of initiation," Keith said.

"That could be almost anything," Maddie said. "Ancient religions had all kinds of symbols—any that could be used in initiation." They paced around the area looking for symbols.

"But Gutenberg only created one set of initiation symbols. And he's the one who wrote the instructions we are following."

"Shield, crescent, lozenge, cross," Maddie recited the basic shapes of the original printer's marks. "Caduceus, pyramid, chalice, scroll." They searched the ground and sides of the huge sculptures. "Sword, diamond, trefoil, star." The climb to the terrace had been rigorous enough that they shed their heavy parkas while they walked, but by noon they had pulled them tight against themselves as the winds whipped in gusts around them and the sky darkened with the threat of a late-season snow. April was unpredictable at best and the two huddled together in the middle of the Western Terrace looking back toward the monuments.

"Antiochus seems to have been into words instead of symbols," Maddie said. "We can't possibly transcribe and read all the inscriptions on these monuments."

"It follows that a shrine that evolved to protect the word would use a lot of words to do it," Keith said. "But we are definitely looking for symbols."

"What did it say exactly?"

"*Stand beside the king and follow the symbols of initiation to the water's edge. There you will find the path to enlightenment*," Keith recited.

"How about that king?" Maddie asked pointing a fallen figure. "You haven't tried him yet."

"You are brilliant, darling," Keith said standing and moving directly to the massive stone lion, king of the beasts. Maddie followed more slowly, examining the ground as she approached.

"Keith, this won't be right. This statue isn't close to where it should be. They've been knocked down just like the heads were. On the western terrace, the lion was up next to the eagle and the thrones."

"They were probably in something close to these positions when Gutenberg was here, though," he said. "The monument is over 2,000 years old. He would have been here maybe 600 years ago."

"Did early Christians knock down the statues as idols?"

"Christians or Moslems or bad weather and abandonment. But I don't find any of the symbols on these statues. I don't get it."

"Does it have to be a statue?" she asked. In front of her was a lion relief on a slab of rock. "This one has stars on it." Keith looked at the lion and became lost in thought. Of all the papers to which the third degree had access, the ritual itself was seen only by the person conducting the initiation, not by the initiate.

"Maddie, you've seen me naked," he began.

"Now we're getting somewhere," she laughed. "That's an image I want to spend some time with."

"Seriously. You said you couldn't see the tattoo Frank put on your shoulder. But you've seen mine."

"Of course. I saw it as soon as it was done in the ritual chamber."

"I assumed that it would be completed with the compositor's setting rule and three stars on the right-hand shield," he said. "But it doesn't feel right. What is the last symbol Frank created?"

"A crescent. Like a new moon. I wasn't expecting a particular symbol there, so I just assumed Frank made them up as he went."

"No. The basic shapes are defined as a starting point. Think now. You saw your grandfather's tattoo. Did it have three stars on it?"

"Yes," she said. "That's why I thought the tattoos were just elaborations of the printer's marks. There are no stars on the Aldine printer's mark that his tattoo and mine are based on."

"Three stars and a crescent," Keith repeated.

"There was no crescent," Maddie said. "Just the dolphin and anchor with the three stars. Is that the symbol of the third degree?"

"Yes," Keith said. "It must be. And your grandfather's tattoo did have a crescent. The anchor is based on the crescent shape." Keith pointed to the side of the lion, engraved with astrological symbols.

"If we stand here beside the lion, the three stars above his back line up with the crescent moon hanging from his neck. The symbols of initiation to the third degree," Keith said. He fumbled in his pack for his binoculars and looked out parallel to the lion's back into the distance. He stood there silently for a moment as he moved the glasses slightly from side to side along the horizon and then focused nearer in. He lowered the glasses and stepped aside, positioning Maddie where he was and handing her the binoculars. He watched as she discovered what he had seen. In a depression about three kilometers away was a lake.

"There are three paths that come up to the mound," Keith said. "One from each of the terraces." Keith pulled a topographical map from his pack and drew their position on it and the path they had taken. "We came up the processional path to the western terrace. That is where most of the contemporary approaches are because of the road. The path from the eastern terrace leads down on the other side. The east and west terraces are duplicates of each other, but the northern terrace was more of a social gathering place. It would be where the feasts were held. According to the topographic map, the path from the northern terrace leads to a spring." Keith drew a line toward the water that followed close to the path before them.

"The water's edge," Maddie said. "That's the beginning of the path to enlightenment."

"That could be where we find the entrance."

"Then let's go."

"The village is the other direction," Keith said. "This is likely to be dangerous. We should wait until morning."

"Down the slippery slope," Maddie said. "It's still early. We can get down there and call Najat to let him know we are camping. Lead on."

This path, in fact, was slippery and difficult. It was used mostly by the summer archaeologists to transport water to their campsite. What was more difficult was that the snow had not melted as much from the northeastern slopes of the mountain and the path disappeared beneath the snowpack. Keith used his compass to keep them on a heading toward where he had spotted the spring, but after about half an hour of treacherous walking down the slope the clouds that had been threatening all afternoon finally let go with a snowstorm.

In the face of the wet stinging snow, they soon realized they were hopelessly off-course.

"Maddie, we have to get shelter," Keith said. "It's not going to be comfortable, but let's set up our tent by that ridge. It should give us some protection from the storm." Maddie silently nodded her acknowledgement and they trudged twenty yards further to an overhang where the wind was slightly less severe.

The tent they bought in Adana was not large. Keith had focused on economy of weight and space over luxury. It did have the convenience of springing into its tent shape from a small bundle without having to fit pieces together. Keith drove a stake into the icy ground at each corner with the side of his ice axe. They weren't really secure, but with the added weight inside of the two people and their gear, the tent no longer felt like it would sail away. Inside the tent, there was barely enough room for the two of them, let alone for them to spread their sleeping bags and stow their packs. Keith had planned well enough to get sleeping bags that zipped together and the two were soon snuggled together in the comparable warmth. They had not counted on the spiciness of the dried lamb strips they had purchased and soon realized they would have to conserve their meager water supply.

As the wind whipped outside the tent, Maddie whispered in Keith's ear.

"Is it true?"

"Is what true?" Keith asked.

"That you conserve more body warmth in a sleeping bag if you are naked?" she asked.

"We can always test the theory," Keith responded, unzipping her parka. It was true enough that the temperature in the tent went up a few degrees.

TWENTY-FOUR

THINGS WERE GOING WELL for Fry. The exchange of information that led to the capture of the three would-be terrorists left both U.S. and Egyptian agents in a cooperative mood. Ultimately one of the terrorists decided to cooperate as well. The group claimed to be an off-shoot of a longstanding anti-government faction that was recruited for the attack via the Internet. They knew nothing about tracking a phone. According to the informant, they had been contacted over a week ago. They were told to stand by for a man to call them and provide what they needed. The man had called the night before and provided $50,000. They were to receive an additional $50,000 when the front of the library was damaged.

"That implies that they knew Drucker and Zayne's planned moves in advance," Fry said to Leroy Anderson as they went over the report. "But according to Drucker, they didn't know where they were headed."

"Which could mean that the bad guys have sleepers waiting in front of libraries all over the world," Anderson replied. "Whoever is coordinating this would just have to sit back and watch a computer screen, then make a phone call when they see where the two are headed."

"That doesn't fit with the bomber in Mainz, though," Fry argued. "If she was the same person who triggered the explosion at the Kane, she had to be following Drucker."

"It's not fitting together," Anderson argued. "If the guy the Egyptians interrogated here is telling the truth, they received a personal hand-off of instructions and money. That still means that the mastermind is traveling to every location."

"Or that they have cells awaiting instructions that are conveniently located near each of their targets," Fry acknowledged. "The question is, how long before they realize that Drucker wasn't in Egypt?"

"They have to already know the attack here wasn't successful," Anderson said thoughtfully.

Officer Salah, the Egyptian agent working with them, came into the room carrying the cell phones that Frank had carried into Egypt. He laid a third phone on the table as well.

"The suspect identified this phone as the one on which he received the call instructing him to proceed with the attack," Salah said without preamble. He pushed the phone toward Fry and then pointed to each of the others in turn. "This is the phone belonging to Keith Drucker and this one to Madeline Zayne. We checked the call history for each phone. We do not have quite the same civil liberty protections in Egypt that you are used to in the United States. We were unable to get information regarding the owners of all numbers as that is controlled by companies in the United States who were uncooperative. However, Ms. Zayne's phone was last used to call a man listed in her contacts as Joey."

"Yes, we were aware that Ms. Zayne called her brother from Indianapolis on the 14th," Fry said. "Did she call him since then?"

"No," Salah answered. "Ms. Zayne is not suspected. However, we used the caller ID log to determine the call to the suspect was made from this Joey's phone."

"Now we are getting somewhere," Anderson said. "I'll get Hu on tracking down Yousef Wadsworth's phone records to see who else he's been talking to."

"That would be a good thing." Salah looked like a man who couldn't believe he'd been doing work the U.S. government should have done already. He sniffed. "Unfortunately, the only other call Joey made while in Egypt was to a prepaid phone. He called it both before and after the incident. We have no record of who owns this prepaid phone or where that person is."

"Wait," Fry said. "While he was in the country?"

"The last recorded location of Joey's phone was at the Cairo International Airport. It was then taken off the grid. We must assume that he boarded a flight. That was at 9:30 this morning," Salah completed. He threw a printed sheet of paper on the table. "This is a list of flights that departed at about that time. Geneva, Paris, Frankfurt, Madrid, Istanbul, Amsterdam. The next cities are domestic flights and since the phone has not returned to our grid, we assume he did not leave the plane again in Egypt." Salah pushed the phones and the flight schedules across the table to Fry and raised his hands in a shrug. "Good luck," he said simply and left the room.

"I think the new era of cooperation with Egyptian Security has just ended," Anderson said. "What next?"

"Gather up the elder Mr. Drucker and get him home at our expense. Fly him First Class, he's been through a lot. But first, make sure he gets a private guided tour of the Library of Alexandria. You should be able to use your new friendship with Officer Salah to arrange things." Fry grinned at his coworker. "I'll call the Chief and tell him what we need in the way of phone records. It looks like Joey is our key player. But he may only be the operative. We need to know who else he's been calling and everywhere he's been," Fry said. "I'd better continue on to Turkey and join the two librarians like I said I would."

"Let's roll," Anderson said. Fry's cell phone rang.

"Agent Fry," said the voice on the other end of the call, "This is Captain Coolidge at Incirlik Air Base. Sir, we have just discovered that the driver we sent to pick up your package was found by Adana City Police. He was murdered. There is no sign of his vehicle or of the two people he was to escort."

"Shit!" Fry exclaimed. "Do you have a track on the GPS signal I gave you?"

"That is also apparently dead," the Captain said.

FRY'S PLANE TOUCHED down at Incirlik U.S. Air Base in Adana seven hours later. The trip to Cairo had been nearly as long as the flight to Turkey and Fry was chafing to be on the road. It was at least five hours more to Adiyaman and they would be lucky to be near Nemrud Dagi by morning. He spent the flight time on the phone, first clearing the mission with his chief and then trying to get support at the air base. The Air Force commander would not send a U.S. helicopter on an unauthorized flight across Turkey. And he was unwilling to send a car and driver until morning.

Fry's Kurdish parents had relatives within a hundred miles of the air base. He had met them only once on a trip with his parents to their homeland, but Fry knew them well enough to call on them for help. They had no fear of traveling the roads at night.

"Agent Fry," the base commander said sternly, "I cannot prevent you from leaving the base, but you need to know that once you cross that boundary, you are no longer under the protection of the United States Air Force. You look like a local and the chance that we would even be contacted in the event of your capture or death is remote. We can clear channels to get an appropriate escort for you tomorrow."

"Tomorrow may be too late," Fry said. "We're operating blind at the moment and I need to be at the site when the sun rises. I'll take my chances with the escort I've arranged, and would encourage you not to contact Turkish authorities with word of my mission. As far as you are concerned, I sneaked off base in the middle of the night and you don't know where I was headed."

"That is not so far from the truth," the commander said. "But off the record, good luck."

"Thank you, Sir."

"And kindly try to be far away before you get killed."

TWENTY-FIVE

EVERYTHING WAS QUIET when Keith woke up. Maddie was still nestled into the crook of his arm, which felt like it might fall off soon if he didn't move it. A stone under the tent floor seemed to be lodged directly under his kidney. He carefully extracted himself from the sleepy embrace and slid his clothes on. The wind had died. When he unzipped the tent flap it was still dark outside but the skies were clear. He slid out of the tent and scanned the area with his flashlight. There was a clean crust of icy snow on the ground and Keith thought absently that it was a shame to spoil it with urine. He found a place against the overhang downhill from the tent to relieve himself as he gazed up at the millions of visible stars. They were scintillating. With no city within a hundred miles to light up the sky, nothing interfered with the clarity of the patterns. It crossed Keith's mind that Gutenberg could have meant charting heavenly stars according to the pattern drawn on the lion. If so, they would not find the treasure on this trip. It had been hard enough to find the moon and star symbols at the tumulus. Regressing a star chart 600 or 2000 years to get the right pattern was not in his mental repertoire. It would require computer software and time that he didn't have right now. He heard a sound behind him and without turning said, "It's beautiful, isn't it, darling?"

"I'm not your darling," said a male voice, "but for what it's worth, it is beautiful." Keith began to spin around, but the voice halted him. "Keep that thing pointed away until you're finished, if you don't mind." Keith zipped himself up and then turned to face the newcomer.

"Who are you?" Keith asked.

"I'm your secret Santa," the man said. The voice was even and cultured, and creepily smooth. The flashlight he held swung toward the tent. "Wakey-wakey, Madeline," he called. "Get your freckled ass out here and talk to papa." There was a frantic stirring in the tent and Maddie's head popped out.

"Derek?" she said, startled.

"Please take time to get dressed, Mrs. Zayne," Derek answered. "It's cold out here."

"So you're Derek Zayne?" Keith asked.

"Yes," the man answered, "and you've been sleeping with my wife."

"Ex-wife," Keith responded.

"Yeah, yeah."

"Go to hell, Derek," Maddie called from inside the tent.

"Be civil, Madeline," Derek responded. "You were supposed to be in the village on the other side of the mountain tonight. Poor Yousef will be worried sick."

"What do you mean?" Keith asked.

"Madeline's brother has been so afraid she would get hurt, what with buildings seeming to blow up wherever she goes," Derek said. "He asked me to please come and find his dear defenseless sister."

"I told you to stay away from Joey," Maddie said as she emerged from the tent pulling on her second boot.

"That is the fastest I've ever seen you dress," Derek said. "We can have our little meeting now and you can tell me where Daddy's long-lost treasure is buried. In the morning we'll all go collect it."

"Why would anyone tell you anything?" Maddie said. "You should be thankful we even came out of the tent. I don't know how you found us, but you are just as stranded out here as we are."

"Madeline," Derek said, "do you really think I would come out here in the middle of god-forsaken nowhere alone? You are the only ones foolish enough to do that." Derek pointed his flashlight to his left over the top of the tent. Maddie and Keith saw Najat standing there with a rifle trained on them.

"You were supposed to come down the other side of the mountain," the driver said.

"You see," Derek said. "We could have had this conversation in comparable warmth and comfort if you had followed the plan. Instead, we had to come out to track you down and rescue you in the middle of the night after the snow stopped. At considerable risk to ourselves, I might add." Derek pointed to their tent with his flashlight. "Now pack up your gear and don't try anything stupid. We have a long walk back to civilization ahead of us and I'm getting cold."

"Poor boy," Maddie sneered. "How did you find us? I'm not carrying my cell phone anymore."

"Oh, has everyone been suspecting dear little Madeline? No one even gives a thought to your traveling companion?" Derek asked, turning toward Keith. "I hope your injuries are healing and that hand isn't giving you any problems, Dr. Drucker."

"You did this to me on purpose?" Keith asked, stunned. "You blew up a library so you could plant a tracking device on me? I don't believe it."

"No one intended you to be injured in the blast," Derek said. "But once you were in the hospital and I was paying for your care…"

"Implanted homing devices are science fiction," Maddie declared. "Don't let him get to you, Keith. He always sounds like he knows more than he does."

"Just pack up your crap and let's get going," Derek snapped, pointing at the tent.

Keith and Maddie looked at each other and silently went about the task of reloading their packs. Keith crawled into the tent and rolled up the sleeping bags one at a time, handing each out to Maddie as he completed the task. As he was loading the food back into his pack, he felt the phone that Agent Fry had given him. He turned the phone on, quietly tapped out the message "SOS" and hit send. He added the phone to the pack, buried at the bottom, and then crawled out of the tent.

Keith pulled the tent stakes out with his ice axe. The driver carefully stayed clear and Keith saw no opening to disable him. The tent collapsed with a twist of the frame. Keith strapped it to the pack and then pulled on his gloves.

"Let's go then," Derek commanded. He led the way back toward the tumulus, uphill and over two kilometers away. The exertion of making the climb in the middle of the night with full backpacks kept Maddie and Keith warm. The driver, rifle still trained on them, brought up the rear.

"What really happened to our first driver?" Keith asked.

"He had an unfortunate accident on the way to pick you up. It happens all the time," Derek said. "The PKK is always kidnapping someone or another. Najat here stepped in to take his place. You were very lucky someone reliable was available."

"Yes, lucky," Keith muttered.

TWENTY-SIX

B Y THE TIME they had regained the Northern Terrace and made their way down the western slope to the village, it was nearly dawn. The village was deserted.

"This is really only a village when there are archaeologists or shepherds about," Derek said. He opened the door to a small shanty. Keith and Maddie dropped their packs inside the door and were pushed onto a narrow bed where they sat. They were inside, but there was no heat in the cabin, so they kept their parkas and gloves on. Derek seemed completely relaxed. "We have the whole village to ourselves." Derek said. "Najat, make us some coffee, would you? We have a lot of talking to do." The driver bristled and Keith could tell he wasn't fond of being treated like a servant, but he moved to heat water at the bottled gas stove anyway.

"Now, tell me where you were on your way to when you got caught in the snow, children," he said condescendingly. "You should have called on me for help in the first place."

"None of your business," Maddie said sharply.

"It's okay, Maddie," Keith soothed. "We're in the middle of nowhere with no support. I'll tell you what you want to know."

"Keith!" Maddie exclaimed. He laid a hand on her leg and gave a gentle squeeze. She calmed and listened to the story he wove.

"We were trying to reach the village of Güngörmüş, east of the mountain," Keith said. "When the snow blew in, we lost the trail."

"Why Güngörmüş?" Derek asked.

"Because it is halfway between the mountain and the water," Keith responded. "We figured we could make it to the water tomorrow, even if we had to shelter in the tent in the village for the night. The instructions for finding the path to enlightenment were to go directly to the water's edge."

"Educated people can be so stupid," Derek said. "You're lucky you didn't drop off the edge of a cliff. You should have come for your driver and he could have driven you to the water in a couple of hours."

"We got too excited," Maddie said, joining Keith's story. "We could see where we needed to go and thought we could make it." Keith squeezed her leg again, thanking her for helping.

"What is at the water's edge?" Derek continued his interrogation.

"The genie," said Keith. "According to the instructions, that is where the path to enlightenment lies, guarded by the fire of the desert—the djinn. I assume there is some kind of carving along the shore that we'll be able to spot when we get there."

"The path to enlightenment," Derek began. "This isn't a metaphorical path, is it? There is some kind of temple, the gates of which are statues of demons, the path to which is lined with gods, or some such, and the entrance is on the banks of the Euphrates?" Derek said. "None of that was in the old manuscript Yousef was carrying around."

"What did Yousef have?" Maddie asked.

"A page of an old letter, apparently 15th century, that your Grandfather had," Derek said matter-of-factly. "Yousef acquired it years ago. I had a damned time getting it into old man Sorenson's collection of old books that was donated to your library. I planted an interesting old catalog of books in his collection when I got him to sign the collection over to the University. The old guy was on my father's board of directors, so he was inclined to take my advice on the donation. I've been following the computer record of what books you were authenticating ever since. When you logged the book out, the computer flagged it to me and I watched you through the security cameras all day. I really thought you were going to steal it." Derek laughed at the implication against Keith's integrity. *Well,* Keith admitted to himself, *I was tempted.*

"So that's where it came from," Maddie said, glancing at Keith. "How did you know what book to put it in and how did you get it?"

"That was another gift from your father," Derek said. "During his years in Iran, Yousef found a cache that his father had hidden. It was when Yousef showed me what he'd found, including a charred page from a manuscript that had been burnt, that I decided it was all worth looking for."

"If you know what we're looking for, you are ahead of us," Keith said. "All we really have are directions to where whatever it is was hidden."

"It's a manuscript that will change people's perception of the world," Derek said. "Neither your father or grandfather could make more out of it than that it was a clue to buried treasure."

"He only had one page," Keith said, guardedly. Errol had certainly known more, but had not seen fit to share that knowledge with either his son or grandson. "And he didn't have the key. It was in a different book entirely." Keith was getting tired. While his wounds had knitted together enough to not be in danger of splitting apart, the stitches in his hand still itched. He no longer wore a patch on his eye, but it was tired, itchy, and watering. They needed food. Maddie asked to go outside to relieve herself and Najat followed her to an outhouse. Keith considered trying to take Derek down while they were gone, but he knew he was no match for the larger man, especially when Derek shifted so that Keith could see he wore a gun at his side. Keith decided on a different tack.

"What's really in this for you, Derek?" Keith asked. "You can't imagine Maddie is going to come back to you after all you've done. You certainly don't need more wealth. Why are you interested?"

"When Maddie sees what I've made possible for her..." Derek broke off, refusing to rise any further to Keith's bait. "You love old books, don't you, Dr. Drucker?" Keith nodded. "You love to feel them beneath your gloved hands. You love to study their bindings. I'll bet you even love the smell of them." Keith nodded again. He couldn't deny any of that. He didn't know a book preservationist or historian who didn't love all the things Derek was describing.

"I really don't care about such things," Derek said. "You can have any book we find if it makes you happy. In fact, I want you to examine and authenticate it. I only care about the contents of the books. The Dead Sea Scrolls have been kept bottled up by the Vatican and other churches for fifty years. Why? Because they expose the sham of religion and question the authority of the church. A few simple words from some previously unknown manuscript can completely change the way we think. But change it how? Who will people trust to tell them their beliefs are clever manipulations of their church in collusion with the government. Fundamental doctrines of the Church will be challenged—and not just for Christianity. The document we are looking for and that you will authenticate, will cast new light, or new doubt, on Judaism, Christianity, Islam, Hinduism, and even national boundaries. We can't let any more ancient knowledge fall into the hands of religious leaders. Or any government for that matter."

"So it's all in the name of altruism," Keith continued to needle him. "We're going to be so much better off with you telling us what to think."

"I'm beginning to not like you," Derek snarled. "You are a typical narrow-minded academic."

Just then Maddie was pushed roughly through the door and collapsed on the bed next to Keith. Najat entered behind her, nursing his hand.

"The bitch bit me," he said.

"Madeline," Derek shook his head sadly.

"He tried to molest me," Maddie said. "Tell him to keep his hands to himself and he won't be bitten." Derek spun to face the driver.

"Is this true?" he snapped.

"It was a misunderstanding," Najat said.

"Ah. A misunderstanding. You see, Madeline? These things happen when we are dealing with different cultures," Derek said smoothly. Keith could see how tightly he was coiled and knew they were moments from a violent explosion. "It's the way wars start—with misunderstandings." Derek turned to face Najat again. "With misunderstandings about one's place in the world. Do you understand me?" Neither moved toward his gun; the tension between the two was palpable. Keith held his breath and placed his arm protectively around Maddie's shoulder. After a moment, the driver turned and left.

"That was close," Derek said, turning toward the two. He frowned.

"He grabbed my breast," Maddie defended herself.

"No doubt," Derek said. "Najat is a conservative. You go about with your hair exposed, so he assumes you are a whore. You keep protesting that you are divorced, so that confirms it, and ups the offenses to adultery. If there were ten like Najat nearby, they would stone you."

"This is Turkey," Keith said. "They don't rule by fundamental Islamic law."

"Najat is not Turkish," Derek said. "Let's just not take unnecessary risks from now on, okay?"

KEITH'S HEAD SAGGED against Maddie's shoulder. He was exhausted and his head hurt. Maybe it had been too early to uncover his eye, but his vision had been improving each time he used it. Maddie looked at him.

"Are you okay, Keith?"

"I need a pain pill," he said, pointing at his backpack.

"Sure," Derek said. "Sorry about your injuries. The blast was supposed to take place after you left the library. The stupid bitch triggered it too early and no one figured you would run back in." Derek rummaged in the backpack while still holding the gun on Keith and

Maddie. He pulled out the bottle of pills and threw them to Maddie who shook two into her hand for Keith to take.

"Why are you blowing up libraries, anyway?"

"Not completely my idea," Derek confessed. "But it worked. Library visits worldwide have fallen 20% since she struck the Kane Memorial Library. I effectively control about 10% of the news sources on the Internet. That might not sound like a lot, but it is enough to determine the slant of any breaking news in the world. The government itself is one of the prime suspects in the bombings and in your death, I might add."

"My death?" Maddie asked.

"He planted stories that you were the bomber at the Gutenberg Museum and that the police killed you," Keith said.

"You knew?"

"Agent Fry showed me the newspapers when I came out," Keith said. "It's why I went through so many diversions to get here."

"See, Madeline," Derek said. "You just can't trust anyone. I'm the only one that's always the same."

"A jerk," Maddie said. She shot a look at Keith and he cringed. The conversation obviously wasn't over, but Maddie wasn't pursuing it yet. "Why libraries?" she asked. "Just to get back at me?"

"And you think I have delusions of grandeur," Derek smirked. "No, not because of you. People trust my Internet news sources more than any other. What they trust more than the Internet, though, is the library. So, if it is no longer safe to go to the library, then people can only depend on me."

"That's why you only attacked the facades," Keith said. "It creates the illusion of the library being unsafe without actually destroying the content. There is still the means to disprove you, but people are afraid to use it."

"If it couldn't be disproven, it wouldn't be a challenge. It was all I could do to restrain her," Derek said. "She wanted to completely destroy the Whit with you in it."

"She?" Derek looked at Maddie and hesitated.

"Sophie," he said at last. "She could never do anything without going overboard. She had no limits, and nothing was ever finished with her." He ran his fingers through his hair.

"Oh, so it's her fault you slept with her," Maddie said bitterly.

"She meant nothing to me," Derek said.

"Do you realize how lame that sounds? You could have sex with a woman who meant nothing to you? I guarantee she thought it meant something," Maddie exploded.

"It's over now," Derek said. "She couldn't get close enough to the Gutenberg Museum to set the charges, so she strapped them to her own body and walked up to it. Even blowing herself up was a failure. Good riddance."

"It's too late, Derek," Maddie warned him.

"We'll see," Derek said.

They were interrupted by the sound of an approaching vehicle skidding to a stop outside the cottage. Najat challenged the newcomer, but quickly fell silent. In a moment, a young man burst through the door.

"Joey!" Maddie exclaimed, rushing to greet him. He stood glancing around the room as if counting to see who was there. His eyes lingered on Keith, but then Maddie had him wrapped in her arms.

"What took you so long, kid?" Derek asked. "You should have been here hours ago."

"Something is happening out there," Joey said. "We're being followed. It looked like Kurds. They tried to stop me about 10 kilometers from here. I had to loop around their roadblock."

"Were you followed?" Derek snapped.

"No," Joey responded quickly. "I mean, I don't know. Maybe. I got lost getting here."

"You have the GPS I left on the plane for you?" Derek demanded.

"Of course," Yousef said, as if just remembering it.

"Joey, you just need to stay calm. I swear, sometimes you can't find your ass with both hands." Joey looked humiliated, not a good thing for a Persian man—even one who was half English and light-skinned. Maddie soothed Joey and looked daggers at Derek. Derek seemed not to notice.

"Okay, if Kurdish rebels are kicking up a fuss in the region, we'd better have a plan," Derek said. "Why the PKK would be interested in this rock in the middle of nowhere, though, is beyond me. We're almost there, Joey," Derek continued, looking at the man. "Didn't I tell you we'd find your Daddy's treasure? Your sister and her boyfriend solved the puzzles and now we're ready to roll."

"But the PKK," Joey said. "They might be the ones who killed my father. If they are here, they must have followed you!"

"Last week you thought it was Islamic fundamentalists and a few months ago you were sure it was the Israeli Mossad," Derek said. "We'll take precautions. Keith and Maddie both know the directions. I'll take Maddie with me. You take Keith. We'll head in opposite directions and meet by the water. But we'd better hurry. Give Maddie and me a couple of minutes to get started. We'll head north around the mountain and draw off anyone who is watching. You take the southern route." Derek was moving almost as fast as he was talking. He hauled Maddie toward the door and grabbed her backpack. Without another word, he pushed her out the door and left Yousef and Keith staring at each other. Keith broke the silence.

"I don't like this," he said. "That still leaves Najat." As if on cue they heard footsteps on the gravel outside and the unmistakable sound of a rifle bolt being shifted. Keith dove for the door, but Yousef hit him from the blind side, knocking him out of the way. Najat burst through the door with his rifle swinging for a target. Keith heard a shot and the guard fell. Keith struggled to turn his head to see Yousef holding a small revolver.

"He was going to have us killed!" Yousef breathed out. "I trusted him. I can't believe Derek was going to have us killed. And now he has Maddie."

"Listen, Yousef, we lied to Derek about the location. He thinks it's by the Euphrates. It's really only about three kilometers from here," Keith said. "We've got to get to him before he finds out and hurts her."

"I'll call Sophie," Yousef said, pulling out his cell phone. "She knows how to track him. I haven't been able to reach her."

"Yousef," Keith said softly. "Didn't you know? Sophie was the suicide bomber in Mainz. Derek planted stories about Maddie to throw you off." Yousef froze and slowly looked at Keith.

"No. He said she…" Yousef swung his gun around to point at Keith. "You're lying!"

"Yousef, he told us just before you got here. I'm telling you the truth." Keith said. "I didn't know you were friends."

"We were going to get married," Yousef said. "As soon as this was over, she said we'd get married."

"Please, Yousef, put your gun down." For a moment Yousef wavered and then lowered the gun.

"My sister loves you," he said simply. "Be careful of the Kurds. I'm going to go kill Derek." With that he picked up the fallen rifle, stepped over the dead guard, and ran to his car. Keith watched him skid down the rutted path toward the road and could see another vehicle approaching from the south. Shots rang out from below and the second car slid to a stop. Two men got out of the car and started up the track toward the village. The car started after Yousef.

Without waiting to see what would happen next, Keith grabbed his backpack and ice axe and headed back up the slope toward the Western Terrace of Nemrud Dagi. As soon as he was a safe distance away, he would call Agent Fry.

Twenty-Seven

FRY TOOK ONE HAND off the wheel to answer his phone and nearly lost control of the Jeep Patriot on the slippery road.

"Robar," said the voice of his cousin at once. "A man has been killed in the village, but he does not look like any of the pictures."

"That means they must have escaped. They've been at that location for more than five hours," Fry said. "Anything else?"

"There was a struggle. This one came in from outside and was shot as he entered. Wait." There was a long pause and Fry could hear a discussion between his cousins. The voice returned to the phone. "There is a man climbing up on the slopes from this direction."

"Can you tell who it is?"

"His back is to us and his parka hood is up."

"Follow him, but don't move in," Fry instructed. "Don't try to apprehend him unless there is a threat. I'll pick you up on the other side."

"It will be good to stretch our legs. I hear the view from the top is wonderful," said his cousin. "See you on the other side." Fry disconnected and dropped his phone on the front seat of the car as he entered another all but deserted village, six kilometers north of the summit. He slowed to a stop and checked the GPS tracking device. The map showed up in brilliant color, but something was wrong. The dot representing Keith Drucker had stopped and Fry went right past him. Fry backed into a narrow space between two buildings and watched the screen. In a few minutes the dot started moving toward him again. If it passed on the main road he would get a look at who was in the car. But the car was not moving along the main road. Instead the dot was moving into the hills behind the town and heading back toward the mountain. Fry checked his gear and got out of his car. Before he could determine his route to intercept the moving dot, his phone rang again.

"Bobby," his chief's voice rang in the phone. "You may have more players than anticipated. The suicide bomber was Sophie Johanssen, a radical who was caught up in all kinds of movements like the WTO riots. She worked for a supercomputer company owned by Madeline Zayne's ex-husband Derek Zayne. He has a clear record as far as we are concerned, but his plane is in Turkey."

"Supercomputers?" Fry asked. "That could explain a lot right there. He probably has access to as much tech as we do. That's probably how he's been tracking Drucker."

"I know that made sense to you," the chief said. "Fill us in when you can make it make sense to the rest of us. What is your status and what do you need?"

"I have local backup and am off the grid as far as the department is concerned," Fry said. "I'm tracking Drucker's signal into the mountains, but it looks like there could be two or three parties converging on this location. I'm about to head off on foot. The driver I contracted in Adana was killed there and another body just showed up in the cabin where Drucker's signal rested after his SOS message. I'm activating my tracking beacon just in case, but don't send the marines into Turkey unless they want to start a war. This is a volatile area."

"Don't make it any worse," the chief said. "I know your family is from that area and there are ethnic tensions. Don't light a fuse."

"I copy that, Chief," Fry answered. "I need to get moving now."

"Roger that. Good hunting."

Fry checked the tracking device again and saw that the dot now had a significant lead on him. He would have to hurry to catch sight of Drucker before anyone else did. He switched his GPS to display a geo-map and set out on an intercept course.

TWENTY-EIGHT

K EITH COULD BARELY move his legs by the time he reached the Western Terrace on the mountain. He'd gained 150 meters in altitude in just over two kilometers and his legs and lungs were near collapse. He looked down from the shelter of the colossal figures that faced out across the valley at the deserted village below. There was movement there. He could make out two figures starting up the hill the way he had come. He ducked his head and moved along the northern processional around the tumulus. He could see the pock-mark in the gravel on the north side where archaeologists had attempted to tunnel into the loose rock to find the burial tomb. In 1989 the Turkish Government made the mountain into a historical treasure and forbade digging in the tumulus, saving it from further damage. The tumulus was over 500 feet across, almost a quarter of a mile around to the North Terrace.

As soon as he was in the shelter of the terrace, he stripped off his pack and began to dig in it for the cell phone Fry had given him. He had to make contact and get help. Maddie was being driven by a madman toward a made-up location with another madman chasing them. He had to get help to her. He pulled a black plastic bag from the pack. *My God!* he thought. *I've got Maddie's pack.* He had equipped the identical packs with food, water, and knives, but that meant Derek had taken his pack with the maps, his notes, and the GPS tracking phone Fry had given him. Keith was completely isolated.

He fought off panic. According to Joey, Kurdish revolutionaries were approaching the summit from the West. He led his pursuers by no more than fifteen minutes and he was already exhausted from the climb. There was no place up here to hide. He could see the beginning of the trail he and Maddie had taken the night before. He knew it should lead to the spring and a kilometer beyond the spring he'd seen another village. He hoped this village was not as seasonal as Kieran. Someone there would surely have a phone.

Keith didn't look back as he followed the ridge away from Nemrud Dagi to the north. The hairs on his neck prickled when he thought of the rebels chasing him. He simply didn't have time to be kidnapped. Maddie could be in danger—no, definitely was in danger—from her unbalanced ex-husband. As he half walked, half jogged down the trail he asked himself repeatedly how her brother fit into the picture. Was he simply trying to protect his sister, or was he, as Fry speculated, the one organizing the attacks? Derek claimed the bombings were all coordinated by Sophie. If so, then Yousef had been elaborately played to take the blame. Derek always planned to get rid of Yousef—and Keith, apparently. And the story of Maddie's death in Mainz meant that she could disappear and no one would look further.

Where the hell is Fry, and what kind of support is he providing? The agent had been willing enough to let Keith and Maddie make the trip to Turkey, promising that he would be nearby to pull them out if needed. But he proved surprisingly ineffective in providing them a safe guide from the airport to the mountain. Now, without the satellite phone, Keith was unable to make contact.

The trail dipped into a split in the ridge and Keith could see where he and Maddie had strayed from it in the snowstorm. *Was that only yesterday afternoon?* Keith found that he no longer had a sense of passing time. Everything was urgently *now*. Time was measured in the steps he took as he dug the ice axe in and slid along icy portions of the path.

Distance was measured in glimpses of a village in the valley at least two kilometers away.

As Keith slid down an embankment, he hit a level ribbon of packed gravel road. He looked back up the trail and could see his pursuers still coming. They didn't seem to be in a hurry to catch him—just strolled down the trail smoking. He looked for a suitable hiding place where he could assess the situation. Keith hurried up the road, keeping an eye on the men uphill. As soon as he was in a hollow where they were not visible, he slipped down off the road and slid—almost out of control—until he stopped at the water's edge. He had found the spring. But there was no place for him to go. Keith could see where the trail continued to his left, but a section about ten feet across had collapsed into the pond. If he followed the trail back the other direction, he would be right back on the path with his rebels.

Keith rummaged in the backpack and pulled out two black garbage bags and a roll of tape. He couldn't trust himself to jump the gap on the uncertain footing. He pulled one bag over each leg, forced as much air as he could out of them, and taped them tightly around his thighs. Then he waded across.

The water was deeper and colder than Keith expected or imagined. He gasped as it hit his waist, but he struggled up to the path on the opposite side. He was wet from groin to waist, and it was freezing cold, but at least his feet and boots were dry. He pushed himself into the vegetation to hide from the men that he could hear on the road above him.

Groping along the edge of the pool, he felt an indentation where the rocks gave way slightly. He dragged himself through the bushes and into a small, relatively dry cave. He was mostly concealed. It took a few seconds before Keith could hear over his heartbeats, thrumming in his ears. The men were on the path. Keith had to move. He pushed himself farther back into the rocky niche and discovered that it continued to open up behind him. He could see the trail of water he was leaving on the rocks, but he was quickly losing light the farther back he went. He rolled over on his hands and knees and began scrambling back into the cave as fast as he could.

The canyons and mountains of Western Asia were honeycombed with caves. It was one of the things that made fighting a war in Afghanistan and Iraq so difficult. Keith knew that the caves provided hiding places for both man and beast, but he didn't have time to worry about that. A rain of gravel hit the bushes outside his haven from above and Keith knew they would be searching the area for him shortly. He reached for the flashlight at his belt and flicked it on. The LED shed an eerie blue light ahead of him and Keith realized that he could now stand and move more quickly along the smooth sandstone walls of the cavern. *With luck*, he thought, *they will decide it's a bad bet to come this deep into the cave and give up*. After looking ahead as far as the beam would show, Keith turned off the light and continued along the dark cave. He would simply keep his right hand against the wall and know that if he followed the same wall back he would eventually emerge at the spring. Before he turned his light on again, he checked behind him. He could see a faint beam projecting into the cave. At first Keith thought it was just the light at the entrance, but then the beam shifted and he knew his pursuers had found his tracks and were following. Without turning his flashlight back on, he kept his right hand against the cave wall and continued deeper into the mountain.

Keith had no idea how far he had come or how long it had been. Each time he stopped to catch his breath, he could hear the shuffling steps behind him or see a glint of the pursuer's flashlight. He hurried on.

Keith had never been particularly claustrophobic or afraid of the dark. He had explored his grandfather's cave in California that went back into the mountain, branching into caverns and tunnels that he couldn't squeeze through. But he had always taken reasonable precautions. With every step he was aware that the pursuer was safer than he was. If there were an accident, Keith would be the first to arrive. Now that his initial panic was wearing off, the fear of falling in the cave was overcoming the fear of being caught by the terrorists. He pulled up short to assess his options and catch his breath. He listened carefully, but there was no immediate sound of pursuit. He no longer saw the bobbing light.

He was alone in complete darkness, except, he realized, for a persistent pinpoint of light that lay ahead of him. For a moment Keith thought he had become turned around in the dark and was seeing the pursuer's flashlight, but this light was small and steady, not bobbing as a person walked. In a flash of understanding, Keith realized that he had to be looking at another entrance to the cave where he could see daylight.

He decided not to risk exposing himself with his flashlight, but proceeded more carefully now toward the light that grew progressively brighter and stronger ahead of him.

Keith gradually picked up his pace, now heedless of the danger of falling, and suddenly burst out into open, blinding light.

TWENTY-NINE

YOUSEF WAS NO STRANGER to being chased through wilderness roads. He had crossed enough factions in northern Iran while investigating his father's death that he'd had to run on more than one occasion. Derek and Maddie thought he was paranoid. But they had no idea of things he'd done. They were after him. Mossad, CIA, Yakuzi, al-Queda. He was an equal opportunity offender. His hand was steady on the wheel and when he blasted through a small village and then south. He pulled up into the foothills on a goat path. He was sure he had missed Derek and Maddie. The roads on this side still had patches of snow on them and there were no other tire tracks through it.

He stopped beneath a ridge and took binoculars from the car, then climbed up to the ridge to look back along the road. The Jeep Patriot he'd wildly shot at when he hit the road came into town slowly, as if checking every alley for him, and then came to a complete stop. After a minute the driver backed into a short tight passage between two buildings. Nothing moved and Yousef used the opportunity to scan the surrounding countryside. From his vantage point he could look over a shallow depression between two ridges that rose toward the mountain. There was movement high above the valley. Yousef could not be sure, but it looked like Maddie's boyfriend rushing down the mountain.

Yousef swung the binoculars back toward the car in the village. A man got out and looked up the valley from the village. Near the top of the valley, the road that circled the summit cut across just above a small lake or pond that still had a crust of ice on it in spots. The man definitely looked native, but something was out of place. This was no opportunistic kidnapper. This man was moving with determination that indicated he was searching for something or someone specific.

Then Yousef saw him check a hand-held device, look up the far ridge, and check the device again. The man headed off toward the ridge, carefully picking his way along, and staying sheltered beneath over-hanging rocks. Yousef looked down the ridge he was on to where he had parked his car. It was barely visible from his location, but he realized that anyone looking through binoculars from the other side would be able to see it clearly. *It's too late to do anything about that now*, he thought. Better to keep out of sight and watch what was going on.

He kept scanning the area. The man he assumed was Keith was struggling on slippery paths high up the mountain. Yousef looked farther up and saw two more figures at the edge of the terrace near the tumulus. One pointed down the trail toward Keith, but instead of hurrying to intercept him, they paused and lit cigarettes. This was definitely not the behavior of rebels on a mission. It seemed that they were content to simply keep track of where he was. As Yousef watched, they began casually to pick their way down the trail.

It took Yousef a minute to pick out the man from the Jeep again. He lay partially concealed beneath scrub 200 meters from the village where he left his car. He was scanning uphill, then checking his device and then looking up again. Yousef followed his line of sight to the top of the opposite ridge. In a moment there was movement. Two figures appeared. It took only a moment to identify Derek and Maddie.

So it wasn't Yousef the stalker was tracking. It was Derek and Maddie. With Keith coming down the mountain, the Zaynes descending from the ridge, and the stalker pursuing from the village, they would all converge at the pond.

For the first time in his life, Yousef felt completely free. No one was pursuing him. Instead, it was he who could pursue the other four. *This is where it will end*, he thought triumphantly. How appropriate that he would put an end to the betrayals, an end to the search, and an end to Derek all at once. It was near.

Yousef watched until he was sure he could pick up the trail of the people converging at the south end of the pond. He scrambled back down the slope to his car. He realized now that the supplies Derek had him bring from the plane in Adana were there for no other reason than to pin the library bombings on Yousef. But Sophie had taught a reluctant Yousef about using explosives. He began assembling the charges—just enough for Yousef and Derek. Just like Sophie showed him. Just enough.

THIRTY

KEITH'S DARK-SENSITIZED EYES began to tear as soon as he came fully into the light.

"Ahch!" he shouted as he shook his head. The wordless expression echoed back at him.

Something was definitely not right about this. He rubbed his good eye to get the water out and blotted his injured eye on his sleeve.

The light was not as bright as his eyes had indicated when he came suddenly into it. It came from a dozen or more torches lit around the perimeter of a large cavern. If there were torches burning, then someone must have lit them and Keith spun around to see who was in the cavern with him.

"Well, well, Dr. Drucker," Derek said as he released Maddie and gave her a gentle push toward Keith. She rushed into his arms. "Not going to the Euphrates after all, are we?"

"Not dead, you mean," Keith answered.

"You just can't get good help these days," Derek said. Maddie grabbed hold of Keith and for the first time Keith began to take in his surroundings.

The roof of the cavern was so high that it disappeared in darkness, out of reach of the torchlight. Fifty feet across the cavern from its entrance were massive doors flanked by the statues of a man and a woman that rose into darkness from the cavern floor. They were dressed in pharaohic garb holding an ankh and crowned by a serpent, barely visible above their heads. The doors were easily ten feet tall and a frieze of scenes that Keith could not quite make out spanned the distance between the figures from the top of the door to as high as Keith could see.

His wet clothes were clinging to his skin and as the adrenalin dissipated, Keith began to shake uncontrollably.

"I'd have to bring an entire team of engineers in here to open that door," Derek was saying, "but I'll bet you know how. Where is Joey?"

"H-he went after you," Keith stammered.

"Keith, you're freezing!" Maddie said.

"D-dry clothes in y-your pack," Keith said.

"Yes, by all means get dry. You're ruining the carpets," Derek said sarcastically. Nonetheless he kicked the backpack across the chamber to Maddie. Keith began stripping off the plastic bags and his clothes as Maddie rummaged in the pack. She pulled his dry trousers out of the pack and as she unrolled them, the satellite phone clattered to the floor of the cavern. She looked up frantically at Keith and grabbed for the phone, but Derek snatched it up.

"What have we here?" Derek asked. Keith risked bluffing.

"It's the tracking phone Homeland Security has been using to follow us. Since you've had it, they've been following your trail. They're not far behind." Somehow his bravado did not sound so brave through his chattering teeth.

"Shut up and put your pants on," Derek snapped. Maddie helped Keith pull on pants and a sweater and then got his boots back on. At least the bags had kept his boots dry.

"Derek, we have to get him out of here and get help," she pled. "He'll die of hypothermia."

"Give him a torch to hold," Derek said. "He'll last." He pocketed the phone and Maddie retrieved a torch from the wall, hoping it would provide a little warmth for Keith. "You sent an S.O.S. message when we found you this morning. That's been twelve hours ago and no rescue. Your phone has no signal down here. If help ever comes, they'll be dragging the pond outside for days before they find this cave."

"How did you find it?" Keith asked. He looked questioningly at Derek and then at Maddie.

"I'm sorry, Keith," she said.

"Oh, don't blame Madeline," Derek said. "It was you who provided the directions. I knew all along you weren't headed to the Euphrates."

"How did you know that?"

"Your instructions are over 500 years old," Derek said. "Ataturk Dam was only finished 20 years ago. There was no water near Acma 500 years ago—at least not more than a stream that wouldn't be visible from the mountain. Then I saw your map."

"What?" Keith asked.

"When I got pain pills out of your pack this morning I saw the map you had so kindly marked your position and direction on," Derek grinned. "I only needed Maddie to identify which cave."

"How did you know which cave?" Keith asked. He had stumbled upon it by sheer luck, himself.

"The stars and crescent," Maddie said. "They are carved in the wall just inside the mouth of the cave."

Derek suddenly dove behind Maddie and Keith, grabbing Maddie from behind and bringing his gun up to point at the entrance to the chamber.

"Come out into the light," he commanded. Keith could now hear a shuffling in the cave. Derek must have been listening for it all along. "Come out, come out, whoever you are," Derek sang. Agent Fry stepped into the light from the cave entrance. "Drop your gun, Agent," Derek commanded. Fry assessed the situation and quickly dropped his sidearm. "Kick it away," Derek said. Fry did so. "Now come on into our little party." Fry joined Keith and Maddie, and Derek herded them toward the massive doors.

"I thought you would still be in Egypt," Derek said.

"Finished there," answered Fry. "Thought I'd come see what the librarians were up to."

"What was in Egypt?" Maddie asked.

"Is Frank okay?" Keith asked at the same moment.

"Your brother bombed the new Library of Alexandria," Derek said.

"Actually, it was local paid guns," Fry said, "and your grandfather is fine, Keith."

"Joey did what?" Maddie exclaimed.

"He was in Alexandria to pay locals on behalf of Derek Zayne," Fry said. "Then he flew out here."

"The library?"

"Is okay," Fry said. "Mr. Zayne's plot was foiled."

"You don't think I had anything to do with the bombings, do you?" Derek said. "Yousef and my assistant hatched the library plot."

"You can quit with the feigned innocence," Keith said. "You've already told us you planned it and Sophie was your executioner. Why would Agent Fry believe something else?"

"Well, that's all over now anyway, and no one was hurt except the stupid twit who blew herself up," Derek said. "The important thing is to open the treasure-chest and see what we've got. Then we can all decide how to live happily ever after. Keith, open the door."

"Open Sesame," Keith intoned at the door. "What do you think I am? It's a locked door."

"I think you are a man with a key," Derek said. "You said so back in Kieran. And I saw it while you were changing clothes, so don't pretend it doesn't exist. Why else would you show up here in front of these locked doors with a huge key around your neck if you weren't going to unlock the door?"

Keith was genuinely startled. Things had been happening so fast that he hadn't even equated his master's key with the locked door in front of him. But on that, the writings were clear. "The master's key unlocks the entrance," the letter had said. It made sense. Gutenberg had the third degree master forge a key that would unlock the secret entrance to Ptolemy's treasure. He created the locked box in the Guild chambers to test the key. But if he unlocked the door now, Derek would just kill them all and no one could stop him from robbing the tomb or library or whatever was behind the doors.

"I don't see any reason to unlock the doors, even if I have the key," Keith said. "You'll just kill us anyway."

"Kill Maddie?" Derek said in amazement. "This is all my gift to her. You love old books, don't you Madeline? They are just on the other side of that door. You can have them all. I only want the words in them. I'm only in this for the knowledge."

"The *control* of the knowledge," Fry said. "Zayne, this has gone far enough, don't you think? You're known now. Homeland Security has already linked you to the library bombings and your plane has been impounded by the Turks. My men are guarding the entrance to the cave and there's no other way out."

"There, you see?" Derek said, waving the gun around. "You have nothing to lose by opening the doors. Now do it." He waved the gun at Keith.

Keith turned toward the door. This was what third degree masters for 500 years had been striving for and now it was in his grasp. The keyhole was above a wrought iron handle with an intricate design of twisted metal, braided with little gaps between the pieces. A tear dripped from his injured eye as Keith suddenly jammed the key into the braided handle and twisted until it snapped.

"Oops," Keith said.

THIRTY-ONE

A MOMENT'S SHOCK was followed by a blur of action. Agent Fry pushed Maddie and Keith aside as he swept Keith's ice axe off the floor and swung at Derek. A shot rang out and the agent spun against the wall with blood from his arm splattering the door behind them. The agent grasped his wounded arm.

"Damn! Why did you do that?" Derek said leveling the gun at the agent again. But instead of firing a second bullet he swung toward Keith. "Why did you do that?" he demanded.

Keith ignored the question and turned his back on Derek. He and Maddie knelt beside Agent Fry to tend to his wound.

"It's not that bad," Fry said.

"There's salve and bandages in my pack," Keith said. Maddie scrambled to get them as Derek kicked the ice axe farther away and continued to rant to no one in particular as they bound the wound.

"Of all the stupid things to do! Idiots!"

"I think it went through the muscle, but it doesn't feel like the bone is broken," Keith said as Fry grimaced under his touch.

"What?" Derek said. "Do you think I want to kill people? Hasn't all this meant anything to you? I'm not a terrorist. Nobody hurt at the libraries. No death threats. You just push until I have to do something and look what happens."

"That sounds like what you said when we were married: 'See what yo made me do?' Well look what you did to Keith," Maddie said.

"And my driver lying dead in Adana," Fry affirmed.

"Those weren't my fault," Derek said. "No one was supposed to be hurt."

"So you let people like Sophie and Najat do the dirty work," Maddie said. "I'm glad Keith broke the key. Now we'll have to just leave and you can surrender to the agents."

"Why did you do it?" Derek asked, turning again to Keith. "You've waited all your life to see what was behind that door. And you ruin the key just to keep me from seeing it?"

"I guess it was the wrong key," Keith said blandly. He and Maddie got Fry back to his feet and stood facing Derek.

"It's a good thing we have another then, isn't it?" said another voice from the tunnel. Yousef stepped out into the light of the room from the shadows where he had been watching with a rifle pointed at Derek. Derek did not lower his gun, but shifted his aim slightly toward Maddie.

"Yousef," he said. "I thought you were lost again."

"Drop your gun, Derek," Yousef said. "I will kill you."

"Do you think you can kill me before I kill your sister?"

"You killed Sophie," Yousef said.

"Sophie?" Derek exclaimed. "Don't be ridiculous. You know as well as I do that no one made Sophie do anything. Sophie chose what she wanted to do."

"I loved her."

"She was crazy. We're all better off without her," Derek said. Keith was certain Derek was making matters worse by denigrating Sophie. If Derek had been talking about Maddie that way, Keith would be furious. Yousef was becoming more agitated.

"She loved me! We were going to get married and get away from you once and for all."

"Sophie was using you."

"You are going to die like she did," Yousef yelled. His voice echoed in the chamber. Derek seemed to figure out that he was making things worse, but his aim on Maddie didn't waver. Keith was trying unsuccessfully to move in front of her, but was afraid any sudden move would cause one of the men to lose control.

"Yousef, I'm sorry old friend. I didn't know. Really," Derek said. "You know I've always tried to do right by you. Look what we've accomplished. We're here. We've found your father's hidden treasure. Let's look at what's behind door number one before we do something crazy. You have a key, don't you?" Derek asked.

"It takes a third degree master to forge a key," Keith said.

"Yes," said Maddie's brother. "Like my grandfather." He pulled a key on a leather thong from around his neck. Even from across the chamber, Keith could see that it was a match for his own broken key.

"Joey," Maddie said, taking a step toward the center of the chamber. Derek's gun did not waver from her, nor Yousef's from Derek. "Please don't do this. We don't need what's behind the door. Don't give it to Derek."

"You thought Gramps was just crazy. But when you went to college, I spent all my time listening to him. I knew all about the Guild by the time I was 17. I knew Gramps had stolen something and he was so ashamed that he couldn't go back there. He kept saying over and over that he'd give me the key if I'd take the map back to the Guild. But he never showed me either one until I was in college. Then I had to promise that I would take them back. It's all he could talk about."

"And you thought Derek would help you," Maddie said.

"He was the only choice I had. Our father lost his life looking for what is behind this door," Yousef said, calm at last. "Our grandfather lost his mind. Now here we are at the door. We can't pretend it isn't there, Maddie." Yousef threw the key to her. "You unlock it," he said. "It's your right as much as his."

"Madeline," said Derek as she picked up the key. "Rest assured that no matter if Yousef kills me or not, if you break that key like your boyfriend did his, I will kill you." Maddie looked at Keith and he could see the tears in her eyes as she reached the door.

"Maddie," he said softly. "For the next generation." She straightened her back and nodded at Keith, understanding. Then she pressed the key to the lock.

"It's the wrong key," she said. "The keyhole is a completely different shape." Keith nodded.

"It's okay," he said before Derek or Yousef could explode. "Take the cord off and use the other end of the key." Maddie struggled with the knot and then Derek held out a knife blade on which she cut the cord. It took two tries to get the key in the slot correctly. The cypher 4 cross slid into the keyhole. There was a long hesitation as she gently slid the key back and forth trying to find the exact spot where it would engage with the mechanism inside. She felt it catch and turn and then move smoothly in the latch as if it were used every day. She pushed on the door, but nothing happened.

"Take the key out," Keith instructed. He had to admit that now that he recognized the futility of his act of resistance, he was excited to see the great doors open. Maddie withdrew the key. Keith gripped the braided handle and twisted it to the left. It slid in a groove and they heard the whisper of air being sucked into the gap that gradually widened as the door swung silently inward.

Keith took a torch from beside the door on one side, and Agent Fry reached a torch from the other side. Together they held the lights aloft as they went into the dark chamber. With all eyes focused on the chamber, Yousef slipped up behind Derek and grabbed the gun out of his hand. Derek spun, but Yousef was already a step away pointing his rifle at him. The chamber was huge, with walls sloping in toward the back and from the sides. Keith and Fry made a circuit of the room, lighting torches as they went.

A marble obelisk near the center of the room rose up out of the floor. At the top, carved in relief on all four sides was a duplicate of the lion with stars and crescents that Keith and Maddie had seen on the terrace. The sides were filled with carved letters in Greek, Latin, Persian, and Egyptian. Keith shone his flashlight at the Greek side. He looked at the text in silence a moment, then translated. "I, Ptolemy Soter, decree the founding of a museum where all the knowledge of mankind will be gathered together," he read.

Maddie, reading along on the Latin side of the obelisk stopped and looked at Keith and then both scanned the remaining text.

"Keith, does this mean what I think it means?" Maddie asked.

"Where's the manuscript," Derek asked. "It's an impressive underground room, but I thought there was a book."

"Not a book," Keith said. "A library." He continued to read and translate the obelisk. "Knowledge is its own nation. It has no... no... It *needs* no king, but it must be preserved. Within the walls of this museum, the Word will be preserved. I have commanded my keepers to build this museum where none will molest it. Not even I know where it is."

"He had this place built to hide the Library of Alexandria!" Maddie exclaimed. "It must never have gotten here."

"It's not quite right," Keith said. "The Library had between 500,000 and a million scrolls. This is a big room, but it wouldn't hold that number of books. And why would Gutenberg be brought to an empty room?"

"It's time for us to go now, Derek," Yousef said softly, jabbing his gun into Derek's ribs and dragging him backward by the collar toward the cave. "We can leave this in the hands of the scholars. Time to finish our business." Keith, Maddie, and Fry turned to look at the two backing out of the chamber into the narrow opening of the cave. Then Derek twisted and knocked Yousef to the ground, his gun skittering away. Yousef's jacket fell open when he hit the ground and everyone could clearly see the explosives strapped to his chest. For an instant everyone froze. Yousef smiled slightly as he looked up at Derek and held up the detonator so he could see it. "For Sophie."

THIRTY-TWO

"JOEY!" MADDIE SCREAMED. Fry charged into Keith and Maddie, knocking them to the floor behind the door as the explosion rocked the outer chamber and the shockwave extinguished the torches. Absolute darkness claimed the space.

"Maddie! Maddie!" Keith called frantically as he groped for her hand in the darkness.

"Joey, no!" she wept. "Why? Why?" Keith caught her hand and soon had her cradled in his arms.

"Maddie, are you injured?" A flashlight flicked on and Agent Fry swept the area toward them with the beam.

"Are you two okay?" he asked at the same time.

"No. Yes." Maddie said answering both questions. "My baby brother." She turned her head and wept into Keith's shoulder.

"I think we're all right," Keith said to Fry. "Shine your light over here. I dropped my flashlight." Fry's beam crisscrossed the area near Keith until it lit on Keith's flashlight. Keith grabbed the light and turned it on. Rubble was sprayed across the floor in front of the door and dust still hung in the air.

"Do you have matches?" Fry asked. When Keith nodded, he continued. "See if you can get a couple of torches lit. I'll take a look at the damage." Fry's left arm hung limply at his side as he moved toward the entry. Keith helped Maddie to her feet and she pulled the flashlight from her belt and helped to look for her lighter. In a moment they had two torches lit. Keith turned off his flashlight and took the torch from the bracket and lit three more to fully illuminate the room. Fry appeared in the doorway once more.

"Ms. Zayne, I'm sorry to say this, but you need to come out here." Keith put his arm around Maddie as they made their way into the outer chamber. He lit more torches as they came. Half way across the chamber, Fry was kneeling beside Derek Zayne.

"Madeline?" Derek whispered. Maddie knelt beside the agent and her ex-husband. "You know what's funny? I never changed my will," he whispered when she touched his hand. "It's all yours now. Everything I built. You won't need this anymore," he said, reaching for the locket that hung from Maddie's neck. Grasping it tightly in his hand he pulled, "I know right where you are now." The chain broke and his hand fell to his chest.

He was no longer breathing. She stood and backed away. Keith caught her as she nearly fell sideways.

"He can't have my sympathy," she said quietly. "He never understood. It's his fault Joey did this." She looked at the entrance to the cave. Rubble filled the opening. Somewhere under the rubble her brother's remains lay buried. With all the people he believed were chasing him, it was his own hand that had proven fatal.

"We're trapped," Maddie said flatly. "There's no way out." She fell to her knees in front of the rubble that blocked the chamber entrance and covered her brother's body.

"Not necessarily so," Fry said. He staggered as he stood and Keith steadied him.

"You're woozy from the blood loss," Keith said. "There's water in my pack." Fry took the offered canteen and moved into the inner chamber. "What are you thinking?" Keith said. He picked the second backpack out of the rubble and dragged behind Fry into the room.

"Look at the shape of this room," Fry said. "You said it wasn't big enough to hold all the books. The wall slopes in from the doors, the back wall is flat. I'd say we are only in the foyer."

"But where is the entry?" Keith said. "Maddie?"

"Could I just have a couple of minutes to deal with my brother blowing himself up?" Maddie yelled at him. "Just a couple of minutes before I have to pretend that I'm all right and here to solve the great puzzle of some ancient practical joker who got us all trapped here."

"Maddie," Keith began.

"Just give me a minute!" Keith started toward her, but Fry caught hold of his arm.

"We can wait," the agent said.

The two began surveying the walls of the room for any sign of a hidden doorway. They were intent on their task and did not hear Maddie re-enter the room. A rock hit the floor outside and both men turned to the doorway. Maddie was scraping the floor with her boot, tossing the larger stones that were in the passage out of the room.

"Maddie, darling, I'm sorry," Keith said going up to her. She leaned against him for a moment as if to accept the apology and then kept sweeping the floor with her foot.

"You could help," she said. Keith began scuffing the rubble out of the doorway.

"What are we doing?" he asked.

"We're getting ready to close the doors," she said.

"If we close the doors, there is no guarantee that we could ever get out of this chamber and no one would be able to get in without the key," Keith said. "If Agent Fry's men come in hunting, they'll try to dig us out."

Maddie pulled her grandfather's key out of her pocket along with the cut leather thong. She re-tied it and hung it from the braided handle.

"There, now they'll have a key. They'll figure out how to use it," she said.

"But why?" Keith asked again.

"Airlock," Maddie said. "Something my grandfather used to say: 'You can't go on until you can't go back.' The chamber can only be opened from one side at a time."

"That's part of the mantra for the Guardian's Ritual," Fry said. "At every stage of the steps, the initiate recites words that roughly translate, 'the only way out is in.'"

Once the floor was clear, they began sliding the doors back closed. They were completely silent when they opened, but now the gravel grated between the bottom of the doors and the floor.

"Well, here goes," Keith said and pushed the door into place. Nothing happened. The back of the door was as ornately decorated as the front had been, however, and Keith explored the carving near where the handle was. Three stars crossed the seam, one split between the two panels. Keith grasped both the outer two and tried turning them left then right. They moved and he could hear the locking mechanism drop into place. A moment after the door had sealed, they heard a second hissing. The torches flickered. On the other side of the obelisk, stones in the wall slid aside. They each took a torch, their backpacks, and flashlights and crossed the room to the darkness beyond.

As soon as they crossed through the passage between the chambers they could hear a difference in the echo of their steps. All three shined their flashlights ahead and could see the beams pick out massive pillars on either side. They glowed, ghostly in the dark, even when they turned off their flashlights.

"I think this room would be big enough for your library," Fry said. His voice echoed in the hollow chamber. As their eyes became more accustomed to the dark, they realized the room was dimly lit. Pillars a yard across and at least 50 feet high stood in rows at least 30 feet apart. The pillars glowed softly. At the end of the central corridor was a colossus figure.

"What are these columns made of?" Keith asked as he approached one and laid his hand on it. Now that their eyes were adjusted to the dim illumination, the three turned off their flashlights. Surprisingly the pillar was not as cold as Keith expected.

"How deep are we?" Maddie asked.

"According to the topo map," Keith said, "the spring where we entered is about 200 meters lower in elevation than the terraces on the mountain. I couldn't tell if we gained or lost any elevation in the darkness between the spring and the first doors."

"Gained," Maddie and Fry both said at once.

"Drainage," Fry said. "The entrances slope away from the main pyramid."

"Pyramid?" Keith and Maddie looked at each other.

"Look at the walls," Fry said. On all four sides of the square chamber, the walls sloped inward. It's what gave me the first clue about the entryway. That wall only sloped in one direction."

"Wait a minute," Keith said, calculating in his mind. "If this room is about 300 feet in each direction, and we are on the ground floor, that would mean that the top of the pyramid is still 200 feet above us. It's not as big as the Great Pyramid of Giza, but that's pretty impressive for an underground structure."

"We may not even be on the ground floor," Fry said. "It just happened to be an entrance level. Very likely there are more entrances hidden around the mountain."

"Are we under the tumulus?" Maddie asked.

"Yes. That must be how it's lit," Keith responded. They were nearly to the colossus at the end of the chamber.

"What do you mean?"

"The tumulus above us acts as a heat sink. The pillars are not exactly warm to the touch, but definitely not stone cold. I don't know what they are made of, but the stored heat must be what makes them glow," Keith said.

"Did you notice, by the way, that we can only see that statue up to about the top of his knees? He must be nearly a hundred feet tall," Maddie said.

"It makes sense," Keith said. "No wonder none of the soundings that have been taken have ever shown anything down here. If a chamber this deep showed up at all, it would diffuse the sounding and they wouldn't get a reliable reading."

"Why is it so empty?" Maddie asked. She was looking around the chamber and it appeared to be little more than rows of pillars extending to a ceiling some fifteen meters above. "Where are all the books?" she asked as she looked down into alcove after alcove.

"We need to decide where we're going," Fry said. "Flashlights won't last forever and we can't count on magical lighting in every chamber. We should bring a couple of torches each, too."

"There are stairs that seem to go up around each side of the statue. Which way?" Keith asked.

"Just a minute," Maddie said, running back down the corridor of pillars. When she was about a hundred feet away she began coming back, looking first at the left pillar and then at the right as she passed each pair. When she had rejoined the men at the foot of the statue she said, "Right," and headed for the stairs on that side of the statue. Keith and Fry were directly behind her as she began to climb.

"Why right?" Keith asked.

"That's where the stacks are," Maddie said. "This is a library. Even one that professed to send the documents out must have had some that were too fragile to move. That's what we keep in the stacks."

"But how do you know?" asked the agent.

"On the pillars," Maddie said as she climbed. "They are all carved like pillars in ancient Egypt. Only the figures on the right get progressively higher on the pillar, like people standing on ladders. On the left, the figures progress downward."

"But both stairs lead up."

"'One long staircase just going up, and one even longer coming down,'" Maddie recited. "It's the one on the right."

"I'm following," Keith said. The stairway disappeared behind the colossus and kept going into darkness. Keith tried to picture the position of the staircase on the other side and was sure that they should cross each other at this point, but instead, the walls closed in on the sides and soon they were going up the staircase sideways, dragging their packs, in order to get through the passage.

When the narrow passage opened into a room, they discovered they were standing facing the waist and torso of the colossal statue. *His head must still be above,* Keith thought. This chamber was significantly smaller than the chamber below and the room was dark. When they flashed their lights around the room, they could see open doorways leading off the central room about every 15 feet around all four sides. Keith began to worry about the lifespan of their lights if they had to explore every room before they found a way out. As if reading his mind, Agent Fry pointed to a torch in a sconce on the wall.

"We'd better go by torchlight when we need it and just by the dim light in the walls when we can," he said. "It will save our batteries."

"It's remarkable that they don't smoke much," Maddie said. "We can hope they don't do too much damage to anything we see." She poked her head through the first door on her right where she took a torch from the wall and gasped.

"What is it?" Keith asked, coming up beside her.

"Not what I thought," Maddie said. "I thought it was a room of mirrors, it's so shiny." They pushed into the chamber together and looked at the flat shining surfaces.

"They are windows," Keith said in awe. He took their torches back outside the room and placed them in the sconces, then went back in. Fry left his outside as well. The windows weren't crystal clear, but it seemed they also radiated a muted light.

"How could there be glass and light in here if this was created in the first century B.C.?" Maddie asked.

"Alchemie," Keith said. "Turning stone transparent. I wonder what the composition is." He tapped the glass. It had a metallic ring.

"Did you hear that?" he asked. "It sounds like transparent metal. And look at the edges. It isn't in a frame. It seems to come right out of the rock."

"And look what you can see," Maddie said, pushing her face right up to the glass. "Books."

"In every chamber," Keith said. "By the looks of it, these books may be a thousand or more years old."

"Sealed in stone," Fry said.

"We've got a lot of work to do down here," Keith said. "How can we get access to the books without damaging the glass?"

"The real question is 'why should you?'" asked the agent. "Maybe they should just be preserved, not shown."

"It's a matter of authentication," Keith said, "—to prove that a concept came from a particular time and individual."

"I'm beginning to understand my responsibility as a Guardian of the Word as exactly that. We're supposed to keep it safe, not expose it to danger," Fry said. Maddie laughed. Both Keith and Fry looked at her.

"It's a little premature to think about getting the books out of here when we don't know how to get us out. I think we should keep going up," Maddie said. "We aren't close to getting out of this place yet. If we find a way out, we can discuss what to do with what we've found."

There was only one staircase this time, the opposite side clearly going down the way they had come. Maddie went first again, dragging her pack behind her and holding her torch in front. It was narrow, but did not get narrower. When they reached the top and came out into another room, they stopped to stare in awe. They were face to face with the colossus. The head rose fifteen feet before its headdress began. It was in perfect condition, having never been exposed to the eroding effects of weather, and like the pillars and the glass, it glowed softly, giving great depth and texture to the carving.

"Spiral once and then once more, until the head is on the floor," Fry said.

"What's that?" Keith asked.

"The chant that goes with the ritual steps," Fry said. "It didn't come to me until we came face to face with the head on the floor. The ritual is a map."

"The chant's in English?" Maddie asked.

"No, but several of us have moved away from our tribes and we decided to do an English translation in case we have children that don't speak the old language," Fry said sheepishly. "It's easier than Farsi."

"Then you can get us out of here," Keith said.

"If what I have is complete," Fry agreed. "Like I said, a lot of the ritual was lost when our people were scattered. There was no one to compare one person's version with. My cousins know the same version I do, but I know of other clans that have different twists."

"Well, before we go following any more of it, come and look at this," Maddie said. She was standing near the center of the room facing away from the massive head. In front of her was a stone dais.

"Did you find an altar?" Keith said.

"I guess you might call it that," Maddie said. Keith and Fry joined her. In the center of the dais was a plinth on which rested a single book.

THIRTY-THREE

THE BOOK WAS NOT A SCROLL, but a bound codex, and Keith could identify quickly that even though it was a manuscript and not printed, it was nowhere near 2,000 years old. *Probably mid-19th century*, he thought as he looked at the beautifully illuminated page open in front of him. Maddie was already digging in her backpack for another pair of gloves. "Get the torches back away from it and shine a flashlight over here," she said. Fry took the torches and retreated a few steps. Keith approached with the flashlight. Maddie carefully tested the quality of the paper to see if it was safe to handle. The paper was high quality and in supple condition. She began to turn pages back toward the beginning of the book.

"I think this is what we were sent here to find," Keith said. They reached the first page of the neatly written Greek. Keith began to read. "'In the year that Alexander died, the seven divided his kingdom. We wept that all his conquering was parted, but only Alexander could rule the world. This book is the testament of Ptolemy Soter of Alexandria, heir to the knowledge and lore of the world's greatest conqueror.'" Keith paused. "I think we've come across the book called *The Wisdom of Ptolemy*. And by the looks of it, it was placed here to be found."

"You think this is the book that the monastery copied?"

"An ink analysis would verify it," Keith answered her question. "There aren't that many manuscripts that were written with cyanide laced ink."

"If you take the manuscript out of here with us," Fry said, "you have to have a plan for releasing it, or you have to guarantee that it is going to be kept secret in your Guild. I may not have understood the role of a guardian before, but I know we have to protect this location."

"I agree, for now," Keith said. "And I have an idea. Maddie, you may not like this."

"We have to have a body in order for me to inherit," Maddie said, already ahead of Keith. "And if we dig him out, we dig Joey out."

"I see where this is going," Fry said. "There is a way that it could work. If the Guardians clear the passage to the front door, they will uncover the bodies. It could be done during the winter when there are few people around. We would also want to arrange it so that it is not quite so easy to stumble upon if you happen to walk around the spring."

"But if the bodies were discovered somewhere in Turkey, say a long ways west of here," Keith volunteered, "they might have died in a spelunking accident. In a few months, after the will is read and Maddie inherits the estate, she could find this moderately old volume among Derek's possessions and donate it to the library where authenticating the volume would reveal its history without revealing anything about the location of this archive," Keith said. "I think this book will reveal Ptolemy's intent for his library and we can work out how to progress from there."

"Now that we know what the Guardians guard," Fry said, "we should be able to keep the site safe. The region is already protected as a national treasure. But if we don't find our way out of here, none of that will make a difference." As if to emphasize his point, one of the torches guttered and went out.

"You know the steps," Keith said. "Maddie, if I didn't use all the plastic bags to wrap my feet in, let's get the book prepared to take with us."

They worked quickly to close the book, wrap it first in cellophane, and then package it in a garbage bag, sucking as much air out of the package as they could with straws before sealing it closed with packing tape. Nonetheless, by the time they were finished, the last of the torches had gone out and Fry held a single flashlight on their work.

"Let's go," he said. "Stay close and we'll use just one flashlight at a time. I've no idea how long this will take."

FRY LED THEM through steps, counting the measures with the ritual words he had learned. When they reached the back of the stone head, they discovered what looked like a fold in the stone headdress concealed a passage inside the head. There, stairs led them still higher. But the maze they entered when they emerged from the passage nearly baffled the agent. He persisted with the steps exactly as he had learned them and eventually they came into a room small by comparison with the scale of the underground pyramid.

"This should be it," Fry said. "At least, this is where the ritual ends." All three turned on their flashlights and scanned their surroundings. In the center of the room stood a massive screw press that would dwarf the replica press in the Gutenberg Museum. The massive timbers stretched from the floor to a stone ceiling. Around the room were typecasting equipment, setting stations, and scrivener desks.

"It's a print shop," Keith said. "It must be where Gutenberg worked out the details of the printing press."

"Yes, but there are no other doors," Fry said. "If this is where the ritual ends, it may be where we end as well. I'm sorry I can't take us any farther." The three circulated through the room and examined all the walls. They seemed solid. The only way out appeared to be the way they had come in.

Keith found himself standing back in front of the press, running his hand along the handle. The screw could apply incredible pressure to the platen below it.

"Keith, we need to find a way out, not be examining another old press," Maddie said.

"I think the press is the way out," Keith answered. Both Maddie and Fry moved to him to examine the press. "Remember, we couldn't get in until we'd closed the door at the entrance. This is the same kind of thing. Most presses of the Gutenberg era were so heavy that a press-man could pull on the handle all day and all the pressure would be exerted down onto the platen. But this press has the extra support of floor to ceiling anchors. If I pull the handle, I could still make a great impression, but look." He pointed to the ceiling. "The top of the screw looks like it goes right through the roof. When I pull the handle, you can see the screw descend from the ceiling."

"Fascinating, but it could just be a design anomaly," Fry said. "No doors opened when you pulled the handle."

"Maybe I'm pulling in the wrong direction," Keith said. He positioned himself on the other side of the press and pulled the handle so that the screw rose into the air. It stopped after a quarter of a turn with the platen just a few inches from the typebed.

"Still nothing," Fry said, shining his light around the walls.

"A screw press this size is capable of over half a ton of pressure if you pull hard enough," Keith said. He propped his feet against the press and heaved against the handle as hard as he could. There was a pop from overhead and the wall opposite the press began to shift. Fry was at the opening shining his light through as the stone moved aside.

"This is it," he said. "The opening is going to cycle closed again. We need to get through." Keith and Maddie ran for the exit. As soon as Keith let go of the press handle the stone began to shift again. Maddie hugged the book in front of her as she dashed out the opening with Keith right behind her. Two steps beyond the portal, the stone snicked closed again. They shone their lights around the entry. Paved with smooth cut stones for about ten feet, the floor became rough as they continued down a passage that was similar to the cave they originally entered from. It was cold in this cave, however.

"We're outside the pyramid," Fry said. "Let's hope that's a good thing because we're not going back in the way we just came out." Maddie pointed at the reflection of the light ahead of them.

"Is that more glass?" she asked as they approached.

"No," Keith said. "It's ice. No wonder it is so cold." They searched the area in front of them, the passage blocked by ice formations.

"There's a passage there," Keith said looking over Maddie's shoulder.

"Are you sure?" Maddie asked. "It looks like a little ice cave to me."

"You were the one who led us up a winding staircase that kept getting narrower and narrower," Agent Fry said. "Let me check it out." From somewhere on his person he pulled a flare that he lit with a tug.

"You had these while we were all in the dark?" Keith asked.

"We had other light then," Fry said. He tossed the flare down the ice passage. They watched it twist and then heard it drop a few feet. It illuminated the base of the passage dimly. "It looks big enough to me," Fry said. "I'll make sure the passage is fully open." With that he went feet first into the passage and they saw the light at the end black out as his shadow came between it and them. There was a muffled crack and crash as ice broke inside.

IT TOOK NEARLY another 30 minutes before the trio had navigated their way to the cave opening, only to find that it was blocked by an iron gate. Fry worked the lock free using more force than finesse to get them through. Finally they stepped out of the cave into the pre-dawn light and looked around.

"It appears we've just emerged from the ice caves on the south side of the mountain," Fry said getting his bearings. Keith recognized a bit of the path they had come up on their first hike up to Mount Nemrud.

"If we head that way we should intersect the processional way and we can head on down from there," Keith said.

"That means my support team is on the opposite side of the mountain," Fry said. "I'll call them around and they can bring a car to meet us at the base," Fry said. He pulled a satellite phone from inside his shirt and turned it on.

So this is it, Keith thought. *We found the library of Alexandria. It is a place where knowledge is kept, not where it is shared. Maybe that is what it means to guard the words.*

They followed the agent, lagging farther and farther behind until he had rounded a corner and then Keith turned to kiss Maddie. She melted into his arms with the book sandwiched between them.

"I know this may not be the best timing," Keith said as he broke the kiss, "but it seems like we've kept waiting for right times to tell each other things all week and those times never get here. I love you, Maddie, and I want you to marry me." Maddie gasped slightly and Keith reached into a side pouch of his backpack. He pulled out a small brown envelope and opened it. A ring shown in the light.

"Keith! When did you ever manage to get a diamond?"

"I confess, it's not a diamond," Keith said. "I think it's more appropriate for us. I had Granddad get it ground and set for me as soon as he got to Mainz. It's a piece of the glass from the atrium of the Kane Memorial Library."

"It's perfect, and yes. Yes, yes, yes," Maddie said.

They kissed again and then headed down the path the direction Agent Fry had gone. Just before they dropped below the ridge, they looked back and could see the crown of the tumulus over the Western Terrace.

"You know I want to come back here," Keith said to Maddie.

"After our daughter is born," Maddie responded. "I think we have enough to keep you busy for a few months right here," she said, handing him the book she still carried. Keith took the book.

"I can't start that until I finish cataloging these," he said, touching a freckle on her nose. They laughed and hurried to catch up with Agent Fry.

ACKNOWLEGMENTS & SOURCES

A HEARTFELT THANKS to the many people who have helped me with this book. Where it shines, it is due to their diligence and help. Where it fails, it is because of my own stubborn bull-headedness. I especially want to thank my wife who read and re-read the story in different drafts and corrected my spelling, grammar, and treatment of women. A second valuable aide was Jason Black, the book doctor, who read the first draft and told me exactly what was wrong, then read it again in time for me to enter it in competition. Should you ever need an editor or book doctor, visit http://www.plottopunctuation.com.

I owe a special thank you to book arts instructor Dan Shafer of Cornish College of the Arts and a member of the Seattle Center for Book Arts for helping with the setup and printing of the original cover art for this book.

Getting input from people who just like to read this kind of book was extremely valuable, and I'd like to thank Jason, Michele, Janet, Nancy, Cary, Steve, Richard, and all those who were pressed into listening to a paragraph or two (or a chapter) to help me get through a difficult spot. Thank you to Gayle Lynds for offering encouragement and taking both my writing and publishing ventures seriously.

THERE IS A LOT OF INFORMATION
available about Johannes Gutenberg and
some of it is apparently accurate. Ferreting
out what part is history and what part is
legend is beyond my simple endeavors. I
took most of my factual information from
The Catholic Encyclopedia at http://www.
newadvent.org/cathen/07090a.htm as it
seemed the most reliable and seemed often
to be the source quoted by other sites.

The printers' marks that adorn the beginning of each chapter
are authentic marks of 15th-18th century printers. The source is
the book *Printers' Marks: A Chapter in the History of Typography* by
W. Roberts, published by George Bell and Sons in 1893. I found
an electronic copy of the work at Project Gutenberg, http://www.
gutenberg.org/ebooks/25663. Project Gutenberg is a repository of
over 33,000 free electronic books created by volunteers from public
domain works, many going back centuries. This edition was produced by Louise Hope, Stephen Hope and the Online Distributed
Proofreading Team at http://www.pgdp.net (This file was produced
from images generously made available by The Internet Archive/
American Libraries.)

Another book that was an invaluable resource from University of
Virginia Library Electronic Text Center was *Forty Centuries of Ink* by
David Nunes Carvalho, Published by Lenox Hill Pub. & Dist. Co.
1904 and scanned by Charles Keller (http://etext.lib.virginia.edu/toc/
modeng/public/CarFort.html). There is more information in this book
on the changes in ink composition over the past 4,000 years than you
will ever want to know!

My historical information on the Library of Alexandria was greatly
enhanced by the book *The Vanished Library: A Wonder of the Ancient
World* by Luciano Canfora, published in 1989 by Hutchinson Radius.
As rich in texture as this book is, however, it is also a great lesson in

not believing everything you read—even in print. Several points in Canfora's book are disputed as to historical accuracy, but it's a great story. Sorting out which pieces a rare books historian would accept and which would be subject to skepticism was a monumental task.

If I could choose one place to visit today, it would be Nemrud Dagi in southeastern Turkey. Most websites regarding the location have used the same source material, so there is very little difference in what they say. Most enlightening was the documentary film *Mount Nemrut: The Throne of the Gods*, directed by Tolga Ornek in 2001. You may have to wait your turn to get the DVD from Netflix, but the views and history are worth the wait.

Of course, there are many other resources I've used, and since this is a work of fiction and not a thesis, I won't do an exhaustive bibliography. The same is true of the people who have helped to make this project come to fruition, including The Gutenberg Museum in Mainz, my wife and daughter, the Pacific Northwest Writers Association, and Book Publishers Northwest. Heartfelt thanks to all of you!

MORE TALES

BY NATHAN EVERETT

The Volunteer. (2014) Journey inside the head of a chronically homeless man. With no frame of reference for his current perception of reality, Gerald Good--G2 to those who see him on the street--is sometimes in the present and sometimes in the past. But he is forever locked in his head.

For Money or Mayhem. (2012) There is a cyber-stalker and computer forensics detective Dag Hamar is just the bad-ass in cyberspace to go after him. But when the young women start disappearing from the streets of Seattle, Dag moves from the safety of his desk into the underground where there is no "undo."

Steven George & The Dragon. (2011) This young adult fantasy follows the journey of Steven George, the village dragonslayer, who discovers that he is poorly equipped to face the world outside his tiny village. He doesn't know what a dragon looks like, where it lives, or how to slay it. Steven trades once-upon-a-times with the travelers he meets and each story leads him closer to the truth about his quest: All roads lead to the dragon.

For Blood or Money. (2010) In this contemporary noir mystery set in Seattle, computer forensics detectives Dag Hamar and Deb Riley discover that hidden files and computer code can be as dangerous as dark alleys and flying bullets as they trace a missing man and the billion dollar fortune that disappeared with him.

Available in print and eBook from major on-line bookstores.